THE DEAD
DON'T TALK

ALEX ROBERT

ALSO BY ALEX ROBERT

Death Sketches

In the misty darkness, nobody heard the screams.

Chapter 1

THE STREETS OF THE city glistened with the cold winter dampness. Thick mist filled the air, an eerie silence only broken by a passing car. York was deserted, the late evening driving all but the hardy indoors. One group stood alone, their presence appearing out of place and yet their purpose was designed to be exactly that. They were there to search out the sinister and find those places where ghostly souls haunt the night. Four lonely creatures were vulnerable in the darkness of the city's dimly lit streets.

They walked down High Petergate slowly. A figure dressed in black spoke softly. His voice was chilling, the unbroken tone matching the fear of the night. Two of the group huddled together, clutching themselves as one for both warmth and reassurance. They were scared, too scared to utter a single word or step away from the safety of those around them.

Progress was slow and almost deathly. A single shuffling step brought the couple closer. A nervous breath was squeezed out by the young lady, her lost face buried within the man's chest. Above, medieval buildings overhung where they walked, bearing down with sinister intent. The feeling of the rooftops closing in was not lost on the frightened couple. This was York at its ghostly best.

Through Bootham Gate, they turned left and saw the road open up. A passing white van made everyone stiffen. Its progress was slow as if looking into the night and searching out the very same souls. Inside, a gaunt face with hollow eyes looked across and examined each of them in turn. The group shuffled forward, oblivious to those watching eyes. On another night, they would have been drawn to it but not when fear was flowing through their veins. Their heads were down and in no mood to offer up their vulnerability.

Only when each face had been noted did the van move a little quicker. A press of the pedal forced the engine into life. It left behind three cold and frightened forms to follow the Gothic creature that led them. Watched in the mirror, they posed no threat to him.

The van slowed once more outside the theatre. The audience had departed into the silence of the night. The driver glanced at his watch and cursed his lateness. There was still time. His victims would be on foot and walking through the city.

As was their routine, the path they followed never changed. In the dim visibility, there was no hint of the threat that was posed. The driver turned right onto Museum Street and noted the lack of witnesses. A cruel grin spread across his face and offered up a missing tooth. Nobody saw it or the cold stare he gave the two elderly figures before him.

For fifty yards, the van accelerated violently. It was brought to a halt with a screeching shudder. Their first instinct was to help and it allowed him to strike with calculated precision. In the misty darkness, nobody heard the screams as two more souls were gathered from the city's streets.

CHAPTER 2

GREGOR BANKS HAD BEEN cleared of all charges. That was the verdict, delivered to a raucous cheer from his entourage. He stood shaking the hand of his counsel, a sickly grin as wide as the Ouse spread across his face. There was back-slapping, waves to the gallery and hugs offered all around him. Worst of all, there was a smug acknowledgement to York's police force that he remained a free man.

DI Jack Husker stood aghast. For several months, he had compiled his case. Insects had been dragged from the cracks, rats persuaded to abandon a sinking ship, all terrified with good old-fashioned detective work. Of course, it wasn't orthodox. They were dealing with crime royalty. Gregor Banks was no ordinary crook. He demanded special attention and, for as long as he could remember, Jack had made it his obsession.

There had been late nights in The Cellars, under the guise of needing time to think. Clandestine meetings had been held with those on the periphery of the underworld. Jack had done it all. He had put in the hard yards, gone the extra mile and now all he had to show for it was a smug gangster who would be waiting for him the moment he turned his back.

DCI Nick Lang's face was thunderous. Repeatedly, he had told Jack the case did not stack up. His witnesses were not reliable and the accusation of coercion would be easy to make. Jack had listened, ignored him and, in a weaker moment, broken him down and convinced Lang the charges would stick. Not only had he been spectacularly wrong but now York's policing standards would be up for independent scrutiny.

It was Lisa who Jack felt most sorry for. Unwittingly, he had dragged her into it. As the replacement DS, Lisa Ramsey was only covering until Dan Millings was back to full strength. It was not even her patch. Her job was in Newcastle and it was Jack who had persuaded her to stay. Now she would be sent back, with a permanent stain against her name. How was he to know his main witness would crumble and two others would go missing the day before the trial? All at the hands of Gregor Banks, a man who claimed to be a businessman and now had an apology from the judge.

Jack sat down on his seat and waited for the courtroom to clear. Above him, the galleries were full of a mixture of Gregor's followers and journalists waiting to fill the following day's papers. Jack could see the headlines already, each one a cruel stab to the chest. His head dropped into his hands. It shut out the bad news until he felt a solid hand placed firmly upon his shoulder.

"Cheer up, Jack. Better luck next time."

Above him stood Gregor Banks, with two sinister-looking men flanking either side. If he could be bothered, he could recognise them, not that he felt in that frame of mind. A dark thought filled his head, to lay Gregor out in the middle of the courtroom. Contempt of court and a few nights in a cell would follow his invitation for the two thugs to strike. No, he would bide his time and avoid giving them a free pass for the violence they craved.

"Cost you much to buy them off, did it?"

"I don't know what you mean, Jack. As I keep telling you, and the judge reminded you, I'm a businessman."

"Yes, and I'm tee-total."

"That's a shame. I thought you might be buying me a celebratory drink."

"You and I aren't finished, Gregor. I'm going to nail you. It's just a matter of time and we both know it."

"Is that before or after the harassment charges stick? I think the judge made that point very well."

Jack swallowed hard when he remembered the words of the judge. He could hardly have been clearer, not that Jack was listening by then. The case was long gone by the time the admonishment started. It had been his trigger to switch off and yearn for the taste of a good pint. Indeed, any pint would do the job, as long as it was wet and semi-cold.

"I'll be seeing you, Jack. Don't ever stop looking over your shoulder."

"Is that a threat?"

"I don't do threats, Jack. I'm a businessman. Now, I'd better be going. I can't keep the press waiting for too long. They might want a joint interview with the two of us."

"Don't push it."

"Or what, Jack? Are you going to press charges? Face it, you're finished."

There was nothing Jack could offer in response to the final barb. He felt beaten and utterly humiliated by the man he despised more than anyone else in the world. Gregor was scum, the epitome of everything he hated about the city. Now walking free and with his apology, he had a VIP pass to unleash his special brand of thuggery and violence across the city. The day could hardly get worse.

As soon as Gregor was gone, DCI Lang walked over. In front of him, Jack stared vacantly at the ceiling of the courtroom. He felt no calmer when his force had been shamed in the public eye. One of his most effective detectives had been called out for his mistakes. Months of work had seen the flimsy evidence shot to pieces in a few short hours. He regretted ever letting Jack persuade him that the case had any merit.

"I know what you are going to say, sir."

"Trust me, Jack, you have no idea. Just do me the decency to look at me when you make your excuses."

Reluctantly, Jack moved his gaze downwards. His blank eyes stared across at his superior. His head was empty, devoid of words that could offer anything to Lang. Out of politeness, he had to say something even if everything inside his head would make the situation worse. What he managed to come up with would have been better left unsaid

"Just admiring the architecture. It's an impressive building."

Lang shook his head and began to walk away. It was his only response to avoid a full explosion in front of a pack of hungry press officers that were loitering in the doorway. The emotion could come later when he was alone with Jack. Then, there would be serious words said.

"Get yourself off home," he told Jack. "I'll see you in the morning and don't talk to anyone, especially the press."

Jack had no plans to speak to anyone. He was done with talking for the next few days. He needed the city to swallow him up and allow him to hide anonymously in its inner reaches. Just a year ago, he had been the hero, the injured officer acclaimed for bringing down York's worst serial killer for many years. Now, he was a dinosaur and a washed-up relic of the past, waiting to be pensioned off. In a strange masochistic way, he was not sure which feeling he preferred.

"Penny for them, Jack."

A kind face looked down. Lisa stood over him and lit up the space. It was his one true regret that he had dragged her into the mess. After the serial killer case, he should have allowed her to go back to Newcastle, but he couldn't. He needed her to provide some sanity in his endless obsession to bring down Gregor Banks.

"You'd be wasting your money."

"What money?"

"The penny you're paying for my thoughts. You would definitely want some change from that deal."

"Can I buy you a coffee instead?"

Jack forced a smile in an attempt to acknowledge her kindness. The truth was he didn't want any. Instead, he needed to fester and get away from everyone even if Lisa was one of the hardest faces to turn away.

"Get yourself back to the station. You don't want to be splashed all over the papers with me. It could ruin your career."

"I'm not sure I care, Jack. We are a team."

"Not for the next few hours, we aren't. I need to do this bit alone."

She took the hint and patted him on the shoulder before heading out of the room. Outside, Jack could hear the scrum of reporters and the general noise seeping into the courtroom each time the door was opened. There were no prizes for loitering in the lobby when a swift exit was the only way to get through the crowd. For now, Jack would wait. He would allow Lisa time to get away and only then would he make his exit.

Nearly ten minutes later, Jack hauled himself to his feet. He felt weary from being dragged through the gutter by the judge. He was physically tired rather than just mentally. To his simple brain, that made little sense.

After two deep breaths, Jack steeled himself for what he was about to face. Outside, the noise had not abated in any way. As soon as he pushed on the door, he was mobbed by flashing cameras. Shutters clicked and questions were thrown randomly in his direction. Not a single one was processed by his scrambled brain.

"DI Husker, have you got any comments for the press?"

"What did you make of the judge's comments?"

"Will you resign?"

"What do you think of the statement from Mr Banks that he will be taking out a civil case?"

"What are you going to do next?"

Suddenly, that question registered. It brought Jack to a standstill, with a throng of recording devices thrust in his face. All were waiting with the hope he would say something that could fill tomorrow's pages. Preferably controversial, for the case had already provided enough material for several days. A good quote would bring the story to life.

"Are you going to retire?"

Jack took a few more steps and then stopped again. His face was drawn to a journalist he disliked. He recognised him as Andy Hutton, a man with whom he had crossed paths before.

"Afternoon, Jack," he smiled, his scruffy appearance consistent with his manner.

There was silence. Jack did not offer a greeting back. It stayed that way until a few of the less dedicated drifted away. They had their pictures. Any quotes could be from anonymous sources, rendering Jack's lack of words immaterial.

"Have you got anything to say for the paper, Jack?" asked Hutton.

Still nothing. Not a single word left his mouth. A brave young photographer stepped across Jack's path to block him until an angry scowl informed him of his mistake.

"I could do an exclusive with you," said Hutton.

"You want an exclusive, do you?" replied Jack.

There was sudden interest from the pack. Journalists that had started to ease away now flooded back around him. One fumbled with his recorder, cursing its shut-down state that left him ill-prepared.

"Yeah, it's your chance to put your side across."

"Well make sure your recording thingy is on. I'm only going to say this once."

The group huddled in. Devices were pushed forward until a dozen surrounded Jack's mouth. In expectation, a hush descended upon the previously noisy rabble. They had lured him in and the man they would rip to shreds in their papers was about to fall into the trap they had set.

"Ready?" checked Jack.

There was a chorus of whispered affirmations.

"Remember, you can quote me on this, word for word."

Eager nods.

"Sod off and leave me alone, you parasitic vermin!"

***

Dan Millings eased himself out of the car. He glanced up at the flat above him. It was still hard to lift his tired body out of the vehicle. It was supposed to be getting easier but it wasn't. At times, he wondered whether he would ever feel okay. It had been twelve months since the shooting and his body was still going through the painful convalescence process. The scars remained, both physically and mentally, and then there was the darkness, which wouldn't go away.

With the taxi driver paid, Dan limped across to the front door. Psychological pain, the physiotherapist had called it and yet it was he who felt it, not her. She only saw him for less than an hour to offer a few cheery words and then moved on to her next victim. The small consolation was her attractiveness. Even that did not make up for the pain of seeing her every week.

Dan walked up the stairs to the first floor. Once more, he was alone. The flat was his place of refuge and yet it felt like a prison cell at times. There was no fun being on your own while convalescing. Each day that passed was like any other that went before it.

The injury had given Dan time to reflect and question whether his career choice was the right one. The sick pay was good, that was for sure, but did he want to sacrifice his life for thankless service to the public? It was a question he had taken plenty of time to ponder. It was also one that a medical assessment might soon decide for him.

He checked his phone. There were no messages. There rarely were, other than a welfare visit once a month. The officer never wanted to come; indeed, they were just ticking a box on a form. For Dan, it broke the monotony of another day that, without the kindly face, would feel even longer. He glanced around at his immaculate flat, almost wishing it was untidy. It would give him a purpose for the rest of the day.

A buzz at the door was both surprising and welcome. With the intercom pushed, Dan pressed his ear to the speaker. It needed to be fixed but that was beyond him. An engineer would need to open up the device.

"Yes, who is it?"

There was a muffled sound. The voice was unrecognisable in between the crackles. Certainly male, perhaps middle-aged, it was hard to distinguish beyond that.

"Sorry, I can't hear you."

"It's..."

Again, the intermittent noise masked any form of recognition.

"Just come up, it's open."

Dan pressed the button to open the door, allowing the stranger into the building. He was beyond caring who it was. Even someone with malicious intent was better than having no visitors at all. He unlocked the door to his flat and wedged it open. Downstairs, he heard the front door close.

"Upstairs," he called out. "Come straight up."

The footsteps on the stairs made the identity of the stranger no clearer. Dan moved to the far side of the room and filled the kettle to the brim. Two purposes went through his mind. Firstly, it put him by the knife drawer. More importantly, it made it harder for them to leave. With coffee being made, the visitor would be obliged to stay and that would break the monotony until the darkness came.

The footsteps grew louder and more solid. Dan could hear them getting closer to his flat. He pulled the knife drawer open and clutched the handle of the largest one he owned. It felt good, with its grip solid in his palm. Just one false move and Dan 'the knifeman' Millings would send a blade flying through the air. It might take four or five attempts but eventually, he would strike his target.

13

"Dan, how are you keeping?"

Jack stood in the doorway. There was barely a grin etched across his face.

"It's been a while, Jack. How's the Gregor Banks case going?"

He would have been better throwing the knife. There was silence as the colour drained from Jack's face. That was the one question he did not want to answer. Jack wanted to forget about it, not that he had thought about anything else from the moment he had left the courtroom.

"Have you been cleaning again? I've seen operating theatres with more dust than this. Am I getting a coffee or a cup of surgical spirit?"

"I can manage a coffee."

"Good. How's the patient?"

"I'm okay. I've been to the physio again this morning. She reckons I'm progressing."

"And the sleeping?"

"That's more difficult. Milk?"

"Yeah and sugar. Plenty of it. Have you tried some brandy?"

"No, I don't want to get...well, you know."

"Like me, you mean."

"I didn't mean that."

"It's fine, Dan. I know what I am."

There was a mutual acceptance of each other's position. They were colleagues, possibly even hinting at friendship. Jack did not have to visit. Unlike the others for whom Dan had been forgotten, a sense of compassion bubbled under the surface.

"Here you go, grab a seat."

Jack took the coffee from him. "Are you sure I won't mess up the neatness of the cushions?"

"Is it that obvious?"

"I'm afraid so. I think we've known each other long enough to tell."

"We have, so you can tell me about Gregor Banks rather than change the subject."

Jack slurped at his coffee. It was too hot. Still, he tried to force it down. Despite great intakes of air, the heat scalded him and yet his body continued to accept the pain.

"Jack, put the drink down. I want to know."

"The case was thrown out."

"What?"

"The judge said it was a personal vendetta."

"And was it?"

"I'm starting to think it might have been."

Jack stayed with Dan for an hour. Reluctantly, he gave him some of the details of the case. Played back, it sounded weak even if he had convinced himself they had everything they needed to lock up Gregor Banks. Dan just listened, offering nothing by way of interruption. At times, he could see the paucity of Jack's evidence but accepted his colleague's words. He had few enough visitors without scaring away one who was willing to come. Dan sat there, watching Jack's torment grow with every piece of information he relayed.

"You need to take some time off, Jack."

"And do what?"

"Take Mary away. You haven't been away once since you two got together."

His mind flitted back to Mary, the sweetheart of his youth. Dan was right. Mary and he had done little together since they began to cohabit. Perhaps it was the case. More likely, Jack's natural defences were keeping her at a distance. Something was wrong and yet his confused mind was unable to determine what it was.

"We'll see. Now, do you fancy a quick one?"

"No, thanks. I'm not supposed to drink. It stops me from sleeping."

"And are you sleeping?"

"Not really."

"That sounds like a well-worked plan. I'm going to The Cellars for one on the way back. If you want to join me, I'll be there for no more than an hour."

"Thanks, I'll give it a miss."

"Your loss."

The two men hugged. It was an unusual display of affection from Jack. It made it obvious to Dan that something was wrong. Jack barely shook hands, let alone offered man-hugs to his colleagues. Dan put on a brave face and wished him well.

Jack left Dan's flat and made the short walk to The Cellars. His mind was full of self-destructive thoughts. To see Dan was difficult when there was a personal sense of guilt within him. Mixed in with the carnage of the lost court case, Jack had a lot going on in his mind.

"Line them up, Alf."

There was never any attempt to keep it to one. A crumpled twenty-pound note was handed to the barman, with a clear instruction to get the beer flowing. Jack did not wait for his change. He sat in his normal place and left the spare monies in the hands of the one man who could offer him some contentment.

Not that he felt like drinking. It was more that he was in the mood to inflict some damage on himself. Drinking was his chosen method, with smoking having been abandoned many years ago. It was too difficult to light up in a politically correct world where one by one the smokers were either dying off or being ostracised from their groups. As for drugs, Jack had never tried them and was sure he never would. He couldn't abide the thought of them, having seen the damage they did to the dregs of society.

Alf could see he had a customer in need. He kept supplying the beer to meet Jack's demands. There were no accompanying shorts. That was too dangerous for the mood Jack was in. As he served him, Alf did not attempt to reconcile the money he had been given. There was no need to with Jack. He would be back the following night and the next and he paid his way. It might take a few days to catch up but Jack would put his hand in his pocket and make sure everything was squared.

Jack's thoughts turned to the case and the obsession that had gone so badly wrong. The sneering face of Gregor Banks haunted his thoughts. He was the smiling kid who had got away with his sins. It had ended with an implied threat on his way out. Jack didn't care. A meeting with him was inevitable, as was a confrontation with his goons. He had one trump card in his favour.

It was just a question of playing it wisely. The Timmy Jackson disappearance was something he would keep in his pocket. It was the one crime Gregor would struggle to walk away from. Jack was just a body away from locking him up for life.

Of course, there had been a gentlemen's agreement. A blind eye had been turned to arrest a serial killer. That was a year ago and both had kept their word. For Jack, the game was now changing. It would be a death sentence to break his promise but it was a price he was willing to pay. Such thoughts were interrupted by a figure looming over him.

"Might be time to go, Jack."

Jack shook his head at Alf, thrust his hand into his pocket and emptied two more tatty notes onto the table. They were swept up. It was credit for another day if Jack did not drink his way through it on this occasion. With a shake of his head, he walked back to the bar and waited for a few moments. It tested whether Jack wanted more beer. Alf had a sense his customer might be leaving, no matter how much he denied it.

Predictably, Alf knew Jack better than himself. The detective rose to his feet, stumbled from the table and was gone. With a brief wave, he left Alf clutching his money, which he deposited in Jack's kitty under the bar. He was ahead by fifty pounds at the moment or a couple of nights drinking at his typical rate.

Out on the street, Jack stumbled along. He lurched from side to side, bumping into the wall on his left. It would leave him with a bruised shoulder in the morning and no discernible reason for it. Always the same shoulder and always the same mystery, Jack blamed it on the way he slept.

Home was not so welcoming for Jack. Mary's harsh words greeted him as he stumbled through the door. She shook her head and folded her arms, offering the same stern look as the previous night.

"Where have you been?"

"I just popped in for one," he slurred.

"I'm sure. Go and get yourself changed. If you want food, I'll reheat some for you."

Jack grumbled to himself. What was it with this fixation about getting changed? Jack didn't have work clothes or non-work clothes, smart or scruffy. They were all the same, just clothes you wore to stop your friends and colleagues from seeing you naked. That was not a pretty sight anymore. Even Jack would admit that. Nobody needed to tell him.

He kicked off his shoes when he entered the bedroom. Mary's words were forgotten the moment he walked in. It smelled nice, with fresh bed linen put on earlier that day. Jack slumped onto the bed and allowed his head to hit the pillow. From that moment on, he slept.

CHAPTER 3

"So, Jack, would you like to explain what happened yesterday? You probably don't need me to tell you it was a difficult day for all of us."

Jack stood silently before DCI Nick Lang, with all the hallmarks of a teacher scolding his pupil. He paused. His head was still filled with thoughts of Mary. She had not come to bed last night, preferring to leave Jack alone. Instead, she had slept in the spare room. It was not a good sign after less than a year of living together.

Something told him she would not be there when he got back. Did he care? He did, making it hard to reconcile his destructive behaviour. She could cope with his abruptness at times, but not the drinking. The way Jack felt this morning, he was not sure he could cope with it either.

"Well?"

For years, he had thought about Mary. She was the lost sweetheart that had nearly slipped from his grasp. Now they were together, he was doing everything to push her away. It was Jack all over. He couldn't do boring and happy. Everything had to be a battle as if a majestic fight of good versus evil. He hardly needed reminding which side each of them sat on.

"Jack!"

Jack's head bolted upwards. His superior was standing in front of him. He had looked angry from the moment he entered the room. Jack had not taken much notice.

"Sorry, I was away with my thoughts. Shall I get some coffee?"

"You've already got one."

He was right. There was an untouched drink in Jack's hand.

"Do you want one?"

"No, I want to know what is going on."

"I'm not sure, sir. I'm just not sure." Jack placed his coffee down on Lang's desk.

"Look, Jack, I can turn a blind eye to some of your unorthodox methods. I can even ignore your drinking. What I cannot have is you being unfit to work and making the force look like a laughing stock."

"I'm not unfit to work."

"Jack, look at you."

Even Jack had to admit he was far from his best. He had slept in his jacket and trousers. As for the socks, he had been lucky to find two that matched lying on the bathroom floor.

"I'll be fine."

"No, you won't. You need to take some time off to sort yourself out."

"Are you standing me down?"

"Not officially. Get out of here until the heat level dies down and I want no more quotes to the press. I heard about your wise words."

"They asked for it."

"It did not need saying. Take two weeks off and I'll see you when you get back."

Jack stood still and gazed around him. The DCI's office was bland. It was hardly something to aspire to as you worked your way up the greasy pole. Not that Jack was going to do so. He had been lucky to make DI, only getting his chance through the untimely death of his boss. That was linked to the Banks family and now the youngest of them all was forcing him to take a sabbatical.

"I'm fine. I don't need a break."

"Jack, you look awful."

"I thought I was the one who was supposed to be blunt."

"Well, you do. Someone has got to tell you the truth. I know you won't listen to anyone but it's for your own good."

"So what case are we working on today?"

"We're not. You're taking a holiday."

Jack walked over to the other side of Lang's desk and picked up a bundle of case notes. He thumbed through them, the contents fairly mundane by recent standards. There was a string of burglaries, all in the Micklegate area. It was a crime and that meant it needed solving. The victims did not care if the police thought it was low-level and not worthy of allocating a senior detective.

"I'll start the door to door."

"Jack, you are not taking the case."

"Are the forensics back from this weekend's break-in?"

"Jack, don't make me suspend you."

"Any witness statements?"

"Last warning."

Jack slammed the documents down and walked around the office like a caged animal. He needed something to get his teeth into, not to go home and spend two weeks in The Cellars.

"I need to keep busy. I understand your position but you also have to understand mine. I could solve this."

"Jack, you are not going back out onto the streets. The press will have a field day with you."

"I'll tell them to sod off."

"That's what I'm afraid of."

"So what do you suggest?"

"You can go on the missing persons' review team."

"You mean you want me to chase the stiffs."

"Call it what you like; it's an important part of what we do."

"And who else is getting added to the team? You know there is no one in there doing anything of worth."

A silence offered a mutual acceptance of one another's point. As two wise owls, they knew it was the departure lounge to retirement. Some did the honourable thing and died early, freeing up a seat for another old copper to spend his last few years. Others sat there and festered.

"At the moment, it is just you. However, if you turn up anything, you will be given access to additional resources."

"In other words, it's a bit like being sent home, isn't it?"

"Jack, that's your choice. It's missing persons or suspension."

"And when will I be allowed out of the naughty corner?"

"When you learn to behave," growled Lang.

Jack never gave DCI Lang a direct answer. He picked up his coffee and threw it at the bin on his way out. Hot liquid splashed across the carpet. There was anger in both of them and any further exchanges would only cause friction. If there was going to be an argument, it was better to allow the passage of time to ease the wounds.

Lisa approached Jack as soon as he was a safe distance from Lang's office. She looked concerned, with a frown etched on her forehead. Jack acknowledged her and then grabbed a fresh coffee from the machine. All the while, his brain processed the information Lang had imparted.

"How did it go?"

He wanted to brush her off, but he couldn't. Lisa had a kindly face and a demeanour that said she genuinely cared. Guilt still flowed through him about dragging her into his vendetta against Gregor Banks. He knew it would be an apology he owed her many times.

"Very well. I've got a new job."

"Really?"

"Yes, Head of Stiffs."

"What's that?"

"Lang reckons it is to do with missing persons. I reckon frozen people count just as much."

Lisa smiled. It eased the tension between them. Gone was the fear of being pushed away by a man determined to suffer alone.

"Come on, let's go and get you a proper cup of coffee. I'm not having a man of your age drinking this stuff."

"Careful, I'm a very important man around here."

"Only to those who are missing," she laughed.

***

York was changing. The Lib-Dems had lost the council to the Tory party and the city was alive with councillors celebrating. No place was safe from the festivities, not even The Cellars, which was packed with a new style of drinker.

David Moss was leading the celebrations. A Tory party member since his university days, he had been set for a life in politics. The Student Union presidency had been his first position and now he had the job he craved. Of course, he wanted to be an MP, but three attempts in a difficult seat had seen him fall short. Today, the honour of being the leader of York council had fallen into his waiting hands.

Any victory would have been sweet but this was especially so. All expert opinions had predicted no overall control and yet victory had been achieved with spectacular results. His great foe and Lib-Dem leader, Nigel Reeves, had only hung on to his seat by the narrowest of margins. Meanwhile, Sandra Reeves, his loyal wife, had lost the safest seat in the council. It could hardly have been better and with his disciples around him, he raised another glass to the sky. It was acknowledged by a raucous cheer.

"Keep it down, lads," instructed Alf. "I do have other drinkers in here."

David Moss was in no mood to heed the barman's words.

"Today, we revel in a great victory. There will be time for solemnness and quieter thoughts. For now, we light up the city!"

"Hurrah!"

Alf knew better than to fight alone. So long as they were just being noisy, he would give them some leeway, conscious that he was in no position to turn away good money. His regulars drank beer; these guys drank expensive wine and champagne. You hardly needed to be an accountant to work out the profit difference between the two.

"More wine, sir. Keep it coming."

"Sure thing."

Bottles continued to be uncorked as thirty or so Tory members circled their leader. The hierarchy was clear, with the younger kids trying to inch closer. Occasionally, an older head placed themselves at the edge of the group and held counsel with the disciples moving around them. Never once did David Moss move from the centre of the throng.

Alf kept uncorking the wine. He placed the bottles on the bar and allowed the group to pour out their drinks. He had a credit card tucked away behind the bar. It would be maxed to the limit before they were finished. Far be it for him to keep the costs down when one pub in York would be taking that money. It was better for Alf that it was The Cellars than another establishment down the road.

"Have you seen any Lib Dems in here?" asked Moss.

"I can't say I have," replied Alf.

"You won't. They're all gone!"

There were great cheers and back-patting at the hilarity of the joke. No matter what he said, David Moss's standing was assured. Back home, Nigel would be licking his wounds and consoling his wife, who now found herself unemployed. It was a day to remember for the Tories.

***

On the other side of the city, Jack's mood was very different. He sat in the chain coffee shop staring at his oversized drink. Lisa knew it was a mistake not to pick an independent the moment she walked into the place. Her superior had slumped down, gazed around at the bland surroundings and made no effort to hide his disgust.

"What can I get you?"

"You mean we have to fetch our own coffees? Impressive."

"I'll get two filter coffees."

Lisa never took her eyes off Jack while she fetched the drinks. She dared not, for fear he would sneak off and disappear into the city. He had a history of not hanging around in places he did not like. This was exactly the type of place he did not have time for.

Thankfully, the young lady serving was quick. She placed two drinks on the counter in a matter of minutes. Lisa added two slices of cake and carried the tray over to the table.

"Here you go," she offered, "I'll get some milk."

"Wow, you have to fetch that as well. I must come here more often, with this standard of service."

"Stop it, Jack. Look, I've bought us some cake."

Jack eyed the cake with a modicum of suspicion. It wasn't a flavour he recognised though something told him not to ask what it was. In time, Lisa would tell him. For now, he would content himself with staring into the hot black drink in front of him. Deep in thought, he watched the steam rise into the air.

Lisa fetched a jug of milk and poured some into hers. She offered it to Jack. He shook his head as he did with the sugar while continuing to look down at his drink. Lisa knew she had a problem. It was just a question of what she could do to prevent the inevitable car crash from happening.

"How's the cake?"

"Good."

"You haven't tried it yet."

"I still know it's good. A slice of cake is always good."

"Have you had carrot cake before?"

Jack screwed up his face at the thought. He struggled with the amount of space taken on his plate by vegetables when he ate. Now, the do-gooding health freaks were putting it in his cake. Were there no pleasures they could not ruin?

"Try it. Do you want a fork?"

"Do I look like the sort of guy who eats cake with a fork?"

Suspiciously, he eyed the slice of brown cake in front of him. He broke off a small piece and held it up. As he took a bite, he waited for the explosion of vegetables in his mouth. It never came and nor did any other taste. The lack of flavour was obvious as was the crumbly texture, which dried his mouth the more he tried to chew.

"Not bad," he lied, somewhat unconvincingly.

"I'm glad you like it," reciprocated Lisa, just as insincerely.

It was followed by a period where they sat in silence. It resembled a couple entering their later years of marriage. It was uncomfortable and awkward in many ways. The impasse only ended when one of the servers felt obliged to break the ice by walking over and asking a benign question.

"Can I get you guys anything else?"

"No," stated Jack. "I better not have too much of this delicious cake. It can't be good for me."

"Oh no, it's very healthy. There's no sugar in it."

Lisa put her hand to her mouth in a bid to contain her smile. She could sense the old Jack returning, with a gullible victim about to become his toy to play with.

"Really, and it tastes so sweet. You must give me the recipe."

"I'm sorry, sir, we're not allowed to. Company policy."

"Oh, that's a shame. I was hoping to bake it myself."

"I'll get you another piece if you like it that much. On the house."

"Please don't."

Lisa could not help but laugh even though the joke was lost on the young lad. He looked puzzled as if wondering what he was supposed to do next. Lisa felt the need to rescue him from the mismatched contest even if the exchange was therapeutic for her colleague.

"What he means is the doctor has told him not to indulge too much. That's the problem with getting older; you have to be careful what you eat."

"I couldn't have put it better myself," added Jack. "Luckily, my mother is here to look after me."

The lad went away content. He was able to see the humour in the less subtle quips. Lisa smiled, happy that Jack appeared to be returning to the world. He picked up his coffee, sat back and pushed his plate away before looking at Lisa with a quizzical look.

"Have we known each other long enough for me to tell you that cake was bloody awful?"

Lisa pushed her plate away to join Jack's.

"Only if I can tell you that I agree. I thought I was doing us both a favour by skipping the chocolate slice. Next time, it is a double helping of sugar for both of us. Now, what happens next?"

"We do a runner before he brings us anymore," said Jack.

"No, I mean with you. What are you going to do?"

"I've told you, I'm now the Head of Stiffs though I might change my job title. How does Chief Stiff Officer sound, or CSO?"

"Perfect. I hope you've cleared it with Lang."

"Hope, Lisa, is just deferred disappointment. Let's keep it our little secret. Come on, finish your coffee and then I'll take you for a real drink."

***

Jack was stunned by how crowded The Cellars was when he walked through the door. Not an inch of floor space was available, with each patch of carpet filled by a smartly dressed man. A few ladies stood on the periphery and had been marginalised. They were not part of anything that was going on. It was a man's world and already, Jack did not like it.

"Excuse me," he growled.

It was not rude and neither was it overly polite. Jack pushed his way through the crowd. Lisa followed, taking the path forged by her companion. As she moved, she nodded a couple of apologies with a half-smile. Briefly, one or two of the throng threatened to react to the intrusion until the fervour of the group reintegrated them.

"Pint of best and a glass of wine, Alf."

"Afternoon, Jack. Is it getting earlier or have you got a date?"

"No, this is work."

"Of course it is."

"Who are these lot?"

"Tory councillors. They've just taken York."

"Taken it where?"

"They've just won a majority."

"Have they?"

"Presumably you didn't vote for them?"

"Was there an election?"

Jack watched Alf pour the drinks with a shrug of his shoulders and a resigned look. He knew there had been an election even though he had not voted. It was difficult to vote for anyone when you believed they were all corrupt and out for personal gain. No, he would allow others to decide and then help pick up the pieces afterwards.

He slipped a ten-pound note onto the bar and swept up the drinks, leaving more coins for his kitty. He was never going to hang around for the loose change. It was too busy at the bar, with too many pretend drinkers who did not know how to behave in a pub. Only out on New Year's Eve normally, today the place was full of these drinking amateurs.

Lisa had taken a seat to the left. It was not Jack's usual space, which put him on edge immediately. If he asked her to move, she would think he was OCD. It left him with his back to the room. That made him particularly uncomfortable, especially with a bar full of people he didn't know.

"What have you got me?"

"Wine."

"What type?"

"White."

It was hard to fathom why she bothered asking. For a brief moment, they sat in silence. Lisa allowed Jack to take two satisfying swigs of his beer. Already, he was halfway down the glass and the drink was slipping down a little too easily for the time of day.

"So, tell me about your new job."

It was said in an optimistic tone as if an exciting opportunity had fallen his way. They both knew the truth of the role, leaving

Lisa wondering what type of response she might get. She smiled and was rewarded with a raise of his eyebrows. It was Jack's way of thanking her for making the effort.

"You mean President of the Missing and the Dead, or PMD."

"As long as it isn't PMT," laughed Lisa.

"It feels like it."

"Seriously, Jack, what are you going to do?"

"The same as I always do."

"You mean, stick your head in the sand and drink...sorry, that wasn't called for."

"It was and it is what I'll probably do. Look, I'll give the job a go and if not, there will always be something out there for Jack Husker. Remember, there is a lot of demand for knackered old detectives, particularly those with a bad attitude."

"You make me laugh, Jack. It's water off a duck's back to you, isn't it?"

"Things move on. A year ago I was a hero. Now, I've been declared persona non grata. In six months, something else will have changed."

"But will you have changed, Jack?"

"No, I'll still be the same grumpy old bastard sat in the corner."

"That I don't doubt. I'd better go, Jack. I'll see you at the station."

Lisa finished her wine and placed the glass on the table. It left Jack sitting alone. He stared into his empty, with a decision looming large. Did he brave the ever-growing crowd or seek an alternative establishment? Already, it felt like he was being chased out of his own pub.

He sensed his hackles rising and a rush of adrenalin flow through him. No one was going to stand in his way, especially a few posh toffs who had no place in his city. Glass in hand, he pushed through them. It brought a couple of complaints and provided the trigger for the altercation he was determined to create.

"Watch it, mate."

"I'm not your mate," barked Jack. "Another pint, Alf."

"You're damn right you're not when you go around pushing people. Have you got any manners?"

"No, but I've got a decent right hook if you fancy trying it."

"Leave it, Jack," chimed in Alf.

"I'm just having a drink."

Jack stepped backwards, knocking a drink from one of the youngster's hands. It crashed to the floor, sending the contents in all directions.

"You'll pay for that drink."

Jack turned and faced the youngster down. He saw fear in the lad's eyes as the kid's bravado shrunk instantly.

"No, I won't, sunshine. Got a problem with that?"

"Jack, leave it!"

Alf's words rang in Jack's ears. He could see the red mist descending on him. A day of frustration was boiling over. As the tension tore through him, Jack's hand twitched, eager to throw the first shot.

"Jack Husker, isn't it? Yes, Detective Jack Husker."

In front of him stood a man in his early to mid-fifties; a well-dressed man who had clearly enjoyed a private education.

Instinctively, Jack did not like him or the disciples who flocked around his sides. Every one of them seemed intent on playing to his ego and treating the man like a God.

"And you are?"

"David Moss, or should I say, David Moss, Leader of York Council."

A raucous cheer went up around the bar.

"Never heard of you."

Jack turned to face Alf who had placed his pint in front of him. He eyed Jack with a disapproving look. He had known him long enough to read the signs that Jack was about to do something he might regret.

Jack picked up his drink and took a sip, taking an inch of froth from the top. It tasted less pleasant than before, with the company having spoilt it. He didn't want it anymore and yet good beer should never go to waste. He would force it down, one way or the other, just to send out a message to those around him.

"Are you going to pay for that?"

Jack bristled at the pompous voice to his left. He felt surrounded as if all the toffs were closing in. The anger boiled inside him, to see them congregating in his pub. York had plenty of sterile wine bars for their type.

"What has that got to do with you?" growled Jack. "Are we good, Alf?"

"We're good, Jack."

"Copper's perks," sneered the man.

Jack spun around to face his accuser. It was David Moss who stood before him displaying the smuggest of grins. The gaggle of worshippers laughed at his barb and seemed to continue for a little too long. Only Jack failed to see the funny side and stared at him through narrowing eyes.

"Don't make me stuff this pint somewhere it will never see the light of day again."

"Those are brave words for a copper on duty. I'm pretty sure you shouldn't be drinking."

"You're right. Luckily, I wasn't planning on drinking it."

Jack lifted his pint and tipped it over the Tory leader's head. It elicited a high-pitched gasp from him and an intake of breath from the hordes. Jack stared them out, daring any of them to make a move. Predictably, none did, preferring to ease a few steps backwards. Jack nodded at Alf before placing his empty on the bar and heading out into the street.

"You haven't heard the last of this, Husker!"

For once, Jack hoped that might be the case. He was ready for David Moss and he was ready for whoever else wanted to take him on. What he was not ready for was what greeted him when he arrived home.

"It's over, Jack. I'm moving out."

Mary was packing her case. It was calm and done without any histrionics. Clothes were folded and pressed neatly inside a large wheelie case. Once the lid was clicked shut, the remnants of their relationship was over.

There was barely a word exchanged between them during the act. There was no need. They both knew the writing had been on the wall for many months. First, the love-making had stopped and then the arguments had started before their two lives had drifted apart. For Mary, that meant throwing herself into her work. For Jack, it involved a lot of drinking.

It was hard not to feel some sorrow. Yet both went about their tasks. Jack put the kettle on and made himself a strong black coffee. Briefly, their paths crossed in the hallway. There was a forced smile and then Mary disappeared out of the front door. It had taken over twenty years for the two of them to come together and less than one for their lives to be driven back apart.

Jack took his coffee, put on some music and sat in his chair by the window. It was one of Mary's CDs if he had cared to notice. He didn't. He sat and stared out into the city while clutching his coffee and enjoying the fact that he was alone.

CHAPTER 4

JACK WALKED BACK TO his chair with a renewed sense of purpose. He clutched a file in his hand and threw it down on his desk. The noise startled those around him and yet not as much as the words that followed. As he sat, his voice filled the office.

"We've got a murder!"

Two of the more gullible officers looked up, their faces excited by the sudden news of a case. Jack sat stoically and stared at the file in front of him, waiting for an unsuspecting stooge to take his bait. He was only an hour into his new job and his mind was already drifting to mischievous thoughts.

"Where?"

"On Coppergate, a stabbing. The assailant approached from behind, grabbed the poor bugger and plunged the knife into his back. He was dead before he hit the ground. The murderer ran off down Piccadilly."

Suddenly, three officers were around his desk, all of whom wanted the facts.

"When did this happen?"

"1976."

Jack did well to maintain a straight face as he pushed the details out in front of him. One of the slower officers took it and began to read. He scanned the text before realising the stupidity of his actions. It was a picture to see his expression change, knowing Jack had got the better of him.

"Yes, very funny. You're looking through the old cases. I forgot."

Jack watched the officers return to their desks and the calm, if not, lifeless office assume its more mundane state. It was hard to imagine anyone enjoying such an environment though there was never a shortage of middle-aged officers wanting a desk job. It was a chance to hide away from the front line and avoid the rough end of policing. Sat in comfort, it was also a way of counting down the days until a pension could be called upon.

Jack reflected on his own time served and how long he had left. Ten, maybe fifteen years with the changes to retirement rules in a post-austerity world. That was a long time to sit and count away the days, especially when boredom had struck in the first hour. He contemplated a coffee, aware that two empty cups already lay on his desk. A third in an hour and he would be heading for twenty by the end of the day. It would be mixed in with the same number of visits to the facilities, which his bladder would insist on. It was better to make a go of the job and find a case to get him out of the office. For now, the 1976 murder could be consigned to the drawer or at least put at the back of what was a healthy filing cabinet of unsolved cases.

He could already feel stiffness in his legs, a result of rising from his desk too quickly. Psychosomatic, no doubt, but it confirmed his thoughts about needing some fieldwork. Carefully, Jack thumbed through the records, pondering whether anyone had disappeared in the current century. Half the people would be dead through old age, offering little of note to follow up on. Finally, he stumbled upon a more recent one, a disappearance just twelve months ago. That would be worth reviewing and would offer a slim chance of success.

Mark Simpson, twenty-four, left his home in Wigginton. He never left a note or ever made contact with anyone again. His phone was found in an alleyway. The name was familiar but the disappearance wasn't, leading Jack to look a little closer.

A search provided an impressive record. Mark Simpson was a low-end criminal, with multiple convictions for dealing in the pubs and clubs of York. He was another of the bottom-feeders, enjoying their brief time as a player before one of the bigger sharks decided to snuff out a rival. It had all the hallmarks of the Timmy Jackson case and that meant his prime suspect would be a familiar foe. Jack smiled, for he had a reason to go rattling Gregor Banks's cage. Better still, he had a reason to go for a drink. He closed down his computer and felt a surge of joy. He was breaking the shackles of DCI Lang and getting out of the office.

"Where are you going, Jack?"

Sergeant Richard Foster, or Dick as he was known for many reasons, never cared about winning friends. He was one of those officers Jack despised most; a time-server ticking down until he was paid off through ill health. Dick was too young to retire and too expensive to get rid of until the next round of cuts came. He had got his desk job off the back of a car accident when he was rammed by a joyrider seven years ago. Dick had milked the system ever since and everyone in the station knew it.

"I've got a lead on one of the cases."

"Give it a rest, Jack. You're going to the pub."

"Never while on duty, Dick. You should know that."

Jack walked past Dick's desk, ignoring the newspaper spread out. It was open at the horse-racing pages and would provide ammunition for a future exchange. Jack exited the office, walked down the stairs and set off into the city. It was a walk that would only take a few minutes.

"Pint of best, please, Alf."

"Not at work, Jack?"

"I am working. I've got a new job, so I need to be flexible."

"Yeah, I bet. Are you paying for this one?"

"Am I in credit?"

"You're four quid to the good."

"In that case, I'll have this one on the tab. It'll be even better for it. While I'm here, do you recognise this guy?"

Jack pushed the photo of Mark Simpson in front of the landlord. He looked puzzled and stared deep into the face. He shook his head and then looked up to see whether he was expected to know him. When Jack did not respond, he took one final look at the features.

"I can't say I do. Should I?"

"No, he never drank in here. I'm just trying to prove I am working."

"Okay, let me know when you plan to do any more of your thorough investigations."

41

Jack picked up his beer and sat down in his favourite corner. Once seated, he took out his notepad from his pocket. The time was duly recorded along with a note of Alf's failed recognition. It bought him twenty minutes in which to savour his drink. It was hard work but someone had to do it and a sneaked pint always tasted better than any other.

Alongside his notes, he jotted down the names of six other pubs. They were all ones where Mark Simpson was confirmed to have visited. Most were seedy establishments, ones that only hardened drinkers or users frequented. Indeed, they were exactly the type of places where Jack enjoyed a drink. They were places to get a good pint and, better still, to meet an individual who might be willing to offer a loose tongue.

***

The route between the six was less than a mile. It was like a delivery run, with a loop of establishments circling the city. It started and finished on the bus route, which would lead the victim home. Except, the individual never made it back to the stop where he departed.

At the first pub, the response was predictably blank. It was early, with only a couple of hardened drinkers having made it through the door. Despite the obvious time on the landlord's hands, he barely glanced at the picture. It was noticeable that he was not prepared to touch the glossy surface.

"Are you sure you don't know him?"

"I've never seen him."

"How long have you worked here?"

"A few years."

"That's funny because he was a regular up to a year ago."

"We get a lot of regulars."

"So I see. If you remember anything, you make sure you call me."

"Of course, officer. Thanks for dropping by. Was there anything else while you are here? I wouldn't want you to have to come back."

"You might need my number?"

"Why? Even I can remember three nines."

"I'll leave it in any case."

The number was in the bin before Jack left. There was too much risk of being seen with a police number in your possession. There were people out there who did not like it; people who could make life both difficult and painful. It was far better not to take any chances and play the tough guy from the outset.

The same routine was repeated until five of the pubs had been visited. Each one delivered the same response. Jack went through the motions and left numbers at each of them. With the last approaching, he decided it was time to try his luck.

Behind the bar stood a middle-aged man with long straggly hair. He had the appearance of a failed band member, someone who had dropped out of conventional life a long time ago. He was dressed in black, from his faded jeans to a cheap plain t-shirt. Perhaps he was once something in the music world but he meant nothing to Jack.

Jack looked around the tatty bar while the barman eyed him suspiciously. There was no way anyone could make a living from the place and remain on the right side of the law. It had to be a front, an empty bar hiding shadier dealings within. Jack smiled, knowing it gave him the opportunity he craved. He slapped the photo down, with the barman feigning indifference to the act.

"Tell me who this is or I'm telling Gregor Banks that you are skimming from him."

There was no response.

"Do you like hospital food?"

Still no response.

"I'll see you in the morgue tomorrow."

Jack turned and walked to the door. He got as far as three steps before a pathetic voice squeaked behind him.

"It's Mark Simpson but I didn't tell you that."

Jack continued to walk. He ignored the quiet words, only for them to be replaced by a scream.

"I told you, it's Mark Simpson!"

Jack turned and walked back a couple of paces while trying to offer a façade of boredom.

"A regular?"

"For a while. He's not been in for ages."

"Don't pull that one. We both know he's dead. The only question is whether you are going to save your skin and tell me where the body is."

"I don't know. Honestly, I don't know."

"You can tell that to Gregor Banks. Hopefully, he believes you more than I do."

Jack turned and walked out quickly. He knew his stunt would be seen through if he stayed for a longer conversation. He had bigger fish to catch, not some dodgy landlord who couldn't hurt a fly. He had thrown out his bait. All he had to do now was wait for it to be taken.

***

Gregor Banks was enjoying his moment in the sun. He had walked free from the court and had been declared an innocent man. It had been done with enough encouragement from the judge to put him in credit for a long time. Words such as 'police vendetta' and 'pursued a personal case against him' were music to his young ears. They were also valuable currency that could be used for future battles to come.

The press interest was what pleased him most. It was always nice to be one up on the police, but to do it with the press onside was better. He was the victim, a law-abiding businessman jealously persecuted by a rogue officer. If the press were stupid enough to believe that, he would be the first to take advantage. His father had told him never to miss an opportunity, shortly before York's so-called finest had locked him up.

The meeting location was sophisticated for Gregor Banks. A small cafe on one of York's bridges felt a little upmarket. He never knew any of their names but it was one the tourists would lap up. He selected a table while his two goons sat separately in the opposite corner. They almost filled the space, with only four tables in the entire place. They had taken two of them and changed the atmosphere in the room.

"I'll have a cup of tea and so will the happy couple over there," announced Gregor.

Two stern faces stared across. They looked ridiculous. Two oversized men were squeezed onto tiny chairs around a table they could barely get a single knee under. Gregor had always told them to blend in. In such surroundings, that was impossible.

"What sort, sir?" asked the waiter.

"Hot tea."

"Do you want Darjeeling, Earl Grey, Lapsang Souchong..."

"Isn't that a dog, boss?"

"No, you clown, it's a Chinese tea. Remind me where I got you from. No, better still, please don't." The waiter smiled politely before Gregor continued. "Have you got Tetley?"

"Tetley?"

"Yeah, Tetley, as in tea bags."

"I'll see what I can do, sir."

You could sense the disappointment in the waiter. Gregor Banks smiled. It was always good to put a posh boy in his place. He had to be the owner to be taking a cup of tea so seriously. The drink only needed to be wet and hot. There was no requirement for fancy names when he just wanted a cup of tea put on the table.

Andy Hutton arrived five minutes later. Like Gregor, he preferred to arrive early, only to find himself gazumped by the man he was meeting. He looked surprised and then immediately clocked the goons. It saw him hesitate in the stone doorway, which was enough to get Gregor's attention.

"Come in, they are on leads and muzzled."

Hutton was still unsure of the surroundings. All his warning systems told him it was not a place to meet. Eventually, he stepped inside and took a seat by the door. He pulled a chair back from the table to create separation between them.

"Tetley for you as well, sir?"

Andy Hutton glanced up at the waiter. A drink was the last thing on his mind when his senses were on edge. He looked across at Gregor Banks and then at the goons, all of whom appeared to be staring intently. His stomach was turning at the thought of self-preservation, knowing one wrong move would put him in trouble.

"Coffee's fine."

"What sort, we have..."

"Just get him a bloody coffee," barked Gregor Banks. "He doesn't give a toss where it comes from."

There was a tone of menace in the voice. Not a man renowned for patience, the waiter had exhausted every bit Gregor had. He took the hint and disappeared behind his counter before the exchange became more fraught. Gregor turned and, with a friendly smile forced onto his face, looked directly at Hutton.

"Sorry about that. He would have flown you over to Colombia to hand-pick the beans. Now, you were interested in seeing me."

"I think you asked to see me, Mr Banks."

"It's Gregor and whatever. The point is I might have an exclusive for you."

Such words made Andy Hutton feel better already. Sources with exclusives were as rare as hen's teeth, especially ones that came to you. He flexed his face in an attempt to relax. It forced the stiffness from it as he picked a voice recorder out of his pocket.

"Do you mind if I record this?"

"Please don't. Let's agree on the parameters and then we'll work out the detail. Everything is off the record until we shake hands."

Hutton nodded. He knew that Gregor Banks was not somebody you would choose to double-cross.

"Okay, what's the proposition?"

"I will give you an exclusive on how the city's police force framed my father and then pursued a personal vendetta to go after me. I can give you witnesses, quotes and the culmination of them being disgraced in court, all from the inside track."

"And in return?"

"I give you a little something to run with on Jack Husker."

"You certainly know how to position a deal."

"Think about it. There's my number. Give me a buzz when you've made up your mind but don't leave it too long. There are other interested parties."

There was nobody else and everyone knew it. It did not stop Hutton from sweeping up the professional-looking business card thrown onto the table.

"Three teas and a coffee, sir."

Gregor Banks took one look at the waiter carrying the drinks on a silver tray. He reached up and placed a twenty-pound note in his top pocket. It was patted twice and offered with a smile.

"Keep them, son. I don't drink cheap tea."

***

Lisa walked into the office to find Jack standing beside a filing cupboard. It shocked her to see him so keen. The office was renowned for being where the oldies waited until they retired. For a few moments, she just stood and watched. She was looking at the man who had been her partner since she had first arrived from Newcastle. It was hard not to be impressed by him at times, only to have your head in your hands for the rest of it.

"Putting on weight, Jack?"

He turned to face her. His immediate reaction was to suck in his stomach. He was carrying a few pounds but was hardly a barrel. Excessive food was never an issue compared to his drinking.

"No, why did you say that?"

"No reason. It must just be the way you were standing."

She had to turn away to stop herself sniggering, her wind-up a direct response to the barbs he had made about her previously. It took him a moment to realise what she was playing at. Even then, he patted himself on the bottom while wondering if he was losing the battle.

"Still an elite athlete, I'm pleased to report."

Jack scowled across the room at a middle-aged copper who was about to butt into their conversation. It would be the only respite he might get from the monotony of his day. Jack felt the same, conscious that Lisa was also his only distraction. She was one he was not willing to share with anyone else in the room.

"What brings you here?"

"I just thought I'd see how you were getting along."

"You mean, you are here to check up on me."

"Perhaps. Before you wonder, I'm here for myself, not on anyone else's orders."

Jack believed her even if he was not prepared to let his guard down straight away. DCIs were masters at such games and able to get people to do their bidding without them even knowing it. There was no way he was going to let her in that easily. Instead, he would keep up the charade and wait for the right moment to play his hand.

"I'm pleased you came. Thank you."

"What are you working on?"

It was a classic DCI question and one that put the shutters straight back down. Two corridors away was Lang; for all Jack knew he could be listening in.

"A couple of cases."

"You don't give much away, do you, Jack?"

"Walls have ears and so do Detective Chief Inspectors."

"I can promise you I'm not bugged. Trust me, I wouldn't have room in this skirt and don't you dare say anything."

Lisa patted her bottom twice in quick succession. She regretted it immediately when the sound attracted the attention of four other officers.

"I wouldn't do that," laughed Jack. "You'll start a feeding frenzy around here."

"I won't hold my breath waiting for someone to rescue me."

Lisa's mobile rang, interrupting the flow of the exchange. She swiped the screen, picking up the call on its second ring. Her face changed to a serious look to end any hint of flirtation. Jack sensed their conversation was coming to a premature end.

"I'll be there in a few minutes, sir. I'm just finishing something off."

"Good case?" Jack asked as she ended the call.

"Sorry, Jack. I'm under express instructions not to share anything with you."

"Lang?"

"I'm afraid so. Now, you never did tell me what you are working on."

Jack thought for a moment and paused. Like Lisa, he was not supposed to share anything around the station. Chinese walls they called it, or was that a takeaway? Either way, he did not care whether he followed any rules.

"Mark Simpson. Heard of him?"

"Can't say I have."

How did a man go missing in York and nobody realised? Indeed, how many others had also disappeared without a trace? It made no sense unless someone was controlling it and that brought him back to the man he was determined to nail.

"You soon will have. The trap has been set and it will catch someone in the next twenty-four hours. I've got one person running already."

"Not illegally, I hope."

"Of course not though I might have rattled him a little."

"Does this involve Gregor Banks?"

"How would I know?"

"Jack!"

Lisa's voice raised as she moved through his name. Her tone emphasised the warning Lang had given him. Jack shrugged as a bit of excitement began to flow through his veins.

"Look, the trap's out. I cannot control who swims into it."

"But you can put a bait out that only one fish likes."

He smiled. Lisa was starting to get it.

"Okay, so what are you working on for the rest of the day?"

"I was about to pick a new case when you came in and started admiring my figure."

Lisa blushed. It was a conversation that she needed to end.

"I better go," she mumbled unconvincingly.

"Why don't you pick a case for me?" offered Jack.

She shrugged and walked over to the filing cabinet. All eyes followed her until Jack's scowl sent distracted heads back to work. Lisa reached into the drawer and then stopped. With her hand poised, she turned towards him.

"Any preference?"

"Pick any. Try to get one from the last few years. I would like someone from my lifetime."

"Okay, any time from the last hundred years it is."

"Remember, I control the sharks in here," warned Jack.

Lisa reached in and pulled at a file. It was a struggle, the drawer packed full to overflowing. It needed emptying ten years ago and yet files had continued to be stuffed in. No matter how hard she pulled, she could only get one corner out, leaving it stuck at a diagonal slant.

"Try that one but you'll have to get it out. I better go."

"No worries. Thanks for popping in to see me. I mean it."

"I know you do, Jack."

Jack watched her walk away. He wished it was the two of them being summoned by DCI Lang. All he had to look forward to was more of the same and a room full of officers waiting to die.

"Coffee, sir?"

It was one of the youngest who was offering. In his early twenties, with a face too fresh for the office, he looked so out of place. Jack refused and then watched how the others took advantage of him. In time, the lad would learn. For now, he would be making all the drinks. The older officers were always looking for someone to do their work and the young kid seemed to fit the role perfectly.

Jack pushed the drawer of the cabinet closed. The raised file prevented it from slamming shut. He tried to force it down but it was wedged. There was no option other than to drag it out. With a sharp tug, the folder flew out, sending sheets of paper and photos up in the air. They landed across the floor, filling the space between the desks.

"Hey, Jack, get the kid to pick that lot up when he's got the drinks in."

Jack ignored the comment and swept everything up in a couple of minutes. He threw it in a heap on his desk, with only half of the papers back in the folder. Then he slumped down onto his chair and put his head in his hands. The reality of his new job hit him like a sledgehammer. There was no hiding it; Jack had been put out to grass.

"I've brought you a coffee. I know you said you didn't want one but I got you one anyway."

Jack parted his hands and looked up. The young lad stood holding the drink. Jack shook his head, smiled and took it from the offered hand.

"Thanks, you're a good lad. You'll do okay. What's your name?"

"Will."

Jack held out his hand and shook Will's with a firm grip.

"I'm Jack. Will, a word of advice. Don't let that lot take advantage of you. If you give an inch, they'll take a mile. Has anyone fetched you a drink yet?"

A shake of the head confirmed what Jack already knew.

"Fine, I'll get the next one. If I'm getting them in, they'll have to take their turn as well. Now, do you fancy giving me a hand with this case?"

Excitement spread across the lad's face. He was just an admin, not someone expected to do real police work. He nodded eagerly. Jack beckoned him to pull up a chair, signalling an end to the mundane tasks that filled his day.

"Where do we start?" Will asked.

"Why don't we go through the file the lady picked?" shrugged Jack.

"You mean the one with the tight skirt?"

Jack smiled. The glint in the kid's eye reminded him of himself some twenty years ago.

CHAPTER 5

THE VICE-LIKE GRIP CLOSED around the man's throat. Words were a struggle to get out when his narrow airway was having to choose between breathing and speaking. Not that he was given the two options. The decision of whether to respond was immaterial to the thug squeezing the life out of him.

"Mr Banks, I've told you everything."

Gregor Banks showed disinterest. He gazed around at the tatty walls of the pub. It cried out for burning petrol, to consign its dowdy interior to history. He looked at a tray of glasses on the bar. Empties from the night before, still not washed and ready to use. There was no pride in the place, no standards maintained. It would hardly be a loss if it went up in smoke. Gregor reached up and tipped the tray off the wooden surface, the glasses splintering into shards as they hit the floor.

"Oops."

"Mr Banks, I didn't tell him, argh!"

The hand tightened around his windpipe, making speaking impossible. He felt dizzy, his head heavy from the lack of oxygen meeting his lungs. Only the strength of the thug held him up. That support was not going to be provided for much longer.

"What shall I do with him, boss?"

Gregor Banks offered nothing. His feet pressed the broken glass into the grubby carpet. He dragged a foot, grinding a piece into dust. With slow footsteps, he walked and gazed around the front room. A small window caught his eye, the dirty pane of glass separating them from the outside world. It was framed by two washed-out curtains.

"You really should do some cleaning around here. I hate working in such an environment. It's not good for my health."

Gregor pulled the curtains closed. The reduction in light was barely noticeable. He took out a handkerchief and wiped his hands to remove any filth he had picked up.

"Ask him again, Bench."

"You heard him. What did you say?"

The ogre's grip eased. Briefly, it allowed a small amount of air to pass into the barman's lungs. The shock caused him to cough, his gag reflex making for some unpleasantness. There were no words, just spluttering. Gregor Banks turned and looked with menace, his face confirming his growing lack of patience.

Slowly, Gregor walked towards him. It was done at a pace designed to unsettle, with his eyes never once leaving his victim. The barman went pale and forced out enough breath to plead for mercy. Just two words came out before Bench squeezed down on his throat for a final time.

"Last chance," whispered Gregor Banks. His face pressed as close to the barman's as he could get without making contact. "I won't ask you again."

A nod to Bench allowed a momentary release. It was only going to be for a second. Bench eased his grip and waited for an instruction to finish him.

"I told him about Mark Simpson. I only gave his name, I'm sorry."

"You told who?"

"The detective guy. Middle-aged, short, stocky."

"And looks like he doesn't give a shit?" queried Gregor.

"That's the one."

"Jack Husker," muttered Gregor. Instinctively, the barman offered a feint nod in recognition. "I can see he and I are going to fall out, big time."

The barman's head bowed, leaving his chin resting on the enormous claw around his neck. Any movement from the ogre and his life would be over. Gregor Banks looked at him and saw a pitiful man begging pathetically. He was not worth it. He shook his head at Bench who allowed his hold to soften. Gregor took a deep breath and dropped the barman with a fearsome punch to the stomach. His legs gave way, the henchman releasing his grip in perfect timing to allow his body to drop to the floor.

"Leave him. It's not worth sullying my reputation with this one. After all, the press reckon I'm the good guy and anyway, we have bigger fish to fry."

***

Jack and Will laid out each piece of information. There were photos, witness statements and even a postcard. They were all offerings of relevance to the case that Lisa had picked out. Will had kindly dragged four tables together, allowing each piece of evidence to be set out. For such a case, there was a surprising amount of information. It was also intriguing, for it was not one person but two disappearances in one night. Jack went straight to the report.

'Pauline and Terry Johnson went missing on the night of the twentieth of February after visiting York Theatre Royal. They were seen leaving the theatre at approximately ten o'clock but never made it home to their house in Fulford. They were reported missing two days later by their niece, Alice Johnson. Alice had been staying with the couple when the disappearance happened.

No record of movements associated with the couple was recorded until the third of May when a postcard was received by Alice and her brother, Jamie, from the Costa del Sol. The postcard was sent by their aunt and uncle.

Subsequent investigations proved inconclusive and the case was held on file, pending confirmation that the postcard had been sent by Mr and Mrs Johnson.'

Jack looked at the summary of events on the front of the file. The names were not familiar, but why would they be? It was a missing persons' case, not a murder. His own life had been too entwined with catching a serial killer when it happened. Missing aunts and uncles were the least of his concern, particularly those who were able to send postcards.

"Will, is any of this familiar to you?"

It was a question Jack knew the answer to. He felt the need to ask, just to make the lad feel important.

"Afraid not. I only joined six months ago."

"Oh good. It sounds like that girl with the tight skirt has picked a cracker for us."

Jack's words brought a blush from Will. He smiled, forcing a grin from the young lad. Already, he had a sense that the two of them might enjoy working together. The lad had more about him than anyone else in the office.

"Shall I get some coffee?" asked Will.

"No, I'll get them. You start reading through what we've got."

Will grew visibly in stature. It was the first drink anyone had fetched for him in his six months at the station. It felt good that someone saw him as more than a waiter.

"I'm getting a couple of coffees for myself and Will. Any of you lazy arses want one?"

There were a couple of mumbled voices though no one lifted their head to acknowledge the offer. It suited Jack and allowed him to make the quick detour for two murky cups of station coffee. It was hardly appetising but it was free for the time being. The Chief Inspector wanted to change that, only to be thwarted in his efforts. No matter how bad it tasted, there was always merit to something that was free.

"Ah, Jack, how's it going?"

Jack turned to see DCI Lang standing behind him. He appeared different as if he had made a little more effort with his appearance. Jack looked him up and down, trying to work out what it was. Lang answered the question that even Jack would never dream of asking.

"Are you wondering why I look less stressed?"

Jack shrugged and said nothing. He didn't need to.

"It's because I'm not managing you anymore. Now, joking aside, can I have a word?"

"If you must. Can I take the coffee back first?"

"You're not pulling that one. It'll only take a moment."

Jack followed Lang into a side office. It was a small glass room with enough space for a table and four chairs. It was similar to an interview room except that it had light. Lang sat on the corner of the table in a manner very unlike him. It hinted at an informal chat. Jack was too savvy to fall into that trap. He chose to stand rather than have his superior tower over him.

"Close the door."

"Oh, one of those words," said Jack.

Jack pushed the door into the frame behind him and leaned back against the glass. He placed his hands in his pockets, offering up the look of a disgruntled teenager. It never suited him and yet it served a purpose, giving the impression he would not accept any form of authority.

"Care to sit, Jack?"

"No, sir. Bit of sciatica playing up, so I'll be better standing."

"Sorry to hear that. I won't be long. I know you've got important work to do. Did I see you with young Will earlier?"

"That's right. I was just showing the lad some basics. He seems a bright kid."

"He is. Just make sure you don't teach him any of your ways."

"I don't know what you mean, sir."

"Let me offer one example to you. I bumped into David Moss at a function. Does the name ring a bell?"

"I can't say it does. I would have to check whether I got an invite to that one."

"You didn't. They don't normally invite people who tip their drinks over people's heads. Does that ring a bell?"

"Are you sure it was me? It seems a terrible waste of a drink."

"He gave a pretty good description of you."

"It could still be anyone."

"And he gave a name. Look, Jack, he isn't going to make a complaint but do me a favour and stay away from him. You're hardly a favourite at the moment here or with the press. Plus, we don't want any grudges with our new council leader."

"Sir, I don't do grudges."

"No, you're too busy having fights to do grudges."

"Something like that."

"Anyway, Jack, how are you keeping...really?"

"I'm okay. I'm bored of shuffling paper already."

"Then give me a reason to bring you back. Jack, you are a good detective but I need a period of calm and having pub rows doesn't help anyone."

"Well, he asked for it. He was being a dick."

"You could turn the other cheek."

"Sir? You want me to point my backside at him?"

"Jack!"

"Is that it, sir?"

"Yes, but remember, I am watching you."

"Then buckle up, sir. You're in for an exciting ride."

When Jack returned with two coffees, Will had sorted all the paperwork into some form of order. The lad looked industrious, with his eyes skimming through the information in front of him. Jack said nothing. He waited for Will to look up until he got a sense that the drinks would be cold long before his concentration had been broken.

"I didn't know what you wanted, so I've got you a white coffee, no sugar."

Will looked surprised at the offering even if Jack had said he would be getting them. He took it from the DI and blew carefully onto the froth. Only then did he take a suspicious sip. It still didn't feel right for someone else to get him a drink.

"That looks like a pretty decent start," said Jack.

"Yeah, there's a lot there. I wasn't sure what to do with it, so I put it in date order."

"That is as good an option as anything. Let's walk through what there is."

Jack lifted each item from the table and scanned it. Will was right, there was a lot to review. Indeed, there was too much. The police notes would make for interesting reading. They offered a copious amount of facts about two people who had simply disappeared.

"Any thoughts on where to start?" asked Will.

"Yes, every good case starts with coffee," smiled Jack.

For the first time in his brief working life, the lad felt relaxed. Perhaps even relaxed enough to take a step backwards and enjoy the drink he had been brought. He had heard about Jack's reputation and yet none of it felt true. To date, he had only found him kind and supportive, rather than the cantankerous grouch he had been told about.

Jack was the first to finish. He scrunched his cup and threw it towards the bin. It missed, leaving a stain on the floor where the remnants of the drink landed.

"I'll get a cloth," said Will.

"No, you won't. Leave it, I'll sort it later. We have proper police work to do."

Will finished his drink and placed his cup in the bin. He picked Jack's up before he could stop him. He left the small mess on the floor but felt better after clearing up the thrown cup.

"Okay, I'm ready," enthused Will. "What are we going to do?"

"We start at the beginning. What's the first thing we've got in date order?"

Will beamed inside. It felt good to be contributing. Jack picked up the report from the night of the disappearance. It contained little more than the summary he had looked at previously. The term 'out of character' was used frequently in the words he read. Already, a missing persons' case seemed an inappropriate term when all the logical conclusions suggested otherwise. Yet no one had reported a murder, nor had any bodies been found. Jack knew it was difficult to conclude foul play without a prima facie stiff to hang your hat on.

"Okay, what's next, Will? That report hasn't got much in it."

"Statements from the people who were there on the night."

"Who have we got?"

"There are a lot of statements from other people at the theatre. The doorman remembers the Johnsons because they were overly polite. We've even got a beggar at the door who they handed some change to and then there is this lot."

Will handed Jack a pack of statements. The set was clipped together to signify a connection. There were pages of it, all neatly typed up, each with a signature scribbled on the bottom. It contained three documents in total, indicating a party linked in some way.

Jack sat down and read through them. They came from a ghost-walking party, all of whom offered a similar account. All three of them were named. Jack noted the people – a tour guide, the son of a Lib-Dem Councillor and a student from a university he knew only too well. Someone was missing. A fourth member of the group was referred to by all but the councillor's son. Her identity was unknown and her statement was missing from the pack.

"Will, are you sure there isn't another statement?"

"Definitely not. They were fastened. Why?"

"These are the statements from a tour group who witnessed a white van in the area. Each of them saw it and all but one of them reference a group of four. Yet only three people are named and provided statements."

"Do you think the fourth has something to do with the disappearance?"

"I think the fourth has something to hide. Mind you, I would be pretty ashamed if I'd spent an evening listening to the drivel they spout on one of those ghost tours."

"I quite like them," said Will. "They do see a lot of ghosts."

"Who does?"

"I was speaking to one of the guides and he says he has seen loads."

"Really? So the one person who needs to see them to make a living sees plenty but no one else does. That would be a tricky investigation. I'll let you work that one out."

"I think I just have," blushed Will.

"Good work. We'll make a detective of you yet. Now, your job is to work out who the mystery fourth person is. I'm going to line up a meeting with the niece who reported them missing. I've got a feeling she might have a fair bit to say."

"Do you want to take this?"

Will offered Jack the postcard. It was handwritten and postmarked from the Costa del Sol. The greeting was brief and confirmed that the couple were well. That card was the only evidence to suggest they were still alive. It felt odd to Jack that it did not appear to have been followed up on.

"Good thinking. I'll see if I can get a cross-reference on the handwriting. Now, there is one other thing."

"What's that?" asked Will eagerly.

"It's your turn to get the coffee. There's always time for another one of them."

***

Jack left the station pleased with his day's work. It felt like the first bright moment since he had been forced into the department. He had a case to get his teeth into; one that patently did not add up. Better still, he had some company to help him on his quest. Maybe Will was not up to Lisa's standards and certainly not as alluring, but there was no doubting the lad's enthusiasm for the job.

He popped in to see Dan as an excuse to leave early. His appointment with the niece was set up for the following day, meaning everything could wait for now. At least his colleague was pleased to see him even if he was tired from another session with his physio. Dan yawned as he invited his colleague into his flat.

"She put me on the treadmill. She's got a bit of a cruel streak."

"Admit it, you love it."

Dan blushed. He found it hard to disagree when his body let him down in his efforts to hide it. A bit older than his normal type, she was more than a distraction for an injured officer attempting to convalesce.

"Coffee?" asked Dan.

"Not got anything stronger?"

"No, it's coffee only, I'm afraid."

Jack sighed in a manner that suggested desperation.

"What are you working on?" Dan asked. It was an encouraging sign in Jack's eyes.

"The disappearance of a couple just after you got shot. Do you remember it?"

"Funnily enough, no. I was in a coma."

They both laughed. It was a stupid question and one which demanded an equivalent answer. Dan never held back. He allowed his frustrations to be released in one short quip. Jack could forgive Dan for not having any recollection. Yet it still seemed strange that two people could go missing and so few people knew about it.

"And how's the convalescing going?"

"Boring. I can cope with the physio; it's the counselling that drives me around the twist."

"Why, is she not as attractive as the physio?"

Dan blushed again.

"No, he isn't. He just thinks everything is a reflex from a childhood experience."

"Even getting shot?"

"It would appear so."

It was the last humorous thought in Jack's head before Dan handed him a coffee. Jack gazed at it with suspicion. Dan's distracted state had seen him hand over something that appeared to be milk with floating granules. Jack smiled and offered his gratitude before starting to examine places it could be tipped. The pot plant was the favourite, a large overgrown house plant that stood to waist height. There was plenty of room under the foliage to lose at least a half cup of the pale milky liquid. For now, he just held it, allowing the warmth to soak into his hands. As soon as Dan turned his back, Jack knew he would strike swiftly.

Dan talked fondly about his time in the station and how close he felt he was to a return. It was an encouraging sign after such a bad injury. He was positive and looking forward to his future, perhaps for the first time, even if Jack could sense some denial in his words.

"Do you want some sugar in your coffee?"

"No, thanks."

Jack cursed his missed opportunity to send Dan to the kitchen. "Biscuit?"

"That would be great."

His disappearance saw half the cup poured into the plant, just before Dan returned.

"Sorry, I've only got digestives."

"That's fine."

Dan leaned over with the packet and looked down at Jack. He seemed shocked by what he saw while Jack wondered what was wrong. A glance at the plant almost gave his guilt away.

"I don't know how you can drink it when it's that temperature. I can't get near mine."

"You know what they say about good coffee. Enjoy it while it's hot."

Jack smiled. It was a good recovery from an awkward moment and bought him time to formulate a plan to dispose of the rest.

"Are you sure I can't interest you in a swift one down The Cellars?"

"I'd better not."

"Don't worry, I'll have one for you."

Jack accepted his colleague's best wishes and shook his hand. He deposited his cup in the kitchen, tipping the last quarter down the sink. It had been good work to get away with two small swigs of the disgusting drink. He never pushed Dan to join him for anything stronger. He always offered but was aware there were barriers. Dan would never return as the officer he once was, no matter how much the young lad tried to claim otherwise. He was lucky to be alive even if Dan had not yet worked that out.

***

The thought of Dan's coffee was a distant memory when Jack walked into The Cellars. He gazed at the beer which Alf poured, his lips longing to encircle the glass and absorb the golden creamy liquid. He smiled, never tiring of that sight. His money was on the top of the bar, waiting to be exchanged for the one form of pleasure in his life. In many ways, that role should have been taken by Mary. Somehow, things never worked out the way they should have done.

"Just the one tonight, Jack?"

"As always, Alf."

A smile of acknowledgement was offered by both sides. Alf knew that Jack spent too long in The Cellars but then so did others. Without that band of hardened drinkers, there would be no pub. Nobody likes a drunk and yet no landlord likes the sober folk who never enter through the door.

"Going to drink this one?"

"Yes, why?"

"Not going to pour it over someone's head? That killed the party, I can tell you. I reckon you cost me a few hundred quid that night."

"Oh, sorry. He was being a bit of a pompous arse."

"Maybe, but he was a pompous arse who was spending a lot of money."

"Sorry."

For once, Jack felt guilty. He liked Alf and respected him for the way he went about his work. He knew when to draw the line without being overly fussy. More importantly, he didn't hold grudges when Jack frequently slipped to the wrong side of that line.

"Anyway, your usual seat is free."

"I might sit at the bar tonight."

That was unusual. Jack hated the bar seats. It came with the inference of chatting with others. He liked solitude; the ability to sit in the corner and watch the room. He preferred to get lost in his thoughts. Tonight, Jack was in a very different mood.

He drank slowly while opening his pad up to go through the timeline. From the night of the Johnsons' disappearance to the postcard sent to the niece and nephew, Jack mentally walked through each of the pieces of information. Twice, he circled the postcard. It seemed so out of place and yet, from the moment it arrived, it had defined the case. Why was it so long before it was sent? He had been on holiday and sent cards. Even the Spanish postal service didn't take that long. He laughed. Sometimes, it did.

"Another one, Jack?"

He looked up to see Alf holding his glass. It was empty and unusual that he hadn't even noticed. Jack looked down at his pad, then up again, before shaking his head. It caught the landlord by surprise.

"No, I'm going to get off."

"Really? Are you feeling alright?"

"I think so. I might take a little walk."

Jack bid Alf goodnight and headed out onto the streets. He sucked in deep lungfuls of air. It felt good to be out in the city, with his head clear of the effects of alcohol. The postcard was on his mind. Instinctively, he patted his jacket to check it was still there. It was and it would be put in front of the niece. It had to be the key. Either the postcard was the defining evidence to prove they were alive or it was the piece that would unlock a sinister outcome.

York was quiet. The usual evening throng was remarkably absent. Sometimes the city could be ghostly for no reason and at other times you could not hear yourself think. It was one of the charms of the place and yet that silence could only last for so long.

"Well, look who we have here. Good evening, Detective Inspector."

Jack looked up to see Gregor Banks flanked by two of his goons. He sighed. He was not in the mood for his rival. Work was occupying his mind and leaving Gregor as an unwanted irritation.

"I heard you were out looking for me."

"No, I've been told to stay away from you. I'm on missing persons now."

"Is that where they've hidden you? Are you finding many of them in the pub?"

"One or two. Everyone likes a drink."

Jack continued to walk, only for the two henchmen to step across his path. He recognised them, both creatures he had run into before. He took a step to the side, as did they, forcing him to stop and look into Gregor Banks's eyes."

"Leave it, I'm not in the mood."

"And I'm not in the mood for you to go throwing your weight about with one of my publicans."

"One of yours?"

"Figure of speech. It's one of the places I like to drink."

"Yeah, right. Even I know you wouldn't be seen dead in a place like that."

"You might be if you go around making wild accusations."

"Is that a threat?"

"I don't threaten people. I'm a businessman, as the judge rightly concluded."

The barb hurt, forcing Jack to take a step back from the argument.

"I'm just following up on a missing person, that's all. It is my job."

"Just don't bring my name into it or you might find yourself joining the list to investigate and before you ask, yes, that is a threat."

Jack bristled. He made an involuntary movement towards Gregor Banks. The path towards him was immediately sealed off. He wanted to punch him and drive his fist through the gangster's face. Gregor had that effect even if the likelihood of it happening was remote.

"Get out of my way or I'll be putting Timmy Jackson at the top of the investigation list."

It was Gregor's turn to recoil. The name hit a nerve. It broke a gentlemen's agreement as something which should never be repeated. The ogres parted, putting the two men nose to nose. Gregor reached for Jack's throat, only for it to be pushed away. One of the ogres took hold of Jack while the other was more respectful with Gregor. As they were eased apart, two venomous sets of eyes never blinked.

The stand-off was broken by flashing blue lights. A police car pulled up, splitting the group apart. Gregor Banks took a few steps away as the henchman released his grip on Jack. It was a poor attempt to present a normal façade.

"Can I help, gentlemen?" asked an officer.

Jack flashed his warrant card and walked clear of the group. Neither Gregor nor his thugs did anything to stop his safe passage.

"Yes, you can. I need a lift home."

"Another time, Jack," muttered Gregor Banks. "Another time."

Chapter 6

THE ATMOSPHERE WAS FROSTY. Jack had never felt so unwelcome in another person's house. Opposite him, sat Alice and Jamie Johnson, their icy stares peering across the kitchen table. It felt distinctly unpleasant. Not even a drink had been offered to suggest that he should get comfortable in their presence.

Jack paused and gazed around the cluttered kitchen. It had all the traits of an older couple, with knick-knacks on every shelf. Items were squeezed in as if they should be treasured for eternity. In many ways, it resembled his own home, which he could not muster the energy to clear up.

"How long did your aunt and uncle live here?"

"They still live here," growled Jamie. He was quick to respond and butted in before Alice could answer.

"Okay, how long have they lived here?"

"Thirty-plus years, I guess," offered Alice. Her voice was a little softer though no less curt in her answer.

"And when did you move in?"

"Not long ago," continued Alice. "We went through this when they were first reported missing."

"And how long is 'not long'?"

"You guys never listen to anything, do you? How many times do we have to go through this? They are not missing. They are in Spain."

It was Jamie who was first to show his frustration. Jack figured Alice would not be far behind. He sensed he would have to do something special to get them onside, probably at risk of bending a few rules.

"When do you reckon they'll come back?"

The question was directed to Alice. It made no difference, for Jamie continued to take the lead with the answers.

"I'm not sure they will. Why would they, the weather's better in Spain?"

"Any thoughts of joining them?"

"No, we don't speak Spanish."

"Do they?"

"How would we know?"

"You are their niece and nephew."

"We were only here for a few months before they left," interrupted Alice.

"Thank you."

A breakthrough. It was a long-winded way to answer the question, but it was a response. Perhaps it was the first direct response to any question he had posed. Jack took out his pad and laid it on the table. Studiously, he looked at the timeline and wondered when he would play his hand.

"Did you say you were putting the kettle on?"

"No," insisted Jamie.

"Could you?"

"Is this going to take long?" snarled Alice.

"Not if my throat isn't dry," smiled Jack.

Alice huffed loudly. Reluctantly, she dragged herself to her feet. She filled the kettle and looked at Jamie, who shook his head to confirm that she was making drinks for one. It made no difference to Jack. A cup of coffee was just as good when drunk alone.

"Tea or coffee?"

"Coffee, just milk."

"I've only got tea," sneered Alice.

"Tea is fine."

Jack read through his notes again. The conversation ceased while his drink was made. He sat back and waited, drowned out by the noise of the kettle. It took a couple of minutes and then a steaming hot cup of something was placed before him.

It did not look much like tea. In the time the tea bag was dunked in and out, it had barely coloured. An over-indulgence of milk had then turned it to a ghostly shade of white. Jack sighed. There was no point having that battle when he was about to start another. It was time to up the ante on the conversation.

"So, your aunt and uncle went missing on the twentieth of February. You heard nothing from them for two and a half months and then a postcard turned up on the third of May."

"That's right," shrugged Alice.

"What did you do between those two dates?"

"I reported them missing."

"Why did that take two days?"

"I left it a couple of days and then, when I had not heard anything, I called your lot. I don't like to interfere in others' business."

"And were you both living here?"

"I was," noted Alice. "Jamie was here two or three days per week."

"And where were you on the night of the twentieth?"

"I beg your pardon. If you're suggesting what I think you are, then you can get out," growled Alice.

"I am asking whether you were here to know if they returned."

A sense of calm returned to the room. It felt like Jack was playing an instrument, their mood swings responding to the words he said. It was time to have some fun with them. It was time to see if they would bite. Jack knew they would and that made it worth being patient.

"So, were you here?" Jack continued.

"Yes," said Alice.

"Were you both here?"

Alice looked furtively at Jamie and then nodded.

"And did they return?"

"No," confirmed Alice.

"What time were you awake until?"

"I don't know. We normally stay up until about eleven and then go to bed."

"At the same time?"

"Yes, but not together if that's what you are thinking," snarled Alice.

The thought was not in Jack's mind until Alice said it. Suddenly, the case had another potential angle. He shuddered at the thought, hoping it was a line of questioning he would never have to take.

"Do you think they could have come home after that time? I mean, once you were asleep."

"No, Alice is a light sleeper," offered Jamie.

A chill spread through Jack's spine. He felt queasy, with his brain wanting to explore areas the rest of him was reluctant to go.

"Okay, let's work on the premise they did not come back. Instead, they went to the theatre and then somewhere else. Did they drive there?"

"No, their car was in the garage," said Jamie.

"So, they were picked up in all likelihood and taken somewhere."

"Yes, to Spain, just as we told you," continued Jamie.

It seems a little odd to go straight after a theatre trip, don't you think?"

"No," shrugged Jamie. "It was probably a late flight."

Jack thought for a moment. He was being led up a dead end and yet something told him it was a path he had to exhaust.

"So, they were picked up and taken to either the train station or the airport," speculated Jack.

"Or the bus station," offered Alice.

"Okay, or the bus station," repeated Jack. His tone hinted at his growing sense of irritation. "Did they take their passports and clothes with them?"

"They must have," said Alice.

"Did you check?"

"Why would we?" interrupted Jamie, continuing the double-edged attack.

"Perhaps because you were concerned about their whereabouts?"

"We got a postcard from them," sneered Alice.

"Not until two and a half months later, you didn't."

"Oh."

Jack noted Alice's reaction. He sensed that she had said something she now regretted. It was obvious she was hiding something, with her evasiveness only matched by that of her brother.

"Do you think I could have a look at their room?"

"It's my room now," said Alice. "We boxed everything up and put it into the attic."

"I thought they might be coming back."

"That's why we stored everything for them."

"Did you happen to notice anything unusual in their possessions?"

"I can't say we did, did we, Jamie?" said Alice.

"No, nothing," he confirmed.

Jack slapped the postcard onto the table. He pushed it forward in front of them. Both gazed downwards and then back up at Jack, waiting for him to make the next move.

"Do you recognise this?"

"It's the postcard we gave you," said Alice. "Is it a trick question?"

"Not really. I'm just intrigued as to why you would get one postcard after two and a half months and then nothing since."

"Who said we have had nothing since?"

Jack sat up. His attention had been grabbed by a revelation that had not made the file. He waited to see if there was anything more forthcoming from Alice. She saw he was expectant as if ready to hear what she had to say.

"We've had other postcards."

"When?"

"Every two or three months."

"Can I see them?"

"We don't keep them. We read them and then throw them away. We're cluttered enough in here without hoarding anything else."

"You kept this one."

"No, we gave you that one to close off the case. Otherwise, it would be in the bin, along with the others."

"Have they sent you an address of where they are staying?"

"Spain," said Jamie.

"Spain is a big place. Was there anything more specific?"

"Costa del Sol, I think," he added.

"Keep going."

"That's it."

"Perhaps they don't want you to follow them," smiled Jack. He waited to see if his goading would create a response. When it did not, he continued. "Okay, one final question for now. How do you guys run this house when everything is in their name?"

"That's easy," said Jamie. "Just before they left they gave us power of attorney over everything."

***

In the council chamber, the noise erupted. A series of insults flew between the main protagonists. In the heat of battle, neither was prepared to take a single backward step. This was democracy York style, with little love lost between the Tories and Lib-Dems.

The adjournment was swift. The session was brought to a close to enable members to calm down. All it achieved was to take the row outside the meeting. The aftermath ignited in the ornate lobby and continued as the councillors walked.

Several younger councillors stepped in. Their attempts to separate bodies only made the affray worse. Each addition to the melee prompted another from the opposition to do likewise. Soon, a dozen councillors were pushing against one another.

The first punch landed on the cheek of Nigel Reeves outside the main chamber. Its impact knocked him to the floor. Voices were raised and another punch was thrown back in the direction of the masses. Nigel sat on the floor dazed and bewildered.

Lisa arrived a few minutes after the first police car. Her proximity to the area and the sensitivity of the matter determined the need for her to attend. When she walked in, Nigel was upright and sat on a chair at the side. His hand was clamped against his jaw. In front of him, the row continued, with two young uniforms struggling to hold back the squabbling councillors.

Lisa took one look at their efforts and knew greater action was required. She found a chair to the side of the room and climbed up to release a bellowing instruction.

"Stop, right, now! This is unacceptable! I am DS Lisa Ramsey and I want silence!"

It had all the traits of a teacher scolding her pupils. It brought an instant calm to the room. Every one of those present obeyed her and allowed their heads to bow in shame. As their eyes turned back towards her, Lisa felt a sense of self-consciousness. On the padded seat, her balance was precarious and the watchful stares did nothing to make her raised position more comfortable. To her relief, a hand reached up from one of the uniforms to help her step down to the floor.

"I want to make a complaint," barked one of the councillors. "Our leader has been assaulted."

"Who by?" she asked.

"Him!"

A hand shot out towards David Moss, who snarled. The fire in his face made it clear that he was going to react.

"Liar! I never touched him, but I would shake the hand of the man who did."

"He punched him!" yelled the accuser.

"Did you see the punch?" asked Lisa.

"No, but I know it's him. He hates him."

"He's right, I do," added David Moss.

"Did anyone else see the punch?" continued Lisa.

"No," muttered the gathering.

Lisa turned to Nigel Reeves, who remained unmoved in his chair. He looked contrite and was still nursing his jaw.

"Did you see who hit you?"

All he offered was a simple shake of his head.

"Are you sure you were deliberately punched?"

"I think so," he whispered, fighting against the pain from talking.

"But you are not sure," sighed Lisa.

"No."

"So, we have a melee, with a punch allegedly thrown. I am presuming that no one is owning up to the punch. In the scrum that followed, someone has gone down to the floor. Tell me, is this a typical day for York's elected elite?"

More heads bowed until one man shouted up.

"Are you going to charge him?"

All heads turned to the young upstart. Dressed in an ill-fitting suit, his shirt appeared torn at the collar. Lisa wondered whether it looked any different when he had put it on that morning.

"For what exactly? For throwing a punch that no one saw or being a member of the opposite party?"

"Your lot are bloody hopeless," he growled.

"Maybe," smiled Lisa. "However, we don't go around fighting in lobbies like children."

It was a point that was hard for anyone to argue with.

"Now, can I suggest you all go back to the important business you were undertaking on behalf of us taxpayers? I would like a word with the two leaders."

The uniforms ushered the throng back into the chamber. Behind them, Lisa took Nigel Reeves and David Moss aside. David looked ruffled and had a spiteful expression etched across his face. Nigel was more passive after the attack.

"I think you two are both old enough to know better."

"I am," snapped David, "but you might need to tell him that. His crowd are lunatics."

Nigel shook his head. He was in too much pain to offer anything back.

"Look, if you prefer, I can take you both in. I will hold you in a cell for twenty-four hours and then release you without charge. We haven't got anything that will stick, other than mud, which will fill the press for a few days. That can't be good for a political career, can it? Or, you could behave like adults and save me the bother."

"I love a strong woman," smirked David. "Have you got any handcuffs to go with that?"

"Sorry, only good boys get that treatment."

***

Jack was saying his goodbyes when the call came in from Will. He felt his phone vibrate in his pocket, providing a welcome distraction from Alice and Jamie Johnson. Hardly forthcoming, they had gone out of their way to make life difficult and had only offered what he could force out of them. That had taken him nearly two hours to achieve.

The power of attorney was the bombshell. It had bounced around in his head from the moment it had slipped out. A ready-made motive had been gift-wrapped and handed to him and yet it gave him nothing. It was still a missing persons' case even if it felt like he had most of the evidence he needed.

"Jack, I'm looking at the copy of the postcard. I think the postmark is Nerja."

"Nur-har? Where's that?"

"On the Costa Del Sol, east of Malaga."

"I'm impressed with your geography, Will."

"You should be more impressed with my ability to use Google maps."

"Just give me a minute to find somewhere to take some notes."

Jack walked away from the Johnsons' house towards the city. It took longer than he hoped to find somewhere to stop. He chose the first flat surface he could lay his notebook on, which was nearly halfway back towards the city.

"How do you spell 'Nur-har'?"

"N-e-r-j-a."

"That's 'Ner-jar'."

"Not in Spanish, it isn't," insisted Will.

"I'll take your word for it. I have enough trouble with English."

"The postmark is from their postal district. I can't tell you any more than that at the moment. I've tried ringing a few numbers but they are not being very helpful. I'll keep going."

"We might need to get someone over there," said Jack.

"I'll go," offered Will excitedly.

"I'm not sure I'll get clearance for that. It'll have to be a couple of officers."

Jack could hear the sigh from Will. He knew that Jack was right even if he did nothing to hide his disappointment. Briefly, Jack thought about persuading the DCI to let him take Mary. It was only a momentary thought before his memory returned and the reality of life struck. Mary was gone and they were no longer a couple. It meant Jack might have to go alone.

"Do you need me to do anything else?"

"No, once you have finished making the calls, you can get on with some other work. I think I've taken enough of your time."

As soon as the call was over, Jack stared at his pad. He pronounced the name of the town over and over again. No matter what he did, he could not make it sound like Will had. It was 'Ner-jar', in the broadest Yorkshire accent he could muster.

Jack scooped up his notepad and pushed it into his pocket. It was less than a mile to get to the city centre. A brisk walk would do it even with no need to hurry. He only had one case on the go, with the disappearance of Mark Simpson pushed to the back of his mind. For once, Jack felt like a man who was not in a rush to go anywhere.

He was less than a quarter of a mile from the station when a car pulled up. A black Mercedes with shaded windows slowed alongside him. It happened in seconds, with Jack's reflexes not as sharp as they once were. His body hit the pavement quicker than he could react. In the flurry of kicks and punches, he recognised no one. Two large well-dressed men did the deed. Jack could taste blood, his lip split from the force of the boots that pummelled him.

Jack's survival instincts kicked in and curled his body into a ball. He covered the back of his head, as well as his face. There was no need, for the beating stopped as quickly as it started. The punishment was just a warning from a foe.

"Compliments of the Guv'nor."

The words were followed by the sound of footsteps retreating to the car. The two thugs left Jack in the street before the Mercedes sped off into the distance. He never moved other than to allow his lips to offer up a name.

"Gregor Banks," muttered Jack as he grimaced and spat out a mouthful of blood.

The next set of footsteps Jack heard were lighter. They approached as quickly as those that went before them. He braced himself, expecting another kick. When it never came, he allowed his body to relax.

"Jack, is that you?"

He looked up. His vision was blurred from the savagery. The voice was familiar even if he struggled to recognise the face. Twice, he blinked, his sight not improving for doing so. Instead, he sat up and stared at the feet in front of him.

"Jack, are you alright? It's Lisa."

Lisa? Lisa? That Lisa! His bravado kicked in as soon as he made the recognition.

"Of course, I'm alright. I just got knocked over. That's all. What are you doing here?"

"I was at the council meeting. Seriously, are you alright?"

Jack pushed himself up to his feet. It was all too quick. His balance was lost, leaving him to crash sideways to the ground.

"Jack, I'm calling an ambulance."

"No, I'm fine!"

His sharpness stopped her in her tracks. It was unusual to hear Jack shout. Indeed, it might have been the first time she had heard him do so. Lisa crouched down, looked at the blood across his face and winced at the injuries she saw.

"I think we need to get you to a doctor. You're covered in blood."

"It's a flesh wound. Head wounds always bleed a lot."

"I wouldn't know."

"Trust me, I would. My first wife packed a mean right hook. The second was hardly a slouch either."

"I never had you down as a battered husband."

"There's a lot you don't know about me, Lisa."

And there was a lot she did. Lisa reached down and helped Jack up to his feet. First, it was onto one knee and then one foot at a time was eased beneath him. She held him firmly until he stood beside her. Jack was grateful for the assistance even if his pride did not allow him to say so.

"Look, I better go and get cleaned up at the station," said Jack.

"You can't go in looking like that. My flat is only around the corner. I'll take you there."

"Only if you promise to take advantage of me," laughed Jack.

Lisa smiled. That was more like the Jack she had begun to know so well.

***

It was a slow walk back to Lisa's flat. Each step was taken carefully, making progress ponderous at best. All the while, Lisa wondered if she was doing the right thing. Not just by letting Jack talk her out of accepting medical treatment but also by allowing him into her private world. They had been working partners for a year and yet it felt like they knew each other so well. From a distance, Lisa had observed Jack and, more recently, his troubles with Mary. Unsuited to any form of stability, Jack was a riddle to solve. So flawed in so many ways; so utterly enthralling in others.

A keypad provided entry to her building, one of many modern blocks that had sprung up around the city. Lisa knew it was everything Jack despised. In his current state, he was hardly likely to complain about the impact it was having on the traditional buildings around it. Jack barely looked up to see the perfect clean bricks and the identical rows of symmetrical windows. They were just a blur for a pair of eyes that were still trying to regain their focus.

"We'll take the lift. I won't drag you up the stairs."

"Thanks, you're all heart."

Even the lift was a pleasant place to be. No smells of dead animals or stale urine were present to greet the nostrils, unlike the older blocks they had to visit. Only a vase of flowers was missing to make the experience complete.

"I can see we're paying you too much," laughed Jack.

"I wish. This place is costing me a fortune. I could pay for the whole block for the same money back in Newcastle."

"Yes, and we both know what the lift would smell of."

"True enough," smiled Lisa.

Lisa's flat stood close to the lift entrance. There were only a few short steps before they entered her front door. It was small, with a tight little kitchen built to the side of the living room.

"Sorry, it's not very big."

"It looks fine to me."

"You cannot see properly!"

"I can see it's tidier than my place."

"Sit yourself down at the table. I'll just go and get changed and then clean you up."

"Are you going to put on your..."

"Don't even say it!"

Jack went silent. He sensed irritation in her tone. He had pushed the boundaries too far, leaving his colleague unimpressed by his words. He needed to get back on Lisa's good side and say something to appease her. They were words Jack knew that he needed to find quickly.

"Shall I put the kettle on?" he called out.

"No, you'll sit there. You'll get a coffee once you are cleaned up."

Lisa was only gone for a couple of minutes. It was long enough for Jack's eyes to begin to clear. She changed quickly, emerging from her bedroom to Jack's left. She wore jeans and a blue hoodie, a simple outfit made to look good in a short passage of time. Jack smiled as his eyes were drawn to her face.

In the time she had been away, Lisa had fixed her make-up. A small amount had been dabbed onto her cheeks and her lips. Her hair had been brushed and then tied back into a ponytail, all things a girl does before she treats the wounded.

"Now, are you taking anything I should be aware of?" asked Lisa.

"What is this, the medical police?"

"I thought you wanted me to play the role of a nurse."

Lisa winked. It confirmed that normality had returned, leaving Jack relieved that he had not alienated a friend.

"It's probably best I tell you what I'm not on."

"I thought as much. Just be thankful I'm not testing your blood."

"I can't have a blood test; I haven't had time to revise."

Lisa took her time, dabbing away the blood on Jack's face. She was slow and deliberate, with a supply of face towels stacked up and dipped diligently into a bowl of warm water. Occasionally, Jack winced, to signify moments of discomfort. Each time, the sting hurt more than the abrasion, not that he would ever admit it to Lisa.

With the blood cleared, all that was left was the bruising. Jack's cheeks were blackened from the blows he had taken. The marking circled the bottom of one eye, inferring the potential for a far more serious injury.

"You are going to have to get that checked out."

"It's fine. If it doesn't improve, I'll get it x-rayed."

"And are you going to tell me how this happened?"

"I told you, I got knocked over. Some idiot barged into me while running through the streets."

"Is that the only version I'm going to get?"

Jack nodded and offered a smile to confirm his words.

"Is there anywhere else that's sore and don't say anything rude or I'll be taking a leaf out of your first wife's book."

"Just my ribs."

"Come on, let's have a look at you," said Lisa as she pulled at the fabric of Jack's shirt.

"What? I'm not undressing in front of you."

"Why not? I'm hardly going to be able to give you a bed bath without you doing so."

She offered another wink. It was a smile of reassurance to put the onus back on Jack. He sighed and then unbuttoned his shirt to offer up his bare chest to his medic. There was no significant bruising, just a little soreness in the flesh on a figure that looked older than its years. Lisa touched it, with Jack's mild groans confirming nothing was broken. She pulled away and stood up to confirm the examination was over.

"What do you think?" asked Jack.

"Not bad for an old man who never eats anything green. Now, do you want that coffee?"

"I thought you'd never ask," smiled Jack.

CHAPTER 7

"COME TO SPAIN WITH me."

They were Jack's first words when he awoke on Lisa's sofa. The day before she had tended to him by dabbing away at the blood caked on his face. She had followed it up by making him a cup of coffee. Jack had never even taken a sip of it. As soon as he sat back, his eyes had dipped closed, forcing Lisa to take the cup from his grasp.

At first, she placed it on a side table. Once she realised he was in a deep sleep, she concentrated on making him comfortable. Carefully, she had taken off his shoes, laughing at the sight of his odd socks. One brown and one black; that was Jack, a man who did not give a damn about how he looked.

With great care, Lisa had lifted his legs to lay him on the sofa in her lounge. He looked so comfortable, with a spare duvet thrown over him, not that there was any shortage of warmth in her modern flat. With a pillow tucked under his head, he was one of her first overnight guests since she had moved to the city. Perhaps not one she was expecting but in an unfamiliar city, she could hardly be choosy.

"And good morning to you too, Jack."

"I've been thinking."

"I hope that is not on my sofa. My sofa is a thinking-free zone."

"Is that coffee I can hear brewing?" he asked.

Lisa scowled at the cheek of the man. Yet when did Jack follow convention? What was that about Spain and what was that about her going? Lisa's head was spinning with the torrent of thoughts that rushed through her mind.

"I'll put it on, no wait, why are you going to Spain? Hang on, let's sort out the coffee first. You should come with a warning. Man in the room; stick to one task at a time."

"No," corrected Jack. "Old man in the room. That means one task and it should be performed by somebody else. Remember, I've had a nasty fall."

"Well, old man, the bathroom is through there if you want to view your bruising. It's not as impressive as I expected."

"I'm sorry to disappoint you."

Lisa set about the task of making coffee. Her coffee machine was still new, a gift from a friend. It was only getting its third outing since it was bought. So far, her efforts had been a disaster. Now, she had a connoisseur to test it and one who would not be slow to offer his critical thoughts.

"How strong do you like it?"

"As it comes."

In Jack's language, that meant strong. Lisa was wise enough to appreciate that. She added an extra spoon of ground coffee and hoped it would hit the mark. Another one followed soon after.

When Lisa finally emerged, Jack was waiting. He was up and had checked his face in the bathroom mirror. His bed had been cleared, removing the reminder of him staying overnight. It had never been his intention. That left a sense of guilt as he wondered how Lisa might treat him. He would drink his coffee and leave quickly, so as not to intrude any longer than he had to.

That was until he took the first mouthful of coffee. It was delightful, the taste like nectar in his sore mouth. He looked up and saw Lisa sipping a drink of her own. Her made-up face was just as attractive as it had been the day before. It was hard not to stare and risk their friendship even if a small part of him sensed some attraction.

"What's the plan?" she asked.

"I'm heading back to the station to follow up on the case I'm working on. Anyway, you never answered. Are you coming to Spain?"

Jack's mobile rang before she had the chance to respond. Its irritating tone spoiled the moment of the conversation. It was DCI Lang, a man Jack had heard little from since his change of jobs. Despite that, he still remembered how to recognise anger in his tone.

"Jack, where are you?"

"I'm just grabbing a coffee."

"Get back to the station. I need to see you immediately."

"On my way."

Jack shrugged and handed the empty cup to Lisa. She smiled, gazing at him a little too long. Her face flushed red to give away her thoughts. It forced her to look away and hurry back to the kitchen with both cups gripped tightly in her hands.

"Great coffee," called out Jack. "Can I come back to this cafe more often?"

Lisa nodded and walked back into the room as Jack made his move towards her and the front door.

"I think I'll squeeze you in. Now go steady."

They almost kissed, only for it to be aborted into a hug. It was a near miss and yet a suggestion that they were more than just colleagues. They held each other for a couple of seconds and then broke apart. Once separated, Jack thanked her and embarked on his walk to the station.

***

Jack went straight into DCI Lang's office when he arrived. His superior stared at Jack for longer than usual. It took him a moment to process his thoughts and less time to say what he was thinking. When he did, it was blunt and offered little compassion in his tone.

"Sit down, Jack. What happened to your face?"

"I was hit by the ugly stick at birth."

"Don't be flippant. Just tell me if I need to know."

"I got barged over in the street. Some idiot was in a hurry"

"And you managed to land on both sides of your face. That's impressive."

"I bounced. I'm not as slim as I once was. I might have to finally admit my hopes of making the Olympic gymnastics team are over."

"Are you sure?"

"Yes, the leotards don't come in my colour."

"I'll put it down as an accident. Does any other part of you hurt? Keep it to the relevant parts."

"Only my pride, sir."

"I don't think that will be a serious wound. That has taken its share of knocks over the years."

"Don't rub it in, sir."

"Anyway, as nice as it is to talk, I've had a complaint."

"I'm sorry to hear that. You are always so careful not to offend."

"Not about me! It's about you, Jack."

"I find that hard to believe."

"Strangely, I don't. It's from the nephew and niece of Pauline and Terry Johnson. They suggested that you were making accusations against them."

"As in Alice and Jamie Johnson?"

"That's them. I take it you know them."

"Not really," shrugged Jack.

"So why are they making accusations?"

"I don't know."

"Care to hazard a guess?" growled Lang.

"A guess," pondered Jack. "Okay, how about this? They could be referring to accusations that they got a power of attorney over their aunt and uncle, then did them in, before covering their tracks by pretending they had gone to Spain. Naturally, I'm speculating and aren't really sure I know what you mean."

Jack's candidness caught DCI Lang by surprise. He had expected a little bit of horseplay before Jack came out with the facts. Instead, he had a blunt response and a man smiling back at him through his bruised face. Once said, Jack did his best to retain a look of innocence.

"Right, and did they do them in?"

"I've got a method and a motive. To be honest, all I'm missing is a couple of bodies. You don't happen to have any spare, do you, sir?"

"Tell me, Jack, didn't I move you over to look after missing persons? I don't think missing persons normally make complaints."

"That's correct. I am investigating their two missing relatives. It's not my fault if I find out they were murdered."

"And I suppose it is just your luck to pick that case. Of all the cases you could choose, it happens to turn into a murder trial."

"Lucky pick, I guess."

"I bet. How sure are you they have been killed?"

"Eighty percent...ish; perhaps a little more."

"And how do we close off the remaining twenty?"

"The answer to that lies in Spain. I need two return flights, please."

"Two?"

"Yes, two. You wouldn't want me going on my own. I could get into all sorts of trouble."

"You're right. It must be far better to have two people getting into trouble. Anyway, about this complaint."

"You mean the one the murderers have put in because they don't like being investigated? That complaint?"

"Yes, that's the one. Okay, if you put it like that, let's file that one. How long do you need in Spain?"

"Two weeks, maybe three."

"You've got two days, maximum. You're not having a free holiday on me," insisted DCI Lang.

"Fair enough, three days it is," smiled Jack.

***

Will continued to trace his way through the evidence. It was in his break, his other work pushed aside for a few minutes. Jack had told him to get on with something else. Yet the case was compelling, as was the chance to work with a man like Jack. He was different to the others, not just in his approach, but also with people. The rest treated him like a serf while Jack seemed genuinely interested in teaching him.

If only he could find one item of note. Just a single breakthrough that Jack would recognise as his. It was not enough to have organised the case. Jack had been through it in minutes and had identified more than he could have established in days. Will picked up the photocopy of the postcard. Beyond the postmark, there was little more that he could do. The next stage had to be done in Nerja, for which Jack had been clear, he would not be allowed to travel.

Frustrated, Will placed the card down and sat back. What would Jack do next? Will scratched his head and thought hard. When the answer came, it hit him like a bolt of lightning.

"Does anyone want a coffee?" he asked.

Four hands shot up in an instant. All were eager for the coffee boy to return to his duties. None of them had followed Jack's lead. Normality had returned even if Will's motives were unclear. He needed a moment to think. He had learned that from his mentor. A trip to the coffee machine should be used to clear one's mind.

"The ghost tour!" he shouted just as the second coffee dripped from the machine.

His loud voice elicited a couple of strange looks from those passing by in the corridor. Will wanted to run back to the office though was fearful of doing so without the drinks. Instead, he waited and watched the brown liquid splutter slowly into the cups. He bemoaned the length of time it took to make a simple drink.

With four coffees poured, he grabbed a cup holder and pushed the beakers into the slots. The first sloshed across his hand, scalding his flesh. Ignoring the discomfort, he dabbed the tear from his eye. Will shook it off and raced back to his desk, declining to get one for himself.

"Coffee is on the table," he announced as he slammed them down at the side of the room.

Again, the drinks spilt over the cups, leaving a sea of coffee surrounding them. There were grumbles at the inconvenience of having to walk a couple of metres to fetch them. Each man forced himself out of his chair and looked at the mess Will had left. In turn, they selected the cup with the most liquid remaining, leaving the emptiest for Dick Foster.

"Bloody hell, lad, where's the other half gone?"

Will said nothing. His scalded hand was rifling through the paperwork. On the other side of the room, there was grumbling and complaints about the coffee. Will was oblivious to it and had turned his attention back to the evidence. He knew he would soon have something that would impress Jack.

One by one, Will jotted down the members of the ghost tour. Each one identified at the time of the disappearance had made a statement. More importantly, they had signed it and left their contact details attached. The file had mobile numbers, which Will set out on the table. Of course, they had all been spoken to before but not by anyone as effective as Jack.

The names meant little to him. Jimmy Niven was the thirty-two-year-old tour guide. He filled his time by running ghost tours along with bar work and other unnamed activities. A former student, he had dropped out of university in his second year, gravitating to casual work before he found his calling. He was considered York's best guide and was the leader of the group on that fateful night.

The information on the others was more limited. Steven Reeves and Sophie Neal were both students, studying at the city's university. Steven was a post-graduate while Sophie was a second-year history student. It was logical to assume they were partners even if there was nothing to confirm that fact. Then, there was the fourth member, of whom no one claimed to know who she was. That was a mystery and one that could not be solved at a desk.

Will rang each of the numbers listed. He paused before the first, knowing he might be stepping across the line. It felt like the right thing to do, to set up a meeting for Jack to question them. He knew his mentor would be pleased even if the approach was a little unorthodox.

Despite his eagerness, Will was thankful that neither Jimmy nor Sophie answered their phones. He breathed a sigh of relief and then panicked, hanging up to avoid leaving a message. He tried Steven, hoping for the same result. The phone rang for what seemed like an eternity, leaving Will to hang up. He was too late, for a voice compelled him to speak.

"Hello."

"Err, hello," muttered Will. "Is that Steven?"

"Who is this?"

He panicked. What did he say when he had no authority to make the call?

"Err, Jack, err, Jack Husker."

"Are you sure?" asked Steven Reeves.

"Yes, it's Detective Jack Husker. I need to see you."

"Why?"

"I'll explain that when we meet."

"Is that the best you can do?"

"Err, yes. He, I mean, I need to see you."

"I'm sure you do."

"No, really I do."

"Well, if you want to see me that badly, I'll be in Flanagan's cafe at about ten o'clock tomorrow. Do you know where that is?"

"Yes," lied Will.

The phone went dead. Will was left with the noise of the dialling tone flooding through his ear. He had no idea where Flanagan's was, but Jack would. Ten o'clock would be a meeting the two men were destined to have.

CHAPTER 8

JACK WALKED INTO FLANAGAN'S cafe at exactly half-past nine. He was deliberately early. He ordered a bacon sandwich and a strong cup of coffee, the perfect tonic for his head. Then, he sat in a corner where nobody could approach him from behind.

The service was quick. Jack had consumed his sandwich before the clock struck a quarter to ten. A second coffee was ordered and placed directly in front of him. As he waited, he gazed at a photo of the lad he was meeting. It was a poor one but the best he could locate in the file. He was thankful to have that, knowing how unusual it was to include a picture of a witness.

At ten o'clock, there was still no sign of Steven Reeves. Jack was struggling to stretch out his drink for any longer. Twice, an aggressive waitress had asked him if he wanted anything else. It came with the implication of him taking up valuable space that could be used by others. Jack gazed around to see just three customers occupying the ten available tables. It was hardly a blockage that was hampering their business. Politely, he refused and sat back, allowing his eyes to drift closed of their own free will.

At ten past ten, a scruffy individual entered, with a series of folders tucked under his arm. His hair was long, unkempt and in need of more than a comb. It matched his clothes, which consisted of a series of oversized items. It implied a nineteen-seventies look that the lad struggled to carry off. In so many ways, it was a classic student image.

Jack glanced at the picture and then back up at the lad. The resemblance had a familiar feel even if it was not particularly striking. The photo looked out of date and held only a passing resemblance. A second look had Jack wanting to ask the question.

"Steven?"

The lad turned around slowly. His full face stared down towards where Jack sat. The facial features matched, his long pointed nose hardly commonplace. Jack smiled, confident he had got his man.

"Yes."

"DI Jack Husker."

"Aha, the mystery man on the phone. I know it wasn't you who called. Have you got someone doing your dirty work?"

It was said with a smile to go along with the implication. Jack thought better than to continue the conversation until he had made peace. He stood up, shook the lad's limp hand and paid for his green tea at the counter. Steven looked shocked that someone would buy him a drink and yet he was not going to refuse. If the police wanted to show their generosity, he would readily accept it.

"Where do you want me to sit for my interview?"

"It's not an interview unless you've done something I should know about," corrected Jack. "I just need to follow up on a missing persons' case. I am going through some of our older files."

"Oh, that one," he sighed.

On the way to his seat, there was a visible slump of Steven's shoulders. The mannerisms were of someone who thought that night had been forgotten. Jack noted it and filed the thought away for the questioning that would conclude their meeting.

"Yes, that one," Jack nodded. "I've read the statements and they make sense. However, it is always better to hear things first-hand. Do you fancy giving me a summary in your own words?"

"If you like. It'll give this a chance to cool down."

Steven wrapped both his hands around his cup of tea, allowing the heat to sink in. They were thin, almost bony and offered the look of someone twice his age. Jack sat quietly and placed his notepad on the table.

"There's not much to tell. I was on the ghost tour that night. I don't know if you've been on it. It's the one where you visit the places where ghosts have been spotted. We hadn't seen anything, which is not that surprising. The tour guide kept saying we would. He was just trying to keep us interested in the cold. I suppose that's his job, but to be honest, most of the group looked as bored as I was."

"Do you believe in ghosts, Steven?"

"Not really."

"So why go on the tour?"

"It was something to do. I think someone had said it was good and I was daft enough to believe them. It was rubbish."

"Can you tell me what you saw?"

"I told you, we all saw nothing."

"I don't mean ghosts."

"Of course, sorry," said Steven as his under-nourished face blushed red with embarrassment. "You mean the van."

"If that's what you saw," shrugged Jack.

"In the mist, we all saw the white van. It was idling along and then accelerated suddenly for a short distance. At the last moment, it screeched to a halt. There was a muffled scream and that was it. We thought it was part of the act."

"And did you see anyone else?"

"Only the couple who walked that way before us. You guys said the two parts were related. For all we know, they just walked off into the night."

"And the van?"

"As I said, it could have been part of the act."

Jack stopped and thought. He believed the lad even if it felt like he was hiding some key information. He had done the good cop bit; it was time to go in hard with some more incisive questioning.

"Were you with anyone?"

There was a notable pause. Nothing was offered in response. Finally, Steven forced a reluctant shake of his head. When that was insufficient, his lips moved softly to confirm his reaction.

"No."

"Who else was on the tour?" asked Jack, allowing no respite before the question.

"There was the tour guide."

"Who else had paid to be there?"

"There were only three of us. I think the other two girls were both students."

"Both girls?"

"Yes, you would know that from the statements."

"Would we? If you remember, we never found out the identity of one of the other girls. One was a student, the other was unknown."

"I think we all told you it was a girl."

"Did you?"

"I'm sure I did," insisted Steven. "Did you check the tickets?"

"Funnily enough, they all paid in cash, so no one ever knew who she was," replied Jack.

"She must have been with the other girl."

"Yes, she must," mused Jack. He pursed his lips and looked directly into the lad's eyes. "Who was she, Steven?"

"I told you, I don't know."

"Yes, you do. You know exactly who she was and you are going to tell me even if I have to drag you kicking and screaming back to the station."

Steven Reeves went silent. He lifted the cup to his mouth to conceal his face from Jack. It was too hot, scalding his lips with the liquid. Steven grimaced and tried to hide his reaction.

"You are going to tell me, Steven. That I can promise you," insisted Jack. He stood up from the table and placed his card alongside the drink, circling his mobile number with a pen. "When you are ready, that's the number to call."

Jack smiled and left the young lad stewing in his wake. He knew his sleep would be punctuated by the thought that the police were closing in. He was never a suspect in the disappearance but he was hiding something. It could be the clue to unlocking the mystery in Jack's file. It would not find the Johnsons, for they were dead, but it would solve the mystery of exactly where they went.

***

Outside the cafe, a pair of eyes were fixed on the meeting and watching closely through the window. They recognised Jack Husker, a familiar acquaintance previously met in unpleasant circumstances. Opposite him, his companion looked worried and had fixed his stare on the drink he clutched in his hands.

The watcher had been on the wrong side of the questioning before. His skills had been tested by the wily old fox he observed. Jack Husker was good at what he did and knew the game too well. That cantankerous approach was designed to unnerve and make undisciplined mouths talk. That was a problem and was the reason the scruffy little git had to be dealt with.

He watched Husker rise and leave something on the table on his way out. It had to be a contact card, with the lad feigning disinterest in it. Everyone knew that as soon as he was alone, he would pick it up and play out the scenarios in his mind. It was inevitable that he would succumb to Husker's game in time. He had to be silenced permanently before he could pick up the phone.

Briefly, Husker loitered to test the lad's resolve. It was almost as if he was waiting to see if he would cave in immediately. Thankfully not, with the conversation over in a matter of minutes. Husker's time would come. For now, he was not the priority. The young lad was the key pawn in the game.

The waiting always came easy to him. It was just a matter of sitting back and allowing events to unfold. When Husker left, the target was only a short distance from being alone. It was too public to go into the cafe when there were quiet streets to walk down. One wrong step and the task would soon be done.

In the cafe, Steven Reeves took an age to finish his drink. He was restless and played with the card in his hand. It was flipped over and over, like a coin being tossed in a game. Each time it landed made it no easier when he feared his secret being uncovered. That secret could finish his father if the information ever leaked out.

Steven slipped the card into his pocket just to get it out of his sight. He could still feel its presence even if it was hidden from view. He smiled at the cafe owner and rose from his seat. His coat was pulled on, ready to set foot in the open air.

Outside, his voyeur watched. Once on foot and alone, Steven became vulnerable. He didn't know it yet but the streets were ready to claim him. Even in the daylight, he was never going to be safe. This was an act to be carried out without being masked by the dark misty streets of that cold York night.

Thankfully, Steven Reeves walked slowly from the cafe. Each step was weighed down by the burden of a conversation with DI Husker. That was good, for his mind was distracted and had forced his defences to be lowered. When the van purred into life, the sound and the movement were not noticed.

For two hundred metres, a stalking approach took place. The vehicle closed the gap between the hunter and the hunted. When Steven made a right turn, the street narrowed into a quiet lane. It was perfect for the act and allowed the predator to make his move. His right foot pressed the pedal to the floor and it finished the act in seconds. In a flash, a hood was dragged over Steven Reeves's head and his body was pulled into the van.

CHAPTER 9

JACK WOKE TO THE sound of his answering machine. Three times, the phone had rung and each time it forced him to cover his face with the pillow. His head pounded, his throat dry from what had been a very late night. It was not his fault and yet even he could see the irony in that argument. Alf had tried to persuade him to go home before finally standing firm with a downright refusal to serve him any more drinks.

His protests had been brief. Jack had only offered a temporary refusal to go. The stubborn devil inside him had to be seen to put up a fight. He had a reputation to hang on to, one of someone who never did as he was told. Now he wished Alf had been more forceful and pushed him out of the door at the first time of asking. It would have made four pints worth of difference. In the morning, that meant a mildly dry throat compared to a raging hangover. Never his fault; it never was.

Jack heaved himself out of bed. The simple movement of his body sent a surge of pain through the back of his eyes. He groaned audibly, wincing with the throbbing inside him. He needed headache tablets and then coffee. Both had to be consumed before he could deal with the answering machine. It beeped again, almost to spite him and as a reminder to Jack of its importance in his life.

Jack gazed downwards. He had managed to undress the night before. That was progress from his last session. One sock had remained on his right foot while the other was in the heap of clothes by the door. He picked up the pile of discarded items, held them up to his nose and accepted they were fresh enough for another day. There was no point wasting good washing powder especially when there was none left in the house. There hadn't been any since Mary left and it would remain that way until it forced Jack to a laundrette.

Again, that same noise penetrated his head with its high-pitched tone. It was still early, particularly so for someone looking after missing persons. Nobody arrived at the station before the official time. That only made the day longer. It was far better to get there a few minutes late, having enjoyed a leisurely breakfast.

The kitchen held no great joys; just a small jar of desperation coffee that had been procured in a corner shop. The unknown brand was the type of powder purchased by students. It needed three heaped spoons to get any semblance of taste. Jack put in four, added hot water and used it to wash down two tablets from his supply. He was rarely short of those. The pharmacy was on his normal route home and, better still, on his way to The Cellars. The brand never mattered; they all did the same job, no matter what they were called.

The coffee was repulsive and it took a real effort to get it down his throat. He would buy some more on his way back along with a few provisions if he remembered. He forced it down and tensed as the second mouthful threatened to re-emerge for a second viewing.

With his eyes still bleary, Jack pressed the button on the answerphone. It was DCI Lang whose mood was worsening with each message he left. It was a summons. Jack's instruction was to get himself into the station as a matter of urgency. It was a directive that was never going to mean positive news.

Jack sighed and wondered if it was a day to defy his boss. He would ponder that while the warmth of the shower brought him back to life. After that, he would find a cafe. His body was crying out for something greasy. Only then, would he be ready to meet Lang.

***

DCI Lang was not amused when Jack walked into his office at nine forty-five. His face was red and seemed to darken with Jack's presence. He went to speak, only to reflect on his words and offer a calmer introduction.

"Where have you been, Jack? I needed to see you first thing this morning."

Jack gazed at DCI Lang. He was sat on his chair, swinging from side to side with the look of a man under duress. His superior's eyes bore into him, with deep pools of anger bubbling inside them. Jack knew he was on dangerous ground even without the need for a warning.

"I came as fast as I could."

"Didn't you get the message last night?"

"Sorry, I only picked it up this morning."

"Did you get in that late?"

"No, I must have gone to bed before you left it."

"What, at five-thirty?"

"You know what they say about early to bed."

"Jack, don't bother. I'm not in the mood."

Jack fell silent. He could see the irritation in Lang's eyes. On a normal scale, this was high by any standards. It told him to shut up and hope his boss's anger began to ease.

"Now, Jack, would you like to explain where you were yesterday?"

"Investigating missing persons, as I'm supposed to."

"Keep going."

"I'm following up on the Johnson case."

"I thought you were going to Spain to do that?"

"I am, but first, I had some investigating to do."

"That was meant to be desk-based. You are not supposed to be doing fieldwork without prior approval.

"Where is this leading, sir? Has something happened?"

"You could say that. I've got Nigel Reeves busting my arse because his son's gone missing."

"Missing? He can't have gone missing. I only saw him yesterday."

"You met him yesterday? What the hell were you thinking, Jack?"

"I wanted to find out who the mystery girl was in my case."

"Jack, for the last time, it is a missing person review, not an investigation."

"I'm afraid, sir, that in this case, it doesn't look like there is much difference."

"You had better pray for your sake there is a difference. If anything has happened to him following your meeting, there will be consequences. Tell me, you didn't put the squeeze on him, did you?"

Jack shrugged.

"Jack?"

"He knows who she was."

"Who was?"

"The final person on the night the Johnsons went missing. She is the key to finding them. If we find her, we find out what happened."

"And in the meantime, what about Steven Reeves?"

"We do what we always do. We get the word out and see who knows what. Someone must have seen him and that someone needs to talk."

"And what happens if they don't and we can't find him?"

"Then we have one less potential suspect to interview."

DCI Lang shuddered at Jack's attitude.

"And what do we do with his father?"

"I'll leave that one to you, sir. I've got a holiday to Spain to organise."

Lang looked stunned at the flippant reply. Even for Jack, it was a new low in terms of inconsiderate responses. Police and politics never mixed at the best of times. With Nigel Reeves still nursing his wounds from his election loss, it was never going to make for a joyful meeting.

"Just stay away from Reeves. I'm going to ask DS Ramsey to investigate this one. I don't want you going anywhere near him."

"But I thought I investigated missing persons."

"Not this one, Jack. Anyway, you're going to be on holiday, as you keep reminding me."

***

Lisa sat at her desk, idly flicking a pen between her fingers. Her mind was racked with uncertainty ever since Jack had visited her flat. She had come close to kissing him; too close for colleagues who were supposed to work together. It left her mind racing through the rumours of affairs in the station.

It was hard not to feel the sense of attraction. The age difference was there but she had dated older men before. And yet Jack was everything she disliked in a man. Something about him put that weakness in her resolve. He felt right for her and no matter how hard she fought it, she was struggling to deny it to herself. Jack was trouble and she had to be professional before he dragged her into his world.

Her eyes returned to her computer screen, reviewing the cases which sat in front of her. None had anything urgent and yet she needed something to occupy her thoughts. She wanted a distraction to put her mind back on the job. Perhaps a simple burglary, which would hardly need much of an investigation.

"So, are you coming to Spain?"

Lisa swung around in her chair. Jack was standing alongside her with a big grin on his face. He smiled, which seemed to dull the bruising on his cheeks. Jack leant on the doorframe, with the cynic in her suggesting that he might need it to stand up straight. Her heart missed a beat and her face flushed red, ridding her mind of all thoughts of work. She needed to focus and offer a response to a man who was getting too close for comfort. Lisa tried and failed. The words were not available in her head.

"I take it that is a yes."

"Err...I don't think I could be freed up. We're very busy at the moment."

"Great, we fly tomorrow. Make sure you bring enough clothes for a good few days and don't forget your bikini."

Lisa blushed. "I thought it was just for a couple of days."

"It is, but you never know what might crop up when we are there. Best be prepared."

"And why do I need a bikini for that?"

"We might need to interview suspects on the beach," smiled Jack.

***

Nigel Reeves walked into DCI Lang's office an hour after Jack had left. It was for a meeting that Lang had been dreading from the moment his son had been reported missing. The revelation that Jack had met him recently only made the situation worse. He had no answer to the inevitable question that would come about a detective Lang could not control.

"I want answers!"

They were the first words offered when Nigel Reeves entered Lang's office. Any calmness normally associated with the councillor was long since consigned to history. His anger was obvious and the slightly scruffy appearance bore all the hallmarks of a man who had not slept. A second-day shirt, tucked into comfortable trousers, was matched with an unshaven look and hair that had not seen a comb for at least two days.

"Nigel, we've known each other long enough for you to be assured that we will be doing everything we can to find your son," insisted DCI Lang.

"Don't give me that guff, Nick. I've also known you long enough to be well aware that is your standard response. That bastard Moss has kidnapped him and your detective is in on it."

"Now, hang on, Nigel, that is out of order."

"Is it? Earlier this week, I got assaulted and your lot did nothing about it, other than to threaten to lock me up."

"Nigel, can we start at the beginning, please? Coffee?"

"No."

"No, you won't start at the beginning or no, you don't want coffee."

"I don't want a bloody coffee. I want to get on with finding my son."

Lang sat forward in his chair to explain the information they had. He looked uncomfortable and nervously shifted from side to side. He could hardly hide Jack's involvement and yet he had no idea whether he had contributed to the disappearance. Either way, it was an embarrassment for a detective who was supposed to be staying out of the field.

Nigel Reeves did his best not to interrupt. He could see the difficulty that Nick Lang was in. He needed Lang to help him and that afforded him the benefit of the doubt. He would do anything to get his son back home.

"When did you last see Steven?"

"In the morning. He popped in on his way to the cafe. He said he had an important meeting to go to, which I found unusual in itself."

"What did he say when you challenged him?"

"I didn't. He shuffled off suspiciously before I could say anything. Of course, now I've found out that he was meeting one of your team. It was a DI something. I'm not sure I got the name."

Lang did not offer it. It would come out in time and he was not about to fast-track the process. Without giving it to him, it would buy him a few hours or possibly days. There was every chance Jack would be in Spain by the time his name emerged. The press would have a field day, once they had a disgraced detective to link to a disappearance. Questions would be asked but at least with Jack abroad, Lang would have the opportunity to seek out the answers first.

"Do you know where he was going afterwards?"

"No. He was due to take his mother to the doctor later that day, so he would have been back. He would never let her down."

"Nothing serious, I hope?"

"That's none of your business. Sorry, no, it's not serious, thankfully."

A brief pause allowed that piece of irrelevant information to soak in. Lang thought for a moment in an attempt to navigate a path through the meeting. Nigel Reeves would have valuable information even if it would require careful extraction. A taste of his anger was a small price to pay to secure it.

"So, we have the meeting with DI...I mean, my colleague. Then, Steven left the cafe and has not been seen since."

"Correct."

"And does he carry a mobile phone?"

"Of course he does; it isn't the nineteen-sixties. It's switched off."

"Okay. I think the next step is to get one of my detectives to trace his steps. Let's see if we can find out who was in the cafe."

"Your officer was in there. I would start with him and, of course, there is David Moss to consider."

"David Moss?" queried Lang.

"Yes, he is the leader of the opposition. Sorry, the new council leader. You know what I mean."

"I know him. Perhaps not as well as you do but certainly enough to question why you think he would be involved. Have you got any theories that might be relevant?"

"Yes, he is a thug. He punched me yesterday and one of your officers did nothing about it. It was lucky she got there or I would have given him a good hiding."

"Nigel, let's keep this to what did happen, rather than speculation. Are you sure it was David Moss that hit you?"

"Of course I am. Everyone knew except your bloody officer who was worse than useless. Now, who are you going to get to find my son?"

Lang thought for a moment and then pressed a button on his phone. It was answered within two rings and offered a friendly voice at the end of the line.

"Yes, sir."

"Lisa, please can you come into my office."

Lang offered a reassuring look to Nigel Reeves. He waited until Lisa had knocked and entered the room. She moved towards the two men and sat down alongside Reeves. The councillor looked shocked and flicked his eyes back and forth between Lisa and Nick Lang.

"Nigel, this is DS Lisa Ramsey, who will be investigating your case."

"I know who she is. Is this some kind of bloody joke?"

"I don't understand."

Lisa smiled and interrupted.

"What Mr Reeves is trying to say is that we've met before. It is good to see you again."

"Well, it isn't good to see you again. Nick, this girl didn't do her job properly last time, so why the hell do you think she will now?"

"I think you will find DS Ramsey is a very capable detective. She will do a good job for you."

"Then why didn't she arrest David Moss?"

"Probably because nobody, including yourself, could confirm he threw the punch and nobody would stand up as a witness," said Lisa firmly, in a manner to bring a smile to her superior's face.

"That aside, he should be in prison. Just for being a bloody Tory!"

"I think you'll find he would plead guilty to that as charged, Nigel," said Lang. "Now, shall we let Lisa go about her work?"

"I suppose," grumbled Nigel Reeves.

"Good. Why don't you give her the details you gave me? It will give her a timeline to work to while you get yourself off home for some rest. We'll be in touch as soon as we have something."

"If I must, though I might take you up on that offer of a coffee first."

"No problem," smiled Lisa. "I'll get some brought in while we take down the details."

***

The meeting between Nigel Reeves and Lisa was brief. Away from DCI Lang, she detected a far softer side to the man. He was sensitive and understandably worried about his son. More so, the trauma of what had happened was playing with his mind. At times, Lisa wondered whether he would be able to hold it together long enough to tell her what she needed.

Clutching his coffee, he looked like a broken man who could give up the fight for life at any moment. Each fact he offered had to be extracted from its wound. All it confirmed was the brief window of time in which Steven could have gone missing.

The rest of the information was limited. Nigel told her when Steven left the house and the time of the meeting in the cafe. After that, he jumped to his son's failure to take his mother to the doctor. Lisa knew that the meeting was with Jack, but, like Lang, had offered no names as part of the process. There was no need to provide that information to the public.

"You will find him, won't you?"

The words were sobbed and pitiful. It was a far cry from the incident she had been called to with David Moss. It was obvious that he was not the aggressor in that confrontation. Yet in front of his supporters, he had to make a show of standing his ground.

At times, Lisa searched for ways to prolong the meeting. She had what she needed though Nigel Reeves was in no fit state to be allowed to go. Background questioning she called it and yet it was very difficult to make it sound like anything other than her accusing him of perpetrating the act. Of all the possibilities, that was the least likely option she had.

After ten minutes of going nowhere, her questions were exhausted. Lisa passed him on to a family liaison officer, leaving the broken man in her capable hands. It felt like the right thing to do when Nigel would need all the comfort he could get. Lisa thanked him and left the room, knowing exactly who she was going to see.

She walked across the main office and surveyed the desks. All heads went down on the assumption she was looking to delegate some tasks. Everybody was always busy when there were shitty jobs to go around. It would always be a junior who made the mistake of looking up and sealing their fate to everyone else's relief.

After a minute of searching, she walked out into the corridor. It was there that she found Jack in the most predictable of places. He was staring at the coffee machine, with a look of disappointment on his face. He studied the buttons as if waiting for divine intervention. Jack knew every option would produce the same lacklustre result.

"Try the tea; that's the nearest to a coffee taste I've managed," laughed Lisa.

Jack turned around slowly. He looked up and offered a smile to his colleague. Lisa smiled back, a welcome distraction to Jack's day. He had Spain on his mind and seeing Lisa only intensified that thought.

"Want one?" he asked.

"I thought that machine made you go blind."

Jack laughed. He remembered his words from when they had first debated the station's coffee.

"You're right. Shall we go out for one?"

"Why not?"

"Any particular cafe in mind or do you want me to find another of York's hidden gems?"

"How about you take me to the one where you met Steven Reeves?"

"There are far better cafes nearby," insisted Jack.

"I fancy that one."

Jack shrugged and allowed Lisa to lead the way downstairs.

The walk to the cafe took place in virtual silence. Jack had sensed the edge in Lisa's tone from the moment she had said the words. Questions would follow, not that he was particularly concerned. Jack's only role was to question a man before he went missing.

Lisa, too, could feel the tension between them. Jack walked unusually quickly through the busy streets. It felt like he was trying to avoid a conversation. With a younger man, she would have been wary of losing him. Jack was different; he was just getting himself to a place where he felt more comfortable talking.

Even by Jack's standards, the cafe was tatty. Peeling white paint on the outside and a window with a small crack across the corner greeted Lisa. It was single-glazed and no effort had been made to make it look homely. It was hard to feel any appetite to consume anything made on the premises.

"Nice," said Lisa.

"Not my choice, remember. I would have taken you to Starbucks."

"I'm sure you would."

"You find a seat; I'll grab the coffee."

Jack was forthright with his words, knowing a table service was on offer if required. It was an excuse to delay the awkward conversation that was coming.

"Two coffees, love."

"I'm not your love," barked the waitress.

Jack looked up to see her scowling through eyes that narrowed above a long pointy nose. If it had been Halloween, he would have made an obvious comparison.

"Okay, please may I have two cups of your finest coffee?" he replied.

"That's better."

An exchanged look of recognition took place. It was the same surly waitress who had served Jack before. Her manners were no different and were unlikely to improve once Lisa started asking awkward questions.

"I'll bring them over."

"No need, I'll wait."

Daggers tore into Jack's flesh. He could see the anger in her eyes from an act of defiance that left her boiling inside. Jack smiled and stood politely until she turned. "Someone out there for everyone," he muttered to himself while wondering if he had found the exception.

"There you are; milk and sugar are on the side."

"Thanks, keep the change."

Jack placed a five-pound note on the counter and swept up the cups. The witch looked more suspicious than before. She eyed the note he had left in front of her in a manner to suggest it would do her harm.

"What for? What do you want?"

"Nothing; it's for the impeccable service on offer."

Jack never caught the full extent of her response, other than to note it ended in 'off'. He had moved away, unwilling to engage with her any longer. Instead, he had Lisa to contend with. The mood written on her face hinted that her manner might be similar to the waitress. The only difference was she had the potential to thaw.

"What was that about?"

"Nothing," smiled Jack. "I was just trying to negotiate one of your fancy coffees. Sorry, I failed again."

"This looks fine."

She took the more insipid-looking cup. Both resembled builders' mugs of coffee; one over-splashed with milk. She left Jack with the one that would be least unpleasant. There was no point falling out over the drinks when there were more serious matters to contend with.

"So, are you coming to Spain with me?" asked Jack abruptly.

His question caught Lisa by surprise. Any thought of being on the offensive was quickly replaced by a backward step. She sat back and pulled her coffee into her. Instinctively, her eyes drifted down towards the drink.

"I'll take that as a no, shall I?"

"Yes, no, I mean, I don't know," mumbled Lisa.

"I do need some help over there," insisted Jack.

It was an olive branch designed to invite her back into the conversation. Lisa looked relieved and breathed more easily. She glanced at Jack and then across at the waitress. Once a sense of calm returned, she drank carefully from her scalding cup.

"It's not bad."

"I told you; it was carefully negotiated. I told her wet and brown and this is what she gave me."

"I think I got lucky given the other options available," laughed Lisa.

Jack smiled. He had broken the ice and could see normality returning.

"Can I put you down for that trip?"

"We'll see, Jack. I've got a little bit of a mess to clear up first. This one isn't wet and brown but could become so if we are not careful. What were you doing meeting Steven Reeves?"

"Missing persons. He was one of the members of my ghost tour and he knows who the fourth person was."

"And now?"

"No idea. I left him in here and I haven't seen him since."

"Who else saw him?"

"Just the pretty young thing behind the counter. I arrived first and Steven came in a little later. We spoke briefly and then I left him."

"And did you threaten him?"

"Lisa, what type of guy do you think I am?"

"One I need to ask the question to. Did you threaten him?"

"No...well, I might have leaned on him a little."

"How little?"

"Possibly quite a lot of little."

"You mean a lot."

"They're your words. You always were better at phrasing things than me."

"And a lot less evasive when asked a simple question."

"Excellent; are you coming to Spain with me? That's a pretty simple question."

Lisa blushed. Her face filled with the embarrassment of being put on the spot. Twice, she blustered, each time the words to respond deserting her. Despite her best efforts, Lisa could not think of anything that would deflect Jack from his line of questioning.

"I can't, I haven't got anything to wear," she blurted out.

"That's even better," grinned Jack. "Now I am looking forward to it even more."

"That's not what I meant and you know it!"

"Are you sure? Look, you go and interview the ice witch and I'll get two tickets booked to Spain. We'll go hand luggage only if you are planning on taking that little."

Lisa's face continued to redden as she lifted her cup in front of her face to hide. There was no getting away from her embarrassment.

CHAPTER 10

NO MATTER HOW HARD Jack searched, he could not find a suitcase. It was hardly surprising when so many women had moved out of his house. Two ex-wives and Mary had packed up and left in a hurry. All three had thrown their belongings into whatever they could find, leaving Jack with nothing but empty wardrobes.

He checked his watch. He had forty minutes until he was due to meet Lisa at the train station. She would be so organised, having packed exactly what she would need. Most likely, it would be in matching luggage. In response, he would throw in a ragbag of what he had clean or passable to wear in public.

He threw his meagre amount of clothes onto the bed. Trousers, shirts, socks and underwear; there was barely enough to fill the smallest case. He would have added some shorts if he had any. Swimming trunks were a memory from his childhood. It was lucky he even had a passport, a leftover from a second wife who was insistent they had a holiday. One week of misery and then four days later she had served him with divorce papers. They were unhappy memories of a holiday that was one final attempt at denial that the relationship had fizzled out.

Jack surveyed the pile. It was unimpressive and yet still too much to fit in a carrier bag. Another check of his watch confirmed time was tight. His best hope was the charity shop five doors down the street. He had seen suitcases in the window. All he needed was one of those modern wheelie cases that sent a message that you were too old to carry a bag. That would do and with any luck, he would be able to put it on his expenses.

Jack hurried out of the house and walked to the shop. Luckily, it was open even if there was nothing suitable on display. With no time to waste, he asked the old lady behind the till. She looked bewildered that anyone would come in wanting something so specific.

"We do get them in from time to time," she mused.

"Have you got one now?"

"We might have, you know."

"Could you have a look?"

"You want a suitcase, do you?"

"A lightweight travelling case, if possible," confirmed Jack.

"We do sometimes get them in."

Jack gave up and chose to make his way to the back of the shop. His eyes were drawn to the right-hand corner where an old case stood on its end. It was huge, perhaps large enough to fit everything he owned inside, plus a spare body or two for good measure. If he was moving house, it would be perfect. For a quick trip to Spain, it was useless.

"Ooh, you found one."

Jack turned to see the woman hobbling down the aisle behind him. She looked even older when released into the freedom of the shop. Excitement appeared to be etched across her face as if she recognised the opportunity for a rare sale. Jack wished he had rummaged harder under the sink. There must have been a bin bag hiding somewhere.

"You did very well to find that."

It was hard to miss. It was half as tall as Jack and wider. It had seen better days, in many ways just like the lady serving in the shop. Jack shook his head and moved on, aware that she was now stalking him.

"Don't you want the case?"

"It's the wrong size."

"Do you want something bigger?"

Jack ignored the question and continued to move around the shop's perimeter. He spied a child's lunch box. For a brief moment, he wondered how much he could squeeze into it. He picked it up and concluded it was not worth the strange looks it would bring.

"I've found another one. You could try this."

Jack hardly thought it was worth the bother of turning around. When the lady repeated the words, he decided to humour her. He was shocked. Her arm was holding up something that appeared suitable. The downside was it was bright blue. Compared to the oversized suitcase, it was perfect.

"That will do. How much?"

"We've had this for a while, so how about three pounds fifty?"

"Call it a fiver and you've got a deal."

Jack pulled a scrunched note from his pocket and walked over to her. She had the look of a woman who had never sold anything before. Glee filled her face. It felt like the shop had been saved from extinction. Just one purchase had staved off the threat of closure for another day.

"Shall I put it in a bag for you?" she asked.

"It is a bag."

"Pardon?"

"No, it is fine as it is."

Jack grabbed the case and hurried back to his house, knowing he had little time to pack and get to the station.

The reality of what Jack had bought only struck him when he threw the case onto the bed. Face up, next to his assortment of clothes, was a shining picture of Thomas the Tank Engine. It was vivid, with the engine's smiling face staring back at him. That face contrasted against the brightness of the blue. Jack's thoughts turned to Lisa and what she would say when she saw it.

Time was too short to worry. Jack threw his clothes into the case. He barely filled half of it. He folded a jacket into the space, not that he had any intention of wearing it. It just made the case a little fuller. He could picture Lisa's perfect luggage with everything neatly folded and fitted into the appropriate place. That brought a smile to his weather-beaten face. He was looking forward to seeing her away from a work setting.

A glance at his watch told Jack he had time to walk. The weather was dry and he could move quickly through the streets. The case stopped him from doing so and forced him into a taxi. It came with a driver who felt the need to comment.

"Nice case."

"It's for a bet," Jack replied.

"I take it you lost," grinned the driver, revealing three missing teeth when he smiled.

"Just take me to the station," growled Jack. All he could think of was punching out another gap in the driver's teeth.

The journey was short. Jack sat in silence until the taxi pulled into the drop-off area. His timing was perfect, with Lisa getting out of the car ahead. Predictably, she pulled a stylish case behind her. In her smart clothes, she could have been a businesswoman heading off to an important conference. In contrast, Jack looked like he had been dressed from a jumble sale.

He tucked the case under his arm. The picture was pressed into his side. It was better to have a big reveal and make a joke of it than allow her to discover it for herself.

"Nice case! Aren't you supposed to be pulling it?"

Her eyes were on it. Already, he felt the shiver of shame. He looked away and took a breath before he met her response with an attack of his own.

"Yeah, it's better than yours. Mine's got a picture of a train on it!" Jack turned the case to face her. The element of surprise took the words from her mouth. It was time to strike and make sure it was done with confidence. "And it has a retractable handle, look!"

Jack pulled it out sharply. It stopped quicker than he was expecting and only went up to a child's height. It forced him to stoop to pull it behind him, offering up a ridiculous charade. Even Jack's restricted height was too much for the size of the case.

There was nothing either of them could do but laugh at the sight of him bending over to drag it.

"Okay, I'll carry it," he growled.

"You could see if any of the station's shops have a case."

"No way, I've spent good money on this one."

Jack and Lisa settled on going for a coffee. It was after the obligatory grumble about the train being late. It was only three minutes but enough to have Jack chuntering. Late was late no matter how anyone tried to present it.

"Sit yourself down," said Lisa. "I'll get them and don't take your eyes off that case. You wouldn't want someone taking it by mistake."

Jack found a table in the cafe on the bridge. Not a usual haunt, it had the benefit of a couple of quiet corners. As he sat, he could see Lisa eyeing up the coffee menu and hoped she was not about to overcomplicate his life.

Another check of his watch told him they had twenty minutes. That provided plenty of time to make a call. He had someone to line up for a meeting as soon as he returned from Spain. Jack took out the number from his pocket, which he had scribbled onto a receipt. He dialled it quickly and waited for the call to be answered. It only took a couple of rings.

"Jimmy Niven, is that you?"

"Yeah, who's asking?"

The voice at the end of the line sounded rat like. The squeaky voice was that of someone who could barely hold a tone. Jack pictured him, with his slender face and pointed nose. He would bet good money that he would have a ponytail. Nobody without a ponytail spoke with a voice like that.

"DI Jack Husker, York police."

"What do you want?"

"I want to meet."

"What have I done?"

Already, the kid was on the defensive and trying to mask his misdoings. He probably had drugs but what did Jack care? That would wait. For now, he needed information. Indeed, he needed the rodent-like kid on his side.

"Nothing, unless you want to offer a confession. I just want to meet up."

"Yeah, right. Do you think I was born yesterday?"

"Okay, I'll get a patrol car around in the next ten minutes. Alternatively, we can meet later in the week. That gives you a bit of time if you know what I mean."

An appreciative noise came through the phone line. Jimmy Niven understood Jack perfectly and could find some common ground.

"Let's go for later in the week."

"I thought you might," said Jack. "I'll phone you when I get back."

"Just text me," insisted Jimmy.

"I think I prefer to phone," confirmed Jack. "We wouldn't want to misunderstand each other."

"Your choice. Could I have a clue as to what this is about? You know, just to make sure we understand each other."

"I'm looking for ghosts, Jimmy. More specifically, I'm looking for ones that went missing about a year ago."

The line went silent before Jimmy Niven hung up.

"Who was that?" asked Lisa as she walked back to the table.

"Nothing, I was just returning a message. Dare I ask what type of coffee you've got me?"

"Just a filter coffee," said Lisa. She looked at Jack and knew he was being evasive.

"And the leaf shape on the top? Any clue?" asked Jack.

"Yes," she smiled. "That is so they can charge an extra pound."

"Good work; you're learning," grinned Jack.

***

David Moss was sitting in his office. For the first time since his election win, he had a clear head. Maybe the celebrations had gone on a little too long. It was worth it, just to enjoy the look of anguish on so many Lib-Dem faces.

It had been forty-eight hours since he had even seen his wife and daughter. During that time, they had become unimportant. Their presence in the house had not registered as he went about the aftermath of the election. He had a bit of back-peddling to do before he got on with the serious matter of running York. It was the victory he had been waiting for and now he had it, he was going to enjoy every minute.

Elizabeth was in her room. She was sitting on her bed, curled up and staring out of the window. She was so innocent about the whole world outside. He wished they talked more, like most fathers and daughters. In recent times, she had been prone to bouts of extreme secrecy. There had to be a boyfriend, not that she would ever admit it. Even to an absent father, there were obvious signs she was hiding someone from him.

"Penny for your thoughts," he said.

"I think inflation has increased it a little," she smiled.

She was beautiful when she smiled. Her long flowing blonde hair and those beautiful blue eyes were radiant. He was proud that he and Jennifer had done such a good job of raising her. She was the poster girl of the pony club and his pride and joy. And yet he had a feeling she was drifting away.

"Are you okay?"

"Yes, I suppose."

David sat down. The bed creaked a little with his weight. She moved up and gave him more space. It offered a hint of her being repelled by his presence. When an arm went around her, she flinched, leaving her body tense to her father's hug.

"Come on, what is really wrong?"

"I don't know."

"Is it the election? Are you afraid you'll see less of me?"

It was an ideal escape from a difficult question. It provided an answer that would satisfy his ego. Elizabeth offered a sigh and followed it up with a nod. With the response, she allowed herself to be drawn into her father's reassuring arms. It was not a place she wanted to be but it allowed her to hide the truth. Her father was not the man she was pining for.

***

Jack and Lisa arrived at Malaga airport in the early evening. The flight over had been quiet, with their seats apart despite them being booked together. Strangely, Jack was pleased about the lack of proximity. It allowed him a couple of hours alone in his thoughts. The only interruption was a couple of babies screaming midway through the trip. Other than that, he had been lost in his own troubled world.

Lisa had felt less relaxed. She was wary of Jack and how she would react to him in the coming days. Her mind flitted back to the closeness she had felt when he sat in her flat and allowed her to tend his wounds. She had to be professional, no matter her feelings. She was there to solve a crime even if the lines felt muddied.

The airport was quiet. Away from the school holidays, there was a mixture of older couples and businessmen. The couples looked like seasoned travellers, a product of regular trips abroad, while the businessmen moved around like zombies. They barely looked up from their phones. It was their life support, their whole reason for existing. Without that small device, they would be lost. Out of habit, Jack checked his. There was nothing, not even a single message or text.

They were met by a man with a board held out in front of him. Their full names including police rank were written up and displayed to every passenger who went through passport control.

Jack's name was most prominent, with Lisa's written under it, only just squeezed on at the bottom.

"So much for arriving unannounced," laughed Jack.

Lisa looked around. It was one of several dozen boards, all held by people with the same vacant appearance.

"Hola," the man called out as they made their way towards him.

Jack looked straight ahead. The frown he offered informed him he only spoke English. The man shrugged, beckoned them towards the exit and then walked silently in front of them.

"See, you've upset him," laughed Lisa. "Now he won't carry your case."

Jack clutched his case tight to his side. Beside him, Lisa wheeled hers stylishly behind her. There was never any danger Jack was going to let anyone take it from him. The embarrassment of it still burned deeply and Lisa was enjoying his discomfort too much.

Their transport was provided by a large silver car. It looked comfortable if too old to be on the road. The driver opened the rear door for Lisa, allowing her to step inside. As Jack followed, a shrug of his shoulders saw the driver walk away. Jack shook his head and threw the two cases into the rear. Once loaded, he walked around and got in next to Lisa. Briefly, he contemplated the front seat, only for the makeshift board to be thrown onto it. It was done with a look that told him that seat was not for passengers.

"I think he's taken a shine to you," grinned Jack.

Lisa smiled. She was not about to fault the driver or the way he had reacted to Jack. He was not the first person who had taken offence with her companion and he would not be the last on the trip.

Once on the move, Jack spent the time staring out of the window and watching the A-7 whizz by. The signs pointed out some of the famous holiday names of the Costa del Sol. He had heard of many of them and seen them in holiday brochures. Never once had he felt inclined to visit.

He was surprised at how built up some of the towns were. He preferred the areas where the road arced towards the sea. In places, it kissed the edge of the ocean. Jack found himself lost in the beautiful blue waves lapping at the beach. They offered glimpses of a place where Jack could one day retire.

Lisa also sat quietly. Occasionally, her eyelids dropped from the tiredness of the journey. She was happy not to talk and drifted away, saving her energy for more important parts of the trip.

"Where are we staying?"

Jack's question startled her. She sat up, her eyes forced open by the interruption. She had the details in her handbag and was irritated at being woken quite so abruptly.

"Can't a girl get some sleep?"

"You've been asleep since we got into the car. We're only a mile or so away."

Lisa was shocked. She had been so out of it. Her mind was lost in a world of deep sleep, leaving her neck sore from being lent against the window. She fumbled in her bag and found the details. Rather than open them, she handed them to Jack. He took one look and engaged a driver who had been happy with the silence.

"Hotel del Nerja, please," said Jack. His pronunciation had not improved.

"Isn't that the name of where the Johnsons were staying?" queried Lisa.

"No, that's Hotel Paraiso del Nerja. It won't be far but that can wait for the morning. Let's get in and grab some food."

Lisa nodded. It was the first reasonable thing Jack had said. She rubbed her eyes as the car turned off the main road. They were quickly into a built-up area and slowed by the traffic. It gave Lisa time to become alert and ready herself for Jack.

"That's it over there," announced Jack.

The driver muttered something in Spanish. Neither Jack nor Lisa understood it and yet the gist was clear. He was the driver and knew where he was heading. He did not need the help of an English policeman to find it.

The car pulled over in front of the hotel. As soon as it came to a halt, the driver got out. He scurried around and opened the door for Lisa, leaving Jack to wrestle with his side. Lisa alighted and was met with her case while Jack's was left in the car.

"Do you need me to carry it in for you?" asked the driver in a perfect English accent.

"No, I'll be fine," said Lisa. "Thank you."

"Don't worry, I'll get my own," said Jack.

His words were ignored. Jack pulled the case out and placed it on the ground. It put it on display and offered too good an opportunity to be ignored.

"Choo-choo!" laughed the driver, shaking his head as Jack muttered an obscenity in his direction.

It was Lisa who guided Jack away. Both pulled their cases behind them in contrasting styles. Lisa moved effortlessly while Jack's case hung above the ground. It was too short to be wheeled and yet Jack was too irate to pick it up.

"I'll check us both in," insisted Lisa. "Just give me your passport."

Jack grumbled and then handed over his document, knowing it was probably for the best. He sat down just inside the door while Lisa approached the reception. His eyes gazed around, looking for inspiration. It came with a sign for the bar. Jack stared at it, almost mesmerised by its presence and felt the taste come to his lips. It occupied him for the time it took for Lisa to check in and walk back over with the keys.

"Here you go," said Lisa. "You're in room 106."

"Is that the penthouse?"

"For the price, I doubt it. How about we meet back here once we have changed?"

"Changed?"

"Yes, Jack, it is what normal people do before they go out."

"Oh, right. How about we meet in the bar instead? If we are going to look our best, we might as well have a drink to celebrate."

"Fine, I'll see you in the bar. Give me thirty minutes."

Jack watched Lisa disappear. She looked immaculate with her case wheeled behind her. Jack waited and then tucked his piece of luggage under his arm. This time, he was careful to face the picture into his body. He was in no mood for any more smart comments. Once clutched, he climbed one flight of stairs and made his way to room 106.

Jack's room was sparse. Police budgets clearly couldn't stretch to anything better. There was one single bed, with a mattress barely thicker than a telephone directory. It creaked. When his hand pressed into it, the mattress slid across the diagonal.

Furnishings were equally poor. A nineteen-seventies laminated dark wood wardrobe was positioned in the corner. It had one wooden chair alongside it and a small rectangular mirror fixed to the wall. Even the bedside table offered nothing to hint at comfort. The room looked as if the contents had been bought from the same charity shop as his suitcase.

Carefully, Jack pushed the door to the en-suite. It was functional and perhaps the highlight of the room. Everything looked like it had been replaced in the last ten years. It even contained a bidet. Jack had never used them for washing anything except his shoes. The room would do for a couple of nights. Jack was not planning on spending much time inside it. He bemoaned Lisa needing half an hour when he had thrown his case down and was ready to go out.

For a couple of minutes, he paced up and down. It gave him a feeling that the walls were closing in. He looked for a kettle. In its absence, he settled on going to the bar. Jack locked his room and walked back down the stairs in the direction of the sign he had seen.

All he saw was a few tables tucked around the corner of the reception, with a small curved worktop to act as the serving point. The one promising sign was the beer tap. Even that did little to appease him. Jack knew that whatever it produced, he was a long way from the comfort of The Cellars.

"A beer, please. Stick it on room 106."

A small glass was washed under a tap and then filled with a light golden liquid. The young barman swilled it around, making a great show of creating an inch-high head. Jack frowned while the lad went about his work, meticulously producing something resembling ice cream. As he finished, he scraped a flat blade across the top to take away any excess.

"Three euros please."

"I've changed my mind. I'll have two beers if they are that size," noted Jack.

He watched a repeat of the whole routine. All that was required was a glass and a flick of a tap. Not for this lad; he was an artist. His greatest work was a glass of beer, which was ready to be displayed in some upmarket gallery.

"That will be six euros."

"Room 106," Jack repeated.

Jack picked up the drinks and walked over to the nearest table, with a glass clutched in each hand.

"Sir, I need you to sign."

"Why? Are they on sale or return?"

"I don't understand, sir."

"Sorry, nothing," offered Jack. He had reached his quota for offending people for one day.

Jack signed the piece of paper with a scribble. He made no effort to ensure it was an accurate signature. It was not important in his life when cold beers were sitting on the table. The lad seemed happy and content to place the piece of paper into a wooden drawer. Whether it would appear on Jack's bill was anyone's guess. Whether the police would reimburse the expense was an even greater question.

Jack sat down and gazed around the featureless room. Even with a wide basis of comparison, it was the most soul-destroying place he had ever drunk in. A cross between a hospital waiting room and an office reception, it had little ambience, not helped by the poor souls trudging in with their suitcases.

The beer was hardly a saving grace. Jack's first sip brought nothing but disappointment. Lacking in taste and over-fizzy, it left him yearning for a proper pint. Suddenly, he regretted buying two of them and having to face another serving of the tasteless liquid, with its froth filling a third of the glass.

"Thirsty?"

Jack was surprised to see Lisa so soon. She looked stunning, with a light top and jacket matching her loose-fitting trousers. How did someone look so good so quickly when she said she needed half an hour to get ready?

"I got one for you," he lied. "I thought we would have a quick one and then wander out."

"Fair enough. Is it any good?"

"I'll let you decide for yourself."

"So, that's a no."

Lisa sipped the suspicious liquid. It was not unpleasant though hardly filled with flavour. After the journey, it was refreshing even if it did not offer much by way of enticement. Jack seemed unimpressed and he was a better judge than she was. As she drank, Lisa's thoughts turned to the way he had looked at her. His eyes had lingered a little too long for a man who was supposed to be travelling with a colleague. Not that Lisa minded; she was just glad she had put on a new outfit.

"It's not that bad."

Jack had drunk his and placed the glass back on the table. Like medicine, he had gulped it down and grimaced with the aftertaste. Lisa felt obliged to do likewise. She finished hers in three mouthfuls and then accompanied Jack onto the streets of Nerja. All food plans were gone as Jack moved swiftly through the town.

"What did you say the hotel was called?" asked Lisa

"Hotel del Nerja. Have you forgotten already?"

"No, the other one."

"Hotel Paraiso del Nerja, why?"

Lisa pointed at a dilapidated building across the street. The stonework was crumbled and its roof had caved in a long time ago. Its windows were smashed where thieves had broken in to steal what little was left.

"That looks better than my room," laughed Jack.

"Yes, but does it look like someone has stayed there recently?"

"Not really. How long do you reckon that's been closed?"

"Longer than the Johnsons have been missing," stated Lisa.

"I tend to agree, which means something doesn't add up. Let's go to the town hall in the morning and see if we can put this to bed early."

"Why the rush? I thought you wanted to stay here for as long as you could get away with."

"That was before I tasted their beer."

CHAPTER 11

JIMMY NIVEN LAY AWAKE in his bed. His mind wandered back to that night one year ago. He had seen the white van clearly and the couple bundled into the back. He hadn't said anything to anyone. Initially, through fear and then the sum of money the Reeves lad had given him had bought his silence. Of course, he knew who the girl was but it would take more than a few police questions for him to name her.

The threat that followed had sealed the deal. One word to the police and he would be joining the couple in a shallow grave. That had been made clear by the hooded man in the balaclava that was waiting for him a few days later. Jimmy knew he was lucky to get away when the cold steel blade had been held up tight against his throat. He had pleaded for his life until his bladder threatened to let him down. That numbness of fear remained in him and would be there for the rest of his days.

Faced with the threat, he had stood motionless and promised the man everything. Long after he had been left alone, he sat down to cry in the damp cobbled alleyway. He had remained there until he shivered uncontrollably, with the coldness leaving his lifeless body unable to move. An old man had saved him by helping him to his feet. He never knew who he was, only that he was kind enough to help him on his way.

To this day, he still had nightmares. Jimmy was too tired to keep his eyes open and too scared to allow himself to sleep. That was when the figures appeared and the lost souls of the city came to haunt him. He would see their shapes against the curtains, dancing around in the glinting light and offering the edge of a knife blade. He shuddered at the thought, knowing no matter what he did, the demons would never go away.

Sweat filled his brow. Even in the cold, dark room, he was boiling up. He felt sick and yet that was not a solution. He would just retch; that was all he ever did until the pain took over. Then, he would stand over the sink and dowse away the fears with icy water.

Jimmy got up. His t-shirt was sodden. The wetness mixed with the cold air sent a chilling shiver through him. The sink was his destination for the next few minutes until he convinced his body there was nothing to dispel. It was the same routine every night and it would be the same again tomorrow. Then, he would sit up and wait out the night or just curl himself into the tightest of balls. There was safety in his foetal position; safety from everything in the world which intended to cause him harm.

A noise at the window caught his attention. It was not a loud noise, just the sound of movement outside. It was in the yard at the back, his Victorian terrace separated from the next row by an alley at the rear. It was piled high with rubbish from a street of individuals who did not care. Mostly students, the alleyway was their dumping ground for the excesses of their life.

Jimmy ducked down into the corner of the room. Again, he curled up to afford himself the protection he needed. Another noise came, this time, scratching at the window downstairs. Then silence, as if an animal had been scared away. It did little to make him feel better. Jimmy knew that whatever was out there was still lurking in the shadows full of terror.

"Go away!" he cried out.

There was no response; nor was there any further noise. Silence returned and remained for the rest of the night. Jimmy hated it almost as much as the noise, for with silence came a hidden threat. Curled up, he rocked himself continually and yet it brought no more than a few minutes of sleep. Always the same; always on edge as he had been since the couple were taken.

Early morning brought welcome relief. The first light offered a sense that he had made it to another day. He was always awake when it arrived, waiting for the first peak of the sun over the top of the buildings. It came with safety that allowed him to leave the house. Others were sleeping in their beds and oblivious to the threats around them. It was hardly fair that he suffered alone.

Jimmy dressed and walked slowly out of his front door. He peered down the street in both directions, spying the rows of cars on either side. They were parked tightly, emphasising the lack of space. Every owner was a master at forcing themselves into the smallest gap. As he scanned the cars, he relaxed a little at the familiarity of each one he saw. Night after night those same cars all fought for the spaces in front of the houses and offered no respect for anyone who returned late.

Mr Williams had got there first. His red Audi was taking centre stage outside his house. Alongside him was Mick's Golf and then the matching Corsas of the twins. They were an eighteenth birthday present from parents with more money than sense. They were the regulars before the usual mismatch of vehicles headed down the street.

Jimmy turned left, noting each car he passed. Every one of them was familiar until he reached a white van. That was new to the street, its presence out of place for the area where he lived. It had a familiar feel of a vehicle he had seen before. Jimmy walked past, wondering who the owner might be.

A crack to the back of his head ended the debate. The pavement rushed towards him at a hundred miles per hour. He could not stop it or the inevitable crash of his full weight hitting the hard surface. His world had taken on a new type of darkness that had permanency that could not be denied. It was a darkness that would never end for Jimmy Niven.

***

Jack and Lisa both woke early. They left their respective rooms and skipped breakfast, eager to follow up from the night before. It was only a short walk and within minutes, they stared at the crumbling building, pondering when it was last inhabited. It looked worse in the day and confirmed what they already knew.

The building had been abandoned and had decayed over time. In its day, it would have been a tourist hotel for the early package holidays. Once the competition grew, the tour operators moved on and were seeking modern facilities on the beachfront.

"Any theories, Jack?"

"Yes, I think the Johnsons must have come here in their younger days."

"And the postcard?"

Jack looked at it closely and pursed his lips. There had to be a clue right in front of him.

"I think it must have been copied from one they sent back in the day. I just don't know how."

"Do you reckon it was sent by the nephew and niece?" asked Lisa.

"Probably. It's our second job of the day to find out."

"And the first?"

"Breakfast, of course, but not in that fleapit of a hotel. I'm famished."

"Fleapit? I quite like my room."

"Really?"

"Yes, they upgraded me to a suite. The guy behind the bar said they had run out of normal rooms."

"Lucky you. Trust me; mine is not a suite."

"You'll have to move in with me. There's enough room for a family in mine."

Lisa blushed as soon as she said it. Inside, she hoped Jack would change the subject and dig her out of the awkward hole she had put herself in. She could see he was tempted to allow her to stew for a moment. Thankfully, the gentleman hidden somewhere inside him persuaded him to let it go.

"Come on, we passed a cafe in the square. We can go there."

"Full English, Jack?"

"No, let's see if they do a good pastry. We've got to fatten you up before we unleash you on the beach."

Lisa did not know whether to blush or punch him. She had a funny feeling she would be doing both before the day was over.

***

The whole investigation, including breakfast, took three hours. Most of it was spent sitting and waiting. At least the pastries and coffee had been good even if they had taken an age to arrive.

"I could have baked them myself in half the time," moaned Jack.

"Would they have tasted so good?"

Jack scowled. It was hard to argue with Lisa's pertinent question. There was no need to hurry and yet the urge to get on was there. It would move the investigation on to the next stage. The delays in service were a barrier to that even if he was pleased to spend time with Lisa.

The hotel had closed sixteen years ago. Its last package tourists had left the year before. For twelve months, they had struggled on before the owner passed away. Then, the heirs to the crumbling fortune spent too long arguing over the closure. In its place, more modern establishments appeared and the loss of one of the older buildings was hardly mourned. To Jack, it felt like a familiar tale, with little nostalgia for anything that failed to move with the times.

The breakthrough came with the postmark. The traditional mark had been replaced with a modern equivalent six years ago. It proved it was fake. The date and postmark were not a valid combination. Whoever had sent the card did not know that. Jack suspected they had not even visited Nerja in the past six years.

The advice at the town hall was to check with the travel companies. They were sound words even if they followed another twenty-five minutes of waiting. Jack nodded and wondered whether the lady was a retired detective. She had all the answers to the questions he was yet to even ask. As they left, Lisa turned to Jack who was still clutching the postcard in his hand.

"What happens now?" she asked.

"I would say we grab another coffee and then ring Lang," replied Jack. "I think we are probably done here. With any luck, the next flight will be in a couple of days and we can hit the beach. Did you bring your bikini?"

"That would be telling," smiled Lisa. "Some things are best left as a surprise."

***

DCI Lang was not amused when the call came. "What do you mean, you are done? You've only been there a few hours."

"One night, actually," corrected Jack. "We've proved the postcard is a fake. We now need to speak to the travel companies."

"I can get someone over here to do that. Is there anything else you need to do over there? Think carefully, Jack, because you are not getting a second holiday at my expense."

Jack looked at Lisa and smiled. The phone was on its speaker and placed on the table between them. Sat in the corner of a quiet cafe, Jack was tempted to make up a list of items. No matter how hard he thought, he could not think of anything work-related to do.

"I could round up some of the old criminals the Met have missed over the years."

"Don't be flippant, Jack. We are not bounty hunters."

"Then I'd say we are done. We'll come back as soon as we've got a flight sorted."

"That might be a couple of days," groaned Lang.

"That's fine; there's no hurry. We'll find something to do in that time."

"I bet you will. I will get you back by tomorrow whether I have to fly a bloody plane over there myself and I expect your reports finished by the time you land."

"I wouldn't go to that trouble, sir. I'm sure there will be a return flight within the week."

"Jack, you are coming back tomorrow and remember, you are on an expense limit."

"I can see that from the hotel you booked."

"And the force does not pay for alcohol," Lang reminded him.

"What do you think I am?"

"A detective who will take advantage of the first opportunity he gets."

"Don't worry, sir, I'll look after him," interjected Lisa.

"I suppose that's a crumb of comfort."

Jack smiled inwardly at the thought of Lisa volunteering her nanny services for him. It was at odds with the façade she often tried to present. She could be one tough lady on the outside and yet soft and mellow underneath. Jack ended the call and sipped his coffee. It was the best one he had enjoyed since they arrived.

"So, what do you fancy doing?" asked Jack.

"I'm thinking shops first and then the beach."

Jack's eyes lifted slowly.

"Why do we need to go to the shops? Why don't we just go to the beach?"

"If you are going to the beach, we need to buy you a pair of Speedos first."

Jack's embarrassment was interrupted by his phone. His face had flushed red in the aftermath of Lisa's words. He tried to hide it behind another sip of coffee. The small Spanish cups did nothing to help him. It had been a long time since someone had done that to him and he was not sure he liked the feeling.

"Jack, I've got you a flight but you need to be at the airport in an hour. Sorry to ruin your holiday."

"An hour?" offered Jack. "But..."

"That's fine, sir," interrupted Lisa. "We might need a little longer on the reports when we get back."

"I'm sure you'll both get them filed in good time. See you when you get back. Safe travels."

The line went dead. Jack could imagine the smile on Lang's face. You could sense his smugness and the contentment he felt at getting one over on Jack. For once, he did not mind. The call had bailed him out of an awkward situation. It had given him time to recompose himself and present the old Jack back to Lisa.

"Oh well, the beach will have to wait," he sighed.

"And I'll have to wait to see you in those Speedos," replied Lisa.

This time, Jack blushed and there was no hiding it. His face flushed crimson red, leaving Lisa knowing she had him on the ropes. She finished her coffee and placed some money on the table. As she stood, she whispered in Jack's ear and walked away before he could respond.

"If you wear yours, I'll wear mine and that's a promise."

***

Jack arrived home at ten o'clock in the evening. He resisted the urge to visit The Cellars on his way back. The flight had been tiring, not helped by being forced into the only available seat. It trapped him in the centre of a row with restricted leg room. Sandwiched between two overweight businessmen, Jack had been left with a perpetual fight for the armrests. Lisa had sat apart, his last gentlemanly act to give her the seat between two ladies.

They had both nodded off to sleep on the train. Jack wished the two of them could have had a little longer in Spain. The tension had been obvious and he wondered whether that might have led somewhere promising. It felt like an opportunity had been lost.

Instead, Jack found himself alone. Sat at home, he felt the absence of Mary for the first time. So far, he had been too busy to miss her. All of a sudden, the house felt cold and isolated. Was it Mary he craved or was he pining for Lisa? He would sleep on it and he would sleep on it alone.

On the other side of town, Lisa felt no different. Her own arrival home had been greeted with a similar gap in her life. Her eyes drifted to the sofa where she had allowed Jack to sleep. She knew how close they had become and she rued the interruption of the early flight.

A sense of conflict filled her. She had no desire to be the subject of station gossip. It was alright for the man; he was the conqueror and able to tell all about his quest. She was the one who would have to suffer the derogatory comments. No matter how strongly Jack resisted, there would be the inevitable discussion about her performance. What was she like and what did she wear in bed? They were all topics that would be fired in his direction. Eventually, he would succumb and offer an answer. They all did, for no other reason than to enjoy a quiet life. Her mind was made up. She had to resist him, no matter how much attraction she felt.

***

Jack's first act of the morning was to text Jimmy Niven. Even before he had reached for the coffee, he was pressing the buttons on his phone. The net was tightening and Jimmy would provide the identity of the fourth person. While he did, Lang's team would close the loop on the travel companies.

No response came back. Jack would call once he got up and the small matter of some coffee and tablets had been downed. He slipped out of bed and went into the kitchen to see nothing but disappointment. There was no coffee and no tablets alongside it. Indeed, there was nothing in the cupboard at all.

Jack texted Lang to say he would be late, citing a couple of leads he needed to follow up on. Thankfully, his boss was happy to see him mid-morning. It left Jack free to start the day as he wanted and that meant his thoughts turned to Lisa. A quick call went to her voicemail service where he declined to leave a message. A breakfast invite quickly became outdated, so he threw on some clothes and walked around the corner to the cafe.

York was miserable that morning. Dark grey clouds loomed over the skyline, with the heavens threatening to open at any minute. The air was damp; the streets still glistening from the rain that had dropped in the night. The only positive was it kept away the tourists.

The businessmen were still there, all suited and going off to their mundane jobs. They would be there during biblical floods or even a plague of locusts. A few drops of rain only brought out their oversized umbrellas. Jack was thankful he was not in their shoes. The flexibility a detective enjoyed was far more to his liking. The new recruits were kept on a tighter leash while a DI in missing persons could come and go as he pleased.

"Sausage, bacon, scrambled eggs, toast and a fried slice, please."

"Anything to drink?" asked a portly woman, who appeared to be using the front of her formerly white apron as a menu.

"Coffee, please."

"How do you like it?"

"That colour, no sugar."

Jack pointed to a stain on her stomach. His smartness was met with a scowl that dared him to say anything else. It was a welcome back to the city he loved. He sat himself down in the corner. It gave him a view of the cafe and better still, it had a discarded paper left on the side.

An article caught Jack's attention. It was a focus on the city's homeless. Did anyone know that fifty people had gone missing in York so far this year? Jack didn't and then wondered how many of them he could trace. That was his job and there were things he could do to find them. He vowed to contact the reporter until he saw the name below the title. Andy Hutton was his least favourite journalist and it was enough to make him turn to the sports section.

"Here's your coffee. Breakfast will be a few minutes."

"Thanks."

Jack smiled. The woman did not. There was irritation written across her face. Jack took hold of the paper, read about the trials and tribulations at the new stadium and sat back contented that nothing ever changed. City had lost and their defence was unable to stop the tidal wave of attacks from the latest visiting team. The concerned fans were bracing themselves for an inevitable relegation. As he waited, Jack sent another text to Jimmy Niven who ignored it as he had the first. Jack huffed in frustration, only to have a greasy plateful put in front of him.

"There you go, love."

It was swimming. Every item was semi-submerged in fat. He would need a lifeboat to rescue most of it from the plate. Jack could feel his arteries hardening, with the breakfast likely to add ten years to his age. He stopped and thought about the healthy alternative, which was enough to confirm it would be eaten. It smelt heavenly and more importantly, it tasted every bit as good.

For the next ten minutes, Jack was fully occupied. His focus was solely on the breakfast before him. It was swilled down with a coffee and a couple of refills to keep him going. There was never a chance anyone was going to interrupt him and it was not until he was on his way out that he gave Jimmy Niven a call. By then, his stomach was groaning from the grease and yearning for something lighter. Jack patted his belly compassionately, knowing it had been the perfect pick-me-up to start the morning.

"Come on, Jimmy, answer it," he groaned.

He didn't. The call was diverted to his voicemail. Jack felt irritated that he could not progress the case. He cursed and made his way back to the station to see Lang.

Jack walked slowly while his thumb flicked at his phone. His instinct told him something was wrong and that he might not be hearing from Jimmy Niven again. Twenty years in the force had given him that feeling and when he got it, he was rarely wrong. He dialled Lang, who picked up the phone within one ring. It was answered in a manner to suggest his superior was waiting for him.

"Morning, are we seeing you today?"

"Yes, I'll be in the station in ten minutes."

"Could this wait?"

"No, I don't think it can. I think we need to get the uniforms out looking for Jimmy Niven. I have got a hunch that something's happened to him while we've been in Spain."

"Evidence or a hunch?"

"A hunch."

"Okay, we'll get onto it. Let's just hope a Jack Husker hunch is more reliable than the last one."

CHAPTER 12

DCI Nick Lang issued the instructions to his officers before Jack had made it back to the station. The description was vague, based on the information they had from questioning Jimmy Niven a year ago. Not that he would have changed much; that type of character rarely did. The sense of urgency was brought on by the concern Jack had offered on the phone.

Jack sauntered in fifteen minutes later, holding two take-out coffees in his hand. The steam rose from the paper cups, leaving the corrugated cardboard sleeves as the only protection from two burnt hands. He looked up while never moving his focus from the drinks. The threat of spillage was enough to occupy all of his available thoughts.

"In your own time, Jack," said Lang.

"I thought you might like a coffee, sir."

Lang looked shocked at Jack's generosity. The surly middle-aged detective was not one to arrive with a peace offering. It made him wary as if the coffee was just an opening gambit of the negotiation.

"You're not having another trip to Spain, Jack."

"Good, I'm still recovering from the last one."

"I hope the alcohol is not on expenses."

"I only had one beer and that was small. It was the crappy hotel and flight that did me in. I can hardly move my back after a night in one of their beds."

DCI Lang laughed and tried not to look too unsympathetic. He took the coffee and lifted the lid suspiciously before pressing it firmly back in place. It certainly looked and smelt like coffee, which made him even warier of Jack's motives.

"It hasn't been poisoned, sir. They were fresh out of strychnine. These modern coffee shops don't carry the stock they used to."

"I'm just wondering what this is in aid of."

"I think it's time you moved me back to being a detective. The Johnson case is anything but a missing persons' case."

"How many confirmed dead have you got, Jack?"

Jack fell silent. They both knew the answer was none. Until there was a body or two, it could only ever be a hunt for the missing.

"Look, Jack, for what it's worth, I've put the word out for Jimmy Niven. We'll know in a couple of days whether anything untoward has happened to him. In the meantime, we continue to follow up on the Johnsons. Did you find what you were looking for in Spain?"

Jack nodded. He told Lang about the dilapidated hotel and its former presence only existing in someone's memory. He felt a new surge of excitement spread through him. That feeling was helped by Lang's acknowledgement of what he was suggesting.

Whether he would admit it or keep up the charade, his case had changed to murder.

"It could just be the wrong hotel."

"It was written on the postcard. How do you explain that?"

"A mistake."

"And the postmark?"

Jack explained the change of postmark that had occurred six years before. It captured DCI Lang's attention and brought a flicker to his eyes. Lang nodded and allowed a wry smile to form across his face. The evidence was getting stronger. It was just a question of whether they had enough to make a move.

"Are you saying that someone has faked the postcard?" questioned Lang.

"Yes," confirmed Jack.

"And you think they must have copied it from one sent more than six years ago."

"It makes sense. If you had an old one floating around the house, that is what you would use."

"Yes," continued Lang enthusiastically. "And the change of postmark is something you would not know about if you had not been there."

"I'm not sure you would know about it if you had."

"Fair point, Jack. So what happens next?"

"I want to search the house."

"Sorry, it is way too soon for that. If we do that and find nothing, we have lost our only bite of the cherry. I think we should do some more digging and see what we can rake up."

Jack sighed, not hiding his disappointment from his superior.

"I suppose I could carry on tracking down the ghost tour party," he offered reluctantly.

"Where are we on that?"

"Steven Reeves is missing. You said you have put a trace out for Jimmy Niven but I think something has happened to him. I've not made contact with the student yet and, of course, we still don't know who that fourth person is."

"We need to find that out."

"Find me Jimmy Niven and we'll get the identity of the fourth person. She had to be with one of the other three. I would say it is pretty unlikely it was Jimmy even if he knows who she was. My bet is she was with Reeves but in his absence, let's see what the other girl has to offer."

***

Lisa had not rested since she returned from Spain. Her mind was a cocktail of thoughts about Jack and the case. Both intrigued her and yet neither made any rational sense. Why would someone go to the trouble of faking a disappearance just to commit murder? Money had to be a primary motive. The beneficiaries could only be the nephew and niece and the unhealthy possibility there was more to them as a pair than a simple family relationship.

She shuddered at the thought and then continued searching through the old case notes. Nerja was mentioned fleetingly as somewhere the Johnsons liked to go on holiday. There was no mention of children. They did not appear to have any. Nor was there any reference to anyone having gone with them. That would be too easy, to discover that the four of them had visited together before. Maybe they were taken there as surrogate children when the nephew and niece were young. It would offer time for a plan to be hatched and for a sinister set of actions to be triggered into motion.

Lisa yawned and wiped the tiredness from her eyes. It was far too obvious to have any likelihood of being true. There had to be more to it than that. Jack had referenced other disappearances that had been far more complex. The Johnsons' disappearance was a case that was becoming more intriguing the longer Lisa cared to study it.

Lang summoned her to his office just after she saw Jack disappear along the corridor. Her eyes had been drawn to him for a little too long. Lisa's head instinctively averted when Jack cast a glance in her direction. No doubt, the DCI wanted to cross-reference something Jack had said or at least get a second opinion on the evidence.

"I'll be right there, sir."

She tidied away the papers in front of her. It was not her desk she was sitting at and it would have another occupant when she returned. Thoughts turned back to the trip to Spain and how she and Jack had worked together. Would she really have got close to him if the chance had arisen? They were thoughts for another time, with DCI Lang awaiting her presence. After a moment of reflection, Lisa rose and made the short walk to her superior's office.

"Ah, Lisa, come in and take a seat."

Lisa noted the empty coffee cups on the table and smiled. It was unusual for Jack to bring two, especially one for someone in authority. It meant something was wrong and it tugged away at the uncertainties inside her. Lisa felt far from relaxed when she took her place opposite DCI Lang.

She sat down in a chair facing diagonally across the desk. She could see it was not the one Jack had sat in. He had left a tell-tale dent in the cushion and the chair at a strange angle. Most would have straightened it when they left. Not Jack; he just left chaos wherever he had been.

"I've been meaning to have a chat with you for a while," continued Lang.

He walked past her and pressed the door shut. Even the quiet sound made Lisa feel uneasy. She had the sense of being trapped and made ready for interrogation. She shuffled and dragged her skirt down, which had barely moved an inch. It was for her benefit rather than DCI Lang's.

"How are you and Jack getting on?"

It was straight to the point. That was what made him the DCI. There was no messing around or dancing around the question. Lang was going for the jugular.

"Fine, why?"

Lisa looked down at her feet. Her shoes needed polishing. She remained fixed on them, allowing her to search out the blemishes. Without making eye contact, she knew his eyes were glaring straight at her.

"How was Spain? Did you get what you were looking for?"

"Yes, the hotel has been closed for years and the postmark was out of date. Did Jack tell you about the postmark?"

"He did."

"Good."

Lisa paused before looking up slowly towards the DCI who had settled down behind his desk. He sat composed, with his hands together in front of him while he tilted back in his executive chair. It looked more comfortable than the upright chair she found herself in. Anything would have felt more comfortable than the position she was in right now.

"And how's Lisa?" he asked.

"I'm fine."

"Not missing the bright lights of Newcastle? We haven't spoken for a while about how long you are staying."

"I'm happy here, unless you are looking to get rid of me, sir."

"On the contrary, Lisa. I do, however, have a little concern."

Lisa's face dropped. A feeling of insecurity filled her. Was her work up to scratch? Had she not lived up to the standards expected of her?

"Have I done something wrong?"

"Not yet."

A quiet sigh of relief was tempered by the word he ended on.

"I have a little concern about you and Jack. He's trouble, you know. I don't want you getting involved."

Lisa's face flushed red. She did not need Lang to tell her what he meant by 'involved'.

"Sir..."

"Lisa, it's none of my business what you get up to outside of work. However, I am concerned if it involves Jack. He's a good detective but he's also a destructive influence. You do need to know that."

"Sir, nothing is going on between us. We are colleagues and friends."

"As I said, that is none of my business. Just make sure you go into it with your eyes wide open. I don't want to see you getting into the sort of trouble Jack has an uncanny knack of finding."

"I won't. Is there anything else, sir?"

"Yes, I want you to support Jack full-time on the Johnson case. Keep going with the search for Reeves, but work on the basis the two are linked. Did Jack tell you that he thinks something has happened to the tour guide?"

"No. I think that's the guy he was trying to arrange a meeting with."

"Oh no," sighed Lang. "That would be the second one he's linked with that we are now looking for."

"You're not suggesting Jack has anything to do with that, are you?"

"Of course not. Jack has many faults but even that is a stretch. As I said, just be careful. You're too good to be dragged down by him."

Lisa nodded and fought to avoid a reaction. She could feel her cheeks burning with the redness they were showing. She hated herself for it and yet it was hard to fight her feelings. Only the relief of being allowed to leave Lang's office offered the chance for the colour to subside.

Her one crumb of comfort was that the desk she had vacated was still empty. In a quiet corner, it allowed her to focus on her work. She spent the morning working through the timeline Nigel Reeves had given for his son's disappearance. Jack's presence loomed large throughout as the bookmark at one end of the passage of events. Something told her that the tour guide's timeline would look surprisingly similar if laid alongside it. They were thoughts she did her best to ignore.

Nigel Reeves had been surprisingly quiet since she had first met him. From such a brusque early response, he had soon melted into the role of a vulnerable father. All he wanted was the return of his son. It was hard not to feel sorry for him. His head would be full of regrets, wishing he had spent more time at home instead of pursuing political glory.

The window of time for the disappearance was short. The event was likely to have taken place shortly after Steven Reeves left the cafe. In York, the river was an obvious point for a mishap but there was no reason for him to go anywhere near it. Well away from his path home, it pointed towards other more sinister factors.

Lisa searched through the records they had for Steven Reeves. His name appeared in two different places. The first was a minor offence in his teens. A small amount of recreational drugs had been found in his possession, an offence for which he escaped with a caution.

The second was the reason Jack and Lisa were working together. In the Johnsons' case, he was one of the four members of the ghost tour party. Jimmy Niven was the tour guide, the same tour guide who Jack now suspected was missing. The party guests included Steven Reeves and a young university student called Sophie Neal. Then, there was the mystery fourth girl. It had been suggested that she was with Steven, but he was adamant that he went on the tour alone.

With two of the roads temporarily extinguished, the remaining path led to Sophie. She was a girl barely mentioned in the investigations to date. She had to be interviewed and not by Jack. Of course, Jack would never allow that, no matter what anyone said.

Lisa flicked through the detail she had for Sophie. It was a year old, from a statement that had been taken at the time of the disappearance. A second-year history student, who would now be in her third year, Sophie had offered little. She had gone on the tour alone and did not know the other girl. Nor had she seen anything untoward on the night, making it understandable that she had been almost forgotten. She could have been lying. Somehow Lisa doubted it even if the lack of information she offered was stark.

Lisa's thoughts were interrupted by a call. She picked up her mobile to see it was Jack. Part of her wanted to ignore it, aware of both her own and Lang's misgivings. She played with it idly and then took the handset to her ear.

"Hi, Jack. How's it going?"

"Okay. Did you get the third degree off Lang?"

"I suppose, a bit."

"And what did you tell him?"

"Just what we saw in Spain. He's asked me to get more involved in the investigation. He thinks Reeves and the Johnsons could be linked."

"He thinks? I bloody told him they were linked and I don't think Jimmy Niven going quiet is a coincidence either. I've had a ring around my eyes and ears on the streets and no one has heard a peep from him."

"So what do we do next?"

"Easy, we have lunch. Meet me at Mellor's cafe in half an hour."

"I'm not sure that's a good idea. We could just meet in the station."

"Nonsense, I'll see you at the cafe. They do a blinding BLT."

Lisa heard the familiar dialling tone of the call being cut off. It was typical of Jack. He never listened to anyone other than himself. She felt a sense of irritation but knew she would not stand him up. If nothing else, she needed to discuss their next move. Lisa hoped that would be enough to occupy them and restrict the conversation to work.

***

Lisa walked into the cafe exactly thirty minutes later. She barked out her words even before she had offered a simple greeting. It was pre-planned and her way of maintaining the focus of their meeting.

"We need to speak to Sophie Neal."

"Not before we've had lunch. Sit down and I'll get you a menu."

"A menu? We must be going up in the world. You've never invited me to a place that was posh enough to have a menu."

"Nothing but the best for you, Lisa."

Lisa felt herself burning up. She could already feel the exchange playing with her mind. It was personal, not just a work meeting and Jack was causing her head to spin. She was grateful for him getting up to fetch the menu and give her a moment to compose herself. That respite was temporary for Jack returned within seconds.

"What do you fancy?"

There was a flippant answer to that, not that Lisa wanted to say it. Inwardly, she scolded herself for her uncertainty. She took the menu from him and opened it wide. Once held, her eyes blurred and she stared at it in silence.

"It might be better that way up."

Jack took it from her and turned it the right way up. Lisa blushed again and prayed that Jack would allow her to recover.

"Give me a chance," she insisted. "I had something in my eye. What do you recommend?"

"I like the BLT. The omelettes are generally okay if you like eggs."

"That does help," she laughed.

"You can even get fancy coffees in here," boasted Jack. "And I don't just mean black or white."

"Wow, you must be pushing the boat out."

Lisa blushed again. It implied that Jack was paying, making it seem more like a date by the second.

"Have you decided yet?" came a pleasant voice.

They stared up at a smartly dressed lady. She was slim, with a white blouse and a black skirt. Most striking was that she was clean, with her blonde hair tied up neatly. It was very different from some of Jack's usual haunts.

"I'll need a minute longer. You go first," said Lisa.

"BLT and a coffee for me, please. Filter coffee is fine."

"And for you?"

"I'll go for the quiche and salad."

"Do you want the quiche warming up?"

"Why not? Let's live a little."

"And to drink?"

"Just a bottle of sparkling water, please."

The waitress nodded. She smiled as she took the menus back. It was all very efficient, giving Lisa a sense of unease.

"Are you okay?" asked Jack.

"Yes, I'm just coming to terms with the fact that this is the first cafe I've been to with you where the waitress fitted in her clothes."

Jack laughed loudly, catching the attention of several other tables.

"I'll let you into a secret. She's new; the normal waitress is off for gastric band surgery."

"Yeah, right. I'm not that gullible."

"No, I'm serious," said Jack. "She's the size of a bus and we are talking a double-decker."

"Not one of those bendy ones?" giggled Lisa.

Lisa's loud laugh brought tuts of admonishment from an elderly lady at the table next to them. Jack leaned over to apologise, offering words that did not come out very often. Lisa just smiled and shrugged her shoulders in a mock apology.

"Let's talk about Sophie Neal," she insisted.

"Yes," nodded Jack. "I think you should go and see her."

It caught Lisa off-guard. Her game plan had been to derail Jack's attempts to exclude her.

"Excuse me?"

"You should go and see her. She might open up more to a lady."

"And that's the only reason?"

"Okay, I might have had my share of university students with all those dead girls from the sketch murders."

Lisa accepted his point, knowing how gruesome the case had been. It had taken a toll on Jack, not that he had been prepared to admit it. He could be difficult at times and too proud to accept any help.

"Okay, I'll see if I can arrange something in the next day or so. I think there is a number on file for her. What about the travel history of the Johnsons? We still need someone to go through that lot."

"Leave that with me."

"I didn't think you liked desk work."

"I don't, but I've got a funny feeling that lad Will might."

CHAPTER 13

THE PEACE OF THE police station was broken by the sound of a shrieking voice. It was enough to wake the dead and turned a series of eyes in the direction it had come from.

"I said, I want to speak to whoever is in charge!"

A stern lady stood at the front desk, her eyes fiery and offering the look of someone with an axe to grind. She was mid-thirties, with her hair tied back into a blonde ponytail, a hint of colouring masking the true shade. She appeared angry and ready to launch a tirade at whoever might cross her. It was PC Dawson that was the first to react.

The young officer at the desk jumped to his feet. His newspaper was pushed aside as the demands of the woman took his attention. He blustered his words, leaving him wrestling with the right thing to say. His only achievement was to sound like a gibbering fool.

"Come on, I haven't got all day," she insisted.

The woman stood with both hands on the desk, her figure looming large. She was not particularly tall and yet the imposing manner with which she presented herself implied someone of impressive stature. She was too much for PC Dawson, his desperation to find somebody of authority obvious. He was panicked and the woman was going to do nothing to let him calm down.

"Let me get someone for you," he said in hope rather than with any expectation it would appease her.

"Just be quick about it," she barked.

Any fear of calling up to the boss was lost in an instant. If it would take away her presence, it was a call that was worth making.

DCI Nick Lang picked up on the second ring.

"Sorry to interrupt you, sir. I've got a woman demanding to see you."

Lang leaned back in his chair, surprised at the unexpected intrusion. He held the phone to his ear while his eyes remained on the incident report displayed on his screen.

"Who is it?"

"I don't know," said PC Dawson.

"Did you think to ask her?"

"Err, no. Just give me a second. Excuse me, madam, what did you say your name was?"

"I didn't and I'm not a madam."

That was a matter for debate thought Lang. He could hear every word of the conversation without the need for PC Dawson to relay it. Whoever had arrived at the station was clearly going to be difficult. It would need the delicate touch of someone who revelled in such confrontations. Lang contemplated finding out where Jack was. Common sense got the better of him and he lifted his frame off his chair to go down to meet her.

"Tell her I'm on my way. Ask her to take a seat."

The relief in the young officer's tone was obvious. He had crumbled in the face of pressure. Lang noted it for future reference. For now, the more pressing matter was a woman causing havoc at the front desk.

"He's on his way," insisted PC Dawson.

"About time. How long will he be?"

"A couple of minutes. Please take a seat."

"No, I'll stand."

PC Dawson knew better than to argue. He was pleased to see the woman take half a step away from the desk. She looked around as if trying to pre-empt which door Lang would walk through. Never once did she suggest her demeanour was thawing.

Her attention was taken when two uniformed officers walked in through the front door. She spun around expectantly, only to dismiss their presence. She knew that the man in charge would not be in uniform. Her fire would be tempered until Lang appeared.

PC Dawson contemplated striking up a conversation with the officers, to keep them close at hand. He backtracked, knowing it made him look weak. After an exchange of nods, he allowed them to pass through to the back of the station. The second officer paused and held the door open. To PC Dawson's relief, it was for DCI Lang, who he pointed in the direction of the lady. Lang acknowledged the young officer and approached her confidently.

"DCI Nick Lang, how can I help you?"

He held out a hand. It was ignored, with her eyes almost sneering at the offer of friendship.

"I want to complain about the behaviour of your officers."

"Okay, we have a complaints procedure which I can take you through. Could I ask your name before we proceed?"

"I suppose so, for what it's worth. I'm Alice Johnson."

Lang recognised the name from the conversations with Jack. Despite the familiarity, his face remained stoic throughout. Where others might have shown excitement, Lang stood without a flicker of emotion. He was too experienced to make that mistake, especially with a lady likely to explode at the smallest detail.

"They will be my officers you are referring to, so I am probably the right person to be speaking to."

She shrugged coldly, offering a picture of indifference.

"Shall we go into the room to your right?" he asked.

"I'm fine here."

"I'm sorry, we cannot discuss confidential matters in front of the main desk. If you wish to make a complaint, it must be done in the right way."

"The right way? That's rich given the behaviour of your so-called detectives."

The term had changed from officers to detectives. That, in all likelihood, meant Jack. Lang shuddered and wondered what he had been up to. Jack's ability to offend was growing by the day.

"I'm sorry, Ms Johnson, there is nothing I can do unless you allow me to do things properly."

Grudgingly, she allowed him to take her into the side room. Alice Johnson's mouth was ready to explode with everything she had. Normally, Lang would have offered her a coffee. Not this time. If Alice Johnson wanted one, she was not going to be slow to ask.

She sat down, banging the chair as she did so. Her manner was aggressive, with her body leaning over the table, ready to go on the offensive. In response, Lang took his time. He repositioned the chair to the side, removing the confrontation. Experience told him that the longer she was there, the calmer she would become. It was always difficult to maintain hostility when time was elapsing in a quiet room.

"Right, Ms Johnson, would you like to start from the beginning?"

A modicum of rage had subsided. The fire in her eyes was still burning but not with the intensity of before. She paused as if allowing the lava to boil up again. Deep down, the anger was still there and Lang was braced to receive it.

"That bloody detective. What the hell is he doing trying to dig up muck on my aunt and uncle?"

"Which detective?"

Lang knew exactly which one she meant. Only Jack was able to exasperate people with such effectiveness. He wanted time to study her reactions before she launched her offensive.

"That aggressive little one. You know, the one who knocks around with the younger girl. Is there something going on between them? You do know they sneaked off to Spain together, don't you?"

"If you are referring to the team following up on a case in Spain, then yes, I know they were over there."

"A case? You mean, they were trying to find my aunt and uncle."

"Who, by all accounts, are still missing."

It was Lang's turn to push forward. It was time to put the focus on Alice Johnson, to see if she would shrink back down. She didn't. Her face burned deeply with anger, which was ready to be fired back in his direction.

"How many bloody times do we have to tell you that they are not missing?" she hissed. "How do missing people keep writing to us?"

"That was a while ago, to be fair. The only card we've seen dates from the disappearance. We haven't got anything to prove they have written to you since."

"Then what the hell do you call this?"

Alice Johnson slapped a postcard down on the table. The handwritten card was marked with a date from last week. It was neat and signed by Pauline and Terry. All it said was how well they were. It felt scripted as if a response to the work Jack and Lisa had undertaken in Spain. Lang surveyed the card and nodded to Alice to confirm his understanding. That small concession was met by a softening of her demeanour from icy to a light frost.

"Well, I would say that wraps that up. I'm grateful for you bringing the card in. I am sure it will allow us to put the case to bed quickly. I know this hasn't been easy for you or your brother but we are duty-bound to keep investigating these matters until we have absolute closure."

Alice almost gave a hint of a smile.

"I just wish I had kept some of the other postcards and we could have sorted this out a long time ago. I'm not going to throw this one away."

"Hindsight is always a wonderful thing, Ms Johnson. Let me grab a copy of the card to put on the closure report and I'll let you get on your way. I'll contact my detectives as soon as we are finished and tell them to come in for a final briefing. As I said, I am very appreciative of you coming in to show us this."

"So is that the end of the matter?"

"That's up to you. Do you still want to put in that complaint? If you do, I will assign a fresh officer to investigate the conduct of my detectives during every aspect of the case."

Alice thought for a moment, smiled, and then declined. The DCI was not fooling anyone with his words.

***

Nigel Reeves sat with his body slumped against the padding of the old threadbare bench. He looked like a broken man. His life was in turmoil, his face withered away from stress. Yet it was the greyness that had taken the firmest hold. His form was that of a man some twenty years his senior.

"I don't know why I'm here," he sighed pitifully.

He gazed emptily across the room. His pint sat untouched, perched in the middle of the table, with a pool of beer surrounding the base. They were spillages from him falling forward onto the table. After two instances, the drink had been moved away as you would react with a young child.

Gregor Banks sat opposite him, offering an unconcerned appearance. His glass of water was placed on a side table, well away from clumsy arms. Behind him, two of his companions kept a respectable distance. There was little chance of either being needed.

"We both know why you are here, Mr Reeves. You want me to find your son."

"Yes, but this isn't the right way. I know it isn't."

"Then I suggest you pay for the drinks and we can both agree that this meeting never took place. I'm sure York's finest will soon find him, dead or alive."

A high-pitched wailing sound dragged itself from Nigel Reeves. The words 'dead or alive' could not be processed. He wanted Steven alive, not as a carcass for him to recognise on a cold slab. Who would have taken him? He was such an inoffensive young lad who had never done anyone any harm.

"I need him found, Mr Banks."

"Look, I don't promise anything. I will shake a few trees and see what drops out. If by doing so I can find him, that's all good for you."

"But you won't hurt anyone, will you?"

"Mr Reeves, I keep telling people I am a businessman. I negotiate and I get results. As long as people don't stand in my way, I go about my normal business."

"What about him?"

A finger pointed up towards one of the men who was standing at the bar. He was massive, with a wide neck and a shirt collar that barely fitted around it. The guy looked like trouble even to the untrained eye. It was not helped when the ogre cracked his knuckles and the room echoed with the noise.

"He's a business colleague. He's one of my top negotiators, aren't you, Bench?"

A grunt was emitted, indecipherable from his normal tone.

"See, I use him for his eloquent use of the English language. Did you know he is fluent in twelve different languages?"

Nigel looked at Bench and frowned. The sound Bench had uttered was unrecognisable to anyone.

"Will you find him?" squeaked Nigel.

"As I said, I don't make any promises. All I can assure you of is that we've got a pretty good track record, haven't we?"

Another grunt came from the bar.

"And what do you want in return?"

"That's the thing. Nothing."

"I don't understand."

"We're just doing you a favour. It costs us nothing to ask around. If we don't find him, at least we can say we tried. If we do find him, at some point you can owe me a favour back."

A sickly grin filled Gregor Banks's face. Nigel Reeves did not like it and yet he was not in any position to negotiate.

"I'm not sure. I'm supposed to be independent, not beholding to anyone."

"Hang on, I only said it would be a favour. Let's not overplay this. If the opportunity arises, you can help me out."

"And if it doesn't?"

"Then you don't help me out. I thought you guys who ran the city were supposed to be the clever ones. Don't make me out to be the brains. I left school with nothing."

"Let me think about it."

"Just don't think for too long. Time is life and death with missing people."

Jack walked through the door just as Gregor Banks rose from his seat. He looked shocked and froze. He glanced at Gregor and then at Nigel whose eyes shied away from making contact.

"We're just doing a bit of business, Jack," said Gregor, a little too keen to get the first bite at the story.

"Nigel Reeves and Gregor Banks. That has to be the most unlikely partnership in the history of business."

"I don't know. If you join us, we would be Husker, Reeves and Banks. That would be a pretty good firm of lawyers."

"Or undertakers," laughed Bench.

All three men scowled at the thug whose face flushed red from the attention. No one said anything, aware of the ogre's capability to lash out. Only Gregor knew he was safe and yet inwardly, he felt nothing but embarrassment.

"Care to elaborate on what this business is?" asked Jack.

Nigel Reeves went to speak. A raised hand from Gregor Banks stopped him. There was no point in arming his foe with more ammunition to fire back. The desire to control the situation was not lost on Jack.

"Funnily enough, no. The first rule of business is you don't go blabbing about opportunities. Anyway, how are you guys getting on with finding his son? Mr Reeves tells me he went missing and you guys are doing nothing about it."

"Mr Banks, that's not strictly true," insisted Nigel.

Jack shook his head. It was hard to believe that Nigel Reeves would enlist the help of Gregor Banks. How did he even know him, their social circles unlikely to cross by natural means?

"We're following up on several lines of enquiries," offered Jack. "Tell me, Nigel, are you aware of the range of criminal sentences available for vigilantism, either directly or indirectly?"

Nigel's face looked worried. Just those few choice words had his eyes flickering with fear.

"Give it a rest, Jack," interrupted Gregor. "Your lot can't even catch a cold. You don't scare either of us."

"Are you sure?"

Nigel Reeves inched away. He excused himself, insisting he needed to use the facilities. Both Jack and Gregor looked to the sky. It was hard to know whether the yellow streak within him came naturally or was genetic. They waited until the councillor was gone and then turned to face each other. The stare they exchanged had Bench inching closer.

"How are the injuries, Jack? I heard you got attacked."

"Yeah, and I wonder who did that."

"I wouldn't know. There are some dangerous streets out there."

"They wouldn't be if you were locked up."

"I think you tried that, Jack. From memory, you made a bit of a fool of yourself. Anyway, how's that lassie of yours?"

"Mary?"

"No, I was thinking of that young detective. The two of you seem to be getting on far better than that old university hag you were knocking around with."

"Don't talk about Mary like that."

"Sorry, I didn't realise that the two of you were still an item. I struggle to keep up with all the disappointed women in your life."

Jack looked directly towards him. Bench edged even closer. One move and the ogre would strike. He only had one task in life and that was to protect his boss. Jack looked to the side, noting his poised position. An argument with Gregor Banks could wait; hospital food was not on his wish list for the day.

"Are you finished?"

"Yes, I'll be seeing you, Jack. If I were you, I'd enjoy that beer. I'm not sure Reeves is man enough to drink it."

For once, Gregor had a point. Jack lifted the beer and downed it in one swift-flowing gulp. He was right about Nigel Reeves. Panicked, the councillor had climbed through the bathroom window, scuttled across a garage roof and was gone.

***

DCI Lang was waiting for Jack when he returned to the station. He looked calm and had a wry smile written across his face. It was enough to put Jack on edge. A contented Lang was something he had learned to be wary of.

"Have you got a moment, Jack?"

Jack nodded and followed his superior up to his office. He wished he had bought some chewing gum on the way back. Inside his mouth, the taste of beer was still fresh.

"Do you want to guess who came to see me today?"

Lang had barely walked into his office before he asked. Jack did the right thing by waiting until the door was closed before offering any indication that he might answer.

"Go on, you've got me intrigued."

"A certain Ms Johnson."

"As in a relation of Pauline and Terry Johnson, I presume."

"The very same."

"What on earth did she want?"

"To put in a complaint about you. She thinks you are rude and aggressive."

"I am, but that's a bit rich coming from her. Did you believe her?"

"Of course I did, Jack. You are rude and aggressive, we know that. However, that is not why I called you in here." Lang pushed the copy of the postcard across the desk. He left it in front of Jack until his eyes were fully focused on it. "Tell me what you make of this."

Jack picked it up. The expression on his face turned to shock. He looked at it a couple of times as if someone was playing a joke on him.

"You have got to be kidding me. When did she claim to have received this?"

"In the last few days."

"That's a laugh. It is postmarked less than a week ago."

"So?"

"Does she know anything about the Spanish postal service?"

Both men laughed.

"It gets better, sir," continued Jack. "The postmark is still the wrong one. She wouldn't know to change it."

Lang nodded. "I'll give her full marks for her front."

"You shouldn't be looking, sir," offered Jack.

"Pardon?" Lang frowned in confusion.

"Nothing, sir. What was she thinking allowing you to copy it?"

"Let's just say you are not the only one with persuasive charms." A sense of smugness went across DCI Lang's face.

Jack said nothing and studied the images closely. Lang went on to tell him that in her eyes the case was closed. The complaint had been withdrawn, leaving Jack and Lisa to go about their work. They had to tread carefully to ensure the nephew and niece were not spooked. This new revelation meant they had a little bit of time on their side.

"Do you know what I'm thinking?" asked Jack.

"I probably do, but go on."

"I think we carry on with our plan to speak to the student. They'll think everything has gone quiet. Let's finish off all the background stuff and then we can move in on them once we are ready."

"Do you want surveillance on the two of them?" asked Lang.

"Not yet. Let's get everything else done without them knowing and then we'll start to tighten the net. I don't want them running scared. Not until we've worked out who that fourth person is. Something tells me if we find that out, we will be close to cracking this one."

"And what about the missing councillor's son and the tour guide?"

"I reckon the Reeves lad will be dead. The tour guide, I'm not so sure. He's just as likely to be on a bender and be passed out on somebody's floor. I wouldn't give up hope on him yet."

"Jack, I haven't given up hope on Steven Reeves either."

"Sorry, you're right. I just have a funny feeling that the lad has found himself in the wrong place at the wrong time. It was obvious he had something to hide when I met him. My mistake was not forcing it out of him the first time."

"Jack, we don't force things out of anybody."

Jack smiled. They both knew what he meant and they both knew it was an opportunity that had been lost.

CHAPTER 14

SOPHIE NEAL WOKE AT ten o'clock. It had been a late night even by student standards. Her mouth felt dry and her head was telling her she needed more sleep. Only the vibration of her phone on the bedside table caused her to stir. It was the same number. The policewoman who had left the message the day before was still trying to contact her.

She reached up and pushed the phone to the floor. The noise cut off in an instant. An improvement, made better by a pillow dragged over her head. Sophie drifted back into her daze. Her body craved her bed and now even more for the interruption.

All too soon, it rang again. This time, Sophie was jolted upright. Why did she keep ringing? Had it really been an hour when it felt like no more than minutes? In the sober light of day, her head was pounding. Sophie eased to the floor and fumbled for her phone. Once found, she swiped to answer and pressed the handset to her ear.

"Yes, what is it?" groaned Sophie.

"Is that Sophie Neal?"

"Speaking."

"This is DS Lisa Ramsey from York police."

"What do you want? It's the middle of the night."

"It's ten past eleven."

"It's still early by my standards."

Lisa smiled. Her mind drifted back to her student days. Nights became days and days became nights at a time when life had less purpose. To be a student again, but with some money to spend, would be an invitation to get into trouble.

"I'm sorry to disturb you, Ms Neal. I need to come over and speak with you."

"Not you as well. You're the second one. Can't you decide what you want?"

"Second?"

"Yes, that guy rang me before."

"May I ask, was it DI Jack Husker?"

"No, it was PC...hang on, I've written it down somewhere. That's it, PC Black. To be honest, he didn't sound much like a policeman. No offence, mind you."

"None taken."

Lisa racked her brain. She was still unfamiliar with all the names in the station. PC Black was another who was unknown to her.

"Did he say what he wanted?"

"Do any of you? He just said it was part of a case he was investigating."

"And where did he ask to meet you?"

"A cafe called Flanagan's or something like that, why? I told him I was not going. Can we talk about this later?"

Alarm bells rang in Lisa's head. Her mind sprung to life with the memory of Steven Reeves. Flanagan's was the last known sighting of him. It was where Jack had met him and from where it was believed Steven had disappeared. None of the thoughts in Lisa's head would offer a good ending for Sophie.

"Where are you, I'm on my way?" insisted Lisa.

"In bed, I told you."

"Get dressed. We're coming straight for you."

"Can't I have another hour?"

"You've got half an hour. What's your address?"

Lisa jotted down the details. She knew she would give her less than ten minutes. It was just long enough to track down Jack, mobilise a support car and arrive unannounced at Sophie Neal's house.

As soon as Lisa ended the call, Sophie got up. She walked to the bathroom and drank a glass of water. Only briefly did she stop to look in the mirror. It afforded her a sight that was best described as not looking her best. She groaned and returned to the bedroom where she slumped onto the bed and threw the pillow back over her head.

Again, the silence was interrupted by her phone. Without raising her head, Sophie's hand reached up. She could not leave it, the phone an unfortunate addiction. She pulled it towards her and, without looking at the screen, accepted the call. The handset was dragged under the pillow.

"What now? I said, come over in an hour."

There was an eerie silence at the end of the line. She could make out the hint of faint breathing. Nothing followed and the caller rang off after a few seconds. This time, Sophie was taking no chances. She turned off her phone and slipped it into the drawer. Five minutes had been wasted; she was not going to lose any more precious sleeping time.

It took Lisa a few minutes to track down Jack. When she told him, his first reaction mirrored Lisa's. Despite the advantage of a long history in the station, the name was far from familiar. There had been a White and a Green. Indeed, there had been enough colours for a game of Cluedo and yet Black was not known to Jack.

"Are you sure she said 'Black'?"

"Yes, I'm certain."

"Hang on," recalled Jack. "We had a guy transfer up from the Met for a case a few years ago. He was called Black. A real smug git, sent up for a big fraud case because it was deemed York couldn't handle it. He was not very popular, I can tell you."

"And could you handle it?"

"No chance, but that's not the point, is it? It was a York case and it should have been managed by York police."

Lisa frowned at Jack's logic and yet it was a strangely familiar tale to her home station. There was nothing worse than an outsider solving a Newcastle case.

"It can't be him," said Lisa. "Are there any others?"

"I'm not exactly the keeper of the personnel records, but no, I don't remember another one."

"So who is this guy?"

"Possibly somebody playing a trick or she has got the name wrong. Either way, I don't think we can take any chances. Let's get down there and pick her up. Remember, she is our last known person on that tour."

Fine, I'll get some uniforms mobilised."

At Sophie Neal's, a large thudding knock offered no chance for her to continue to sleep. She rolled over and pulled the pillow tight to her ear. It made no difference for the hammering on her door only got louder.

"For crying out loud, I said an hour!"

Sophie rose from her bed and threw a dressing gown over her shoulders. Her head still hurt and had been made worse by the constant interruptions. She paused briefly to tie off the belt around her waist. The sight of her was already scary enough without the need for anyone to see more of her.

She was at the top of the stairs when the thundering knock sounded once more. It surprised her, for the sound was coming from the back door. It came again, sending the vibration through her fragile head. As her eyes blinked closed, the pain throbbed across her temple.

"Police, open up!"

"I heard you! Give me a minute!" she bellowed.

Sophie walked to the bathroom and filled her hands with cold water. Twice, she submerged her face into her palms. She shuddered. It was unpleasant and a rude intrusion, no different from the police who were threatening to knock down her door. She looked terrible. There were huge black bags under her eyes, hovering above a gaunt-looking face. Her mother had always said she should eat better but it was the drinking and the lack of sleep that did the damage. Despite her appearance, there was no hiding the fact that she felt even worse than she looked.

Another knock on the back door greeted her when she reached the bottom of the stairs. This time, it was firmer. Sophie feared the loss of her security deposit. The frame was rotten and if the police forced the door open, she would be paying for the damage.

"I said, I'm on my way!"

As she approached the door, she could hear movement outside. It made little sense to approach from the rear of the house. The front door was perfectly serviceable and faced the street. Indeed, the only purpose of the back was to sneak people in and out without being noticed. Sophie smiled and remembered the one-night stand she had slipped out through the back, just as her boyfriend had knocked at the front. They were fun memories from a time when she cared less about morals and when sleep was of no importance.

Carefully, Sophie unbolted the back door. It seemed pointless when the bolts were not fixed to anything solid. They offered comfort rather than a physical barrier to keep people out. There were two latches, top and bottom, and neither made the door secure.

"Right, what do you want?" demanded Sophie. "Hang on, you're not the police."

A single blow to the side of her head knocked Sophie to the floor. She recoiled to her left and plummeted downwards. Her senses faded to the brief sighting of a hooded man. He was unfamiliar and the memory was soon lost in her descent into a darkened world.

***

Jack and Lisa arrived at the house fifteen minutes after Lisa had called. It was quiet, with a solitary light left on in the bedroom. The front door was locked and the curtains were drawn downstairs, offering the suggestion that nobody had got up.

"Keep knocking," said Jack. "I'll go and have a look around the back."

"If nobody answers, I'll try the neighbours," added Lisa.

Jack walked to the end of the street. He turned and followed the narrow path down to the rear alley. It was cobbled and just big enough to drive a vehicle down. That was if it was left clear. He gazed down and then bent over for a closer look. Wet tyre marks appeared fresh and two bins were pushed onto their side. It hinted that a vehicle had been in the alleyway not that long ago. And yet there was every chance it was not related.

"Three, four, five..."

Jack counted the houses on his way back along the terrace. He opened the correct gate and entered the yard. Inside, the rear door was closed. Jack looked at it and gave it a gentle kick, which was enough to send it swinging inwards. He slipped on his gloves and looked into the building, knowing anything could be inside.

"Police, identify yourself!" he called out.

The house was silent

"I'm coming in," insisted Jack.

There was still nothing. The eerie state of the house left Jack concerned. He moved slowly, hoping someone would stir. At least a burglar would try to get away. It was somebody hiding in the shadows he feared; someone with more to lose than he had.

Edging forward, Jack noted the grubby state of the house. It was not unlike his own, long since loved by anyone. At best, functional, there was little to like about the place. Jack's eyes scanned carefully, looking for anything unusual as his senses told him something was wrong.

The house was empty. He moved into the lounge and was greeted by a musty smell. In front of him was a collection of tatty old furniture and stale beer cans, some of which had been used to collect ash. It was squalid and smelt damp. To Jack, it was a reminder of his student days. It paid homage to a time he thought was lost.

His attention was taken by a knock at the front door. His body stiffened and then relaxed when he heard Lisa's voice. It was soft and familiar, its welcoming tone a relief. Jack moved slowly towards it, let out a deep sigh and opened the front door.

"Found anything?" she asked.

"Tyre marks at the top of the alley and an unlocked back door. Downstairs is a typical student fleapit. Do you want to have the honour of leading upstairs?"

"The honour?"

"Yes, I thought we would share the full experience. It's a rite of passage along with some of the cafes I take you into."

"Thanks. Is there anyone up there?"

"Just three dead bodies and an axeman. After you," smiled Jack, holding his hand out towards the stairs.

Lisa bristled and narrowed her eyes before deciding it was no time to argue.

"Come on," insisted Lisa. "Let's get it searched. After all, those bodies might have another appointment in their diary."

"And the axeman?" queried Jack.

"He's with me. He's probably the best chance I have of dating someone my parents would approve of."

Lisa marched up the stairs. Inside, her heart was pounding even if she would not admit it. When Jack did not follow immediately, she slowed her pace. Thankfully, he soon caught up and they moved together. Both were braced for someone to fly at them on their way to the back door.

Upstairs was the equal of the ground floor. Three bedrooms had been left in a mess and were accompanied by a bathroom riddled with mould. The beds were unmade. Lisa found Sophie's and placed a hand on the mattress. It was still warm, suggesting she had left in a hurry.

"What do you reckon?" asked Lisa.

"She could be at lectures," shrugged Jack. "Let's go back to the station and give the university a call."

"Or she could have been abducted," offered Lisa. "Actually, given the state of the house, that might improve her living conditions. Tell me, do people live like this?"

Jack blushed and reached up with his hand to hide his face. Already, he had made a mental note to himself, Lisa was not getting an invite to his house.

***

At the station, DCI Lang was sat in his office. He was enjoying a quiet moment in the run-up to lunch. He leaned back and relaxed his eyes. The tiredness in him caused the lids to drop for a few precious seconds. It jolted him awake. Fear ripped through him that someone would see him asleep. It was not the done thing for the chief to be sleeping while others were working hard in the field.

As he forced himself upwards, a junior popped in to drop off a report. Thankfully, his eagerness to get out of the office meant Lang's drowsy state went unnoticed. He was relieved it had not been one of the wiser owls who had seen him. That small advantage would have given them an edge for months.

He needed a holiday. It was a repeated message from his wife. This time, she had taken it a stage further by booking a trip to Italy. Not his first choice, but she had given up waiting for him to act. She had taken the matter into her own hands. He smiled. He needed that break even if it was a few weeks away.

A knock at the door interrupted his thoughts. It was Jill Baker, a young officer who was making quite an impression in the station. Her police work was thorough and her appearance had not gone unnoticed. Lang had seen the attention she got and yet the girl seemed to handle it with aplomb. Nobody took liberties with Jill and that impressed him.

"Sorry to disturb you, sir. We've got a call for you from someone called Dr Larkins. He's a lecturer at the university. He wants to report a missing student."

"Okay, you had better put him through."

Lang waited for the phone and accepted it after the first ring. It felt strange to be talking about missing students a full year after the sketch murders. Not that there hadn't been a few scares along the way. There had been too many false alarms from students getting themselves into drunken escapades only to turn up a day or two later.

"DCI Nick Lang speaking."

"Hello, this is Dr Larkins from the university. I want to speak to you about one of our students. She has gone missing. She was due to turn up to a tutorial this morning but didn't show up."

Lang turned up the volume to allow himself to stand up and walk around his desk as he spoke. He no longer felt tired and the thought of Italy had been banished.

"Surely that isn't unusual for a student."

"It is in this case. She texted to say she would be late because the police wanted to speak to her first. That was the last we heard from her."

"Can you give me her name?" asked Lang.

Before Dr Larkins could respond, DCI Lang's door flew open. In walked Jack who interrupted his superior by calling out, "Sophie Neal." He was followed in by Lisa, who was struggling to keep up behind him.

"Excuse me a moment, Dr Larkins."

Lang was furious. He pressed the mute button and turned to Jack with a face like thunder.

"What the hell do you think you are doing barging in like that? I'm being told a student is missing and, hang on, how do you know her name?"

"We've just been to her house."

Lang's jaw dropped visibly. It created a chasm that a small bird could have flown into. He remained like that until he regathered his composure, which was accompanied by a rise in his blood pressure.

"Why is it that you are involved in every bloody disappearance in this city?"

"Just unlucky, I suppose."

"That had better be the case. Sit down and let me finish the call."

Jack sat down while Lisa took the seat alongside him. Opposite, Lang returned to his chair and picked up the handset. It was a deliberate attempt to not allow Jack to hear what was being said. He offered an apology to Dr Larkins, regretting the rude interruption to the call. As the details were given, Lang jotted them down and nodded. The call ended with the promise that an officer would be sent to see him.

Lang placed the handset down solemnly. His face had a ghostly appearance, having been drained of colour. To Jack and Lisa, he looked scared. It was the same look he had offered when the sketch killer had been at the peak of his spree.

"Sophie Neal?" asked Jack.

Lang nodded.

"So, that's Steven Reeves and Sophie Neal officially missing. Meanwhile, Jimmy Niven has gone to ground."

"That's about the long and short of it," confirmed Lang.

There was another knock on the office door and another apology from Jill Baker.

"Now is not a good time, Jill."

"This is important, sir."

"Is it about Sophie Neal?"

She shook her head.

"Then, no, it isn't important right now. Come back later."

Jill Baker stood silently. She was not sure whether to offer her information. Lang waited and stared impatiently, expecting her to turn and leave. She never moved, leaving Jack to interrupt when he recognised the uncertainty on her face.

"Just tell us. It will be quicker."

"A man called Jimmy Niven has just been reported missing. I thought you'd want to know."

Lang slumped to the desk and allowed his face to sink into his hands. This time, it was Jack's turn to look fearful.

The news forced silence in the room for nearly twenty seconds. In that time, Jill turned and left. Both men took a moment to regain eye contact before Lisa felt the need to speak.

"I'll get some coffee," she offered.

Both Lang and Jack sat staring, with their eyes piercing through each other. Either might as well have not been there. They were lost in their thoughts and knew they had a problem. It was a problem that was growing out of control.

Finally, Lang broke the deadlock. He scribbled a few words onto a piece of paper. They were a memory jogger, a method of getting the facts out in front of them. Neither of them needed it when the names were etched firmly in their minds.

"Ignoring the Johnsons, we are looking for Steven Reeves, Sophie Neal and now, Jimmy Niven. All three of them were on that ghost tour you spoke about along with another mystery person. Each of them potentially witnessed Pauline and Terry Johnson disappearing and all three are now missing."

"That's about right," confirmed Jack.

"And what else do we know?" queried Lang.

"We know that as soon as we started investigating, a forged postcard turned up from the Johnsons," added Jack.

"Is it fair to say that all roads lead to the nephew and niece?"

"I would say so but we have nothing to pin on them that would stick," said Jack.

"What about the vehicle?" asked Lang.

"We went down that route when the Johnsons went missing. No van was linked to them."

"Which means they have somewhere to hide it."

"Exactly."

"And what about the fourth member of the tour?"

"Still nothing. We need to identify her and then we have to move fast."

"You're right, Jack. Once we know who she is, we don't let her out of our sight until we have the case solved."

"Or we use her as bait," smiled Jack, in a way that did nothing but trouble his superior.

"Coffee," announced Lisa with a smile, trying to lighten the mood as she walked through the door. The reaction she was given by both men told her it might be a bad time. "Shall I go away again?"

"No, sit down. We might have the beginning of a plan."

***

Gregor Banks was leaning back in his chair. His hands were entwined, allowing his thumbs free-reign to move. He circled them around each other, dancing his digits in front of his quarry. He was having fun at the expense of a man who needed him.

"I didn't think you were interested in my services, Mr Reeves."

"I need my son found, Mr Banks. Do whatever it takes to find him."

"Do you really mean 'anything'?"

Nigel Reeves shuddered when the question was turned back towards him. His hand gripped around his pint glass a little harder. There was tension in his body and a feeling that all his problems had come together. Reluctantly, he nodded even if he was unable to force out the words.

"Careful with that glass, you'll break it."

The councillor's knuckles were white. His grip had tightened around the base. It forced Gregor Banks to lean over to prize the glass from his hand. There was no point spilling good beer even in the hovel they sat in. Gregor glanced down and noted the grotty carpet. A few more stains would make no difference.

Gregor Banks had chosen the location for a reason. In the corner sat a shadowy man. He said nothing. All the while, he monitored the two of them, with a baseball cap pulled down over his face. He never looked across. Instead, he sat and listened to every word. There was no need to make notes. His mind retained everything and it would be filed away until he needed it.

"How long will it take?" asked Nigel Reeves.

"How long does anything take?" offered Gregor with a shrug. "Hours, days, weeks, who knows? These things take as long as they take. It's the result that counts."

"I won't do anything illegal in return."

Gregor Banks reeled back with indignation. It was hard to tell if it was for show or whether he was genuinely offended. He played the mortally wounded card well, allowing just long enough for the reaction to be noticed.

"How many times do I have to tell people I am a businessman, not a gangster?"

"I'm sorry. It's just your father; well, you know."

"You mean my father who was framed by that excuse we have for a police force in the city. He's not the first and he won't be the last unless you can do something about it."

Briefly, a flicker of excitement appeared in the voice of Gregor Banks.

"I don't think the power of a councillor runs quite that deep. We are not above the law."

Gregor released a sigh in an overplayed effort to show his disappointment.

"Look, Mr Banks. You know if you find my son, I'll do anything I can to help you. I just want him found."

It was music to his ears and more so, to the shadowy man who smiled into his pint.

"I can assure you I will be doing everything I can to help."

Nigel Reeves got up, leaving his half-drunk pint behind. He looked gaunt as if age had played a trick on him since his son went missing. Gregor sipped at his drink contentedly, pleased that the councillor was not staying for a longer chat.

"Not finishing that?" he asked.

"I can't. I'm so worried," came the reply.

"Look, I've got your number. I'll call you when I have some information. Go and get some sleep."

Nigel Reeves went to respond with a message that he couldn't sleep. Already, Gregor Banks had lost interest. His eyes were staring at his phone, perhaps looking at contacts to track down his son. Nigel paused for a moment, then turned and exited the bar. Gregor waited until he was sure he had left the building.

"Did you get all that?"

"Every word," smiled the man in the shadows. "I can see the headline now. City councillor is seen offering favours to a local businessman."

"Very good, Mr Hutton. We'll make a journalist of you yet. Now, you never gave me an answer to my proposition. Are you going to run my exclusive in return for a bit of meat on Jack Husker?"

Andy Hutton sat with a dead-pan expression, trying to think of a way to let Gregor Banks down gently. He had no intention of being his public mouthpiece. Hutton's bosses had warned him off when he first floated the idea.

"Our main men don't want to run with it. I'm still keen but there's a lot of convincing to do."

Gregor shook his head at the journalist.

"What a load of rubbish. Admit it, you're too yellow-livered to stick your neck out. Let me know when you grow a backbone."

Gregor rose from his stool and left a ten-pound note on the bar. He was fuming and somebody was going to pay.

CHAPTER 15

LISA LOOKED UP AT the impressive university buildings. It was a far cry from her education, a time she had spent in far less salubrious surroundings. There was a busy throng of youngsters outside. Intertwined, was the occasional older interloper, with their clothes rather than their age making them stand out from the crowd.

It was hard to comprehend that one of their pack was missing. Sophie Neal should have been among them. She would have been crisscrossing through the melee in front of her, heading to her lectures that afternoon. Among her peers, she would have been anonymous and able to blend in unnoticed. Lisa studied the faces, hoping that she was one of them while reflecting on the probable sad outcome. The longer she was missing, the chances of finding her were diminishing.

Lisa glanced at the details on her phone. All she had was what she had photographed before she left. It read, 'Dr Larkins, 3rd floor, Jorvik Building, 3 pm'. She was ten minutes early and it afforded her enough time to look around.

The university felt like a strange place. A mixture of old and new, it now seemed to be fighting for its identity. For Lisa, it was her first real look at it. Her year in York had not allowed her much time to go there. Jack had led on the sketch murders. He was the one with the university contacts and, of course, there was Mary. That was another reason for Jack to visit and for Lisa to stay away.

"Can I help you?"

Lisa turned to see a woman in front of her. In her mid-forties, she was not unattractive and fitted the description of Mary. Lisa smiled, with a somewhat embarrassed response. Surely it was not her, not that she had any intention of revealing her identity. What if Jack had mentioned her to Mary and now their paths were about to become linked?

"I'm looking for Dr Larkins."

"Try the second building on your left when you go under the walkway. You will need to go around the back to get in."

"Thanks."

Lisa walked away before the conversation could continue, leaving the exchange as a brief interaction between two random strangers. Maybe it was somebody else and her mind was trying to play tricks on her. Either way, she walked on quickly. There was nothing to be gained from finding out.

The directions were good. The building met the description and more importantly, the reception was at the back. A prim-looking lady greeted her, one whose hair had been set to perfection. Lisa noted the contrast to herself. Every part of her appeared dishevelled, a product of the breeze outside.

"Hi, I've got an appointment with Dr Larkins."

"Ah, DS Ramsey, he's expecting you. It is a terrible business about Sophie, isn't it? What do you think has happened to her?"

Lisa knew better than to engage in idle chatter at the front desk.

"Is he in his office?"

"Yes, of course. The lift is over there. Do you think she's been abducted?"

"Third floor?"

"Yes. Do you know who took her?"

"I'll see myself up."

"Okay, DS Ramsey."

Lisa felt relieved to extricate herself from the receptionist's clutches. Not that she felt anything sinister, the lady simply craved information. Maybe she knew her or maybe she was just a lonely old gossip. Either way, she was getting no tittle-tattle on her watch.

Dr Larkins was sitting in his office. Studiously, he tapped away at a computer. Books of text were laid out in front of him and were being used actively. The sign on the door informed Lisa of his specialism in ancient history. He hardly looked the sort. His appearance was that of a science teacher but what did Lisa know? She was simply judging him based on first impressions.

A quiet knock saw her beckoned in. Dr Larkins barely glanced up from his work. He stared at the textbooks and a couple of manuscripts alongside them. With each line he read, his head shook and was accompanied by sounds of admonishment. To

Lisa, it felt like being back at school following a summons from the headmaster. She could feel the butterflies dancing inside her.

"Unbelievable!" he announced abruptly.

Just a single word was offered and then nothing to follow. When he fell silent, his finger traced along the line of text. Lisa waited to be formally invited to sit down, aware she was in the presence of a busy man.

"Does he think we are stupid? Oh, I'm Dr Larkins, pleased to meet you."

He stood up. A hand was offered along with another series of tuts in the direction of the papers. Lisa offered her introduction. She was unsure whether he had heard it. She sat down and waited for his attention, knowing she might have to get heavy-handed to get his full focus.

"Sorry," he announced suddenly. "I'm just very disappointed."

"I'm not sure I follow," offered Lisa. "I'm here to talk about Sophie Neal."

"Oh yes, I'm sorry."

He shook his head and then glanced back at the screen. The lure of whatever had distracted him kept pulling him back. It felt strange for Lisa to play second fiddle when Dr Larkins was the one who had called her in.

"Do you want me to come back later?"

"No, I'm so sorry. Let me turn this off. Give me a minute and we'll go somewhere else. I'm in a bit of a state in here."

Lisa glanced around. There were stacks of papers everywhere. Each of the items was laid out to suggest it was current. The mess was hardly a problem. The office looked lived in, a bit like most of the desks back in the station.

"This is fine. I'm sorry to intrude. Is everything okay?"

"Yes, actually no, it isn't. I've been teaching this lad for three years. He's one of my brightest students and then he puts this in. Look!"

Dr Larkins thrust a document into Lisa's hands. It was a piece on ancient history, either a large essay or a thesis. Her eyes scanned it and yet she had little to offer. It felt like she was expected to provide a critical eye.

"I'm not sure I can help much. I didn't get very far with history. It looks a fair piece of work to me."

"Of course, sorry, it's the job. I start to think everyone knows the subject as well as I do. The work is plagiarised. Large passages have been copied. I was trying to identify the source when you came in."

"And have you found it?"

"I think so. I recognised it from my own time studying. I did a thesis on the same subject and remembered the work. It's all in there, you know."

Lisa smiled as he tapped his head.

"Will he get into trouble?"

"Trouble? He'll be lucky to leave with a degree. We'll put him in front of the committee and he can explain himself. If he's got enough about him, he'll cite some form of stress. Committees are suckers for a good sob story. He will probably need the death of someone close or something similar to turn this one around."

"Or a disappearance?"

"Ah, the matter I called you about. Sophie Neal, a most unfortunate occurrence. That won't help him. They barely knew each other."

Lisa spent nearly an hour with Dr Larkins. In that time, she did her utmost to keep him on track. At first, his ease of distraction was quaint. By the end, Lisa wished she had agreed to go to another room. He constantly referred his facts back to his computer as if it acted as some form of electronic comfort blanket. Dates, times and even the stage of her studies were all checked back to his records. There was no doubt he would make a reliable witness.

Beyond the timeline and his insistence that Sophie would never miss a tutorial, he gave little of use. There was a reference to the meeting with the police. Even that was checked on the computer. Lisa took the details and vowed to follow up on the number she had called from, knowing it was likely to be Sophie's.

"Sorry, I can't be of more help," sighed Dr Larkins.

"You've given us plenty to go on. I'll let you get back to your work."

"I can't believe something like this has happened."

"We don't know anything has happened to her yet."

"Who would have thought," he continued, "that a student of mine would be passing off someone else's work as their own? It's just wrong."

He was back in his trance and mumbling to himself. All the while, his hands traced feverishly across the passages of text. Lisa thanked him quietly and got up, knowing he had not heard her. It allowed her to slip out of his office without being noticed.

***

Jack recognised Bench as soon as he arrived at the restaurant. His suited appearance did little to hide what he was. His neck bulged over the collar of his shirt, his hands slipping in and out to show his discomfort. At best, he looked like a bouncer; at worst, a thug squeezed into a suit.

For once, Jack had the edge, thanks to a tip-off from a favour he was owed. His approach had been through one of York's snickelways. It twisted and turned through a narrow cobbled alleyway, only opening up into the square at the last minute. That gave him a side view of the thug. Jack contemplated saying nothing and using his advantage to surprise the ogre from behind. Self-preservation stopped him. It would give Bench freedom to strike out in self-defence. It made more sense to enjoy a moment of fun.

Jack got as close as he dared and then shouted, "Afternoon!"

The ogre was startled and spun around. It was unlike one of Gregor Banks's goons to be caught off-guard. Fearing it was his boss, he stiffened until he recognised Jack's appearance. Only then, did he begin to breathe more easily.

"What do you want?"

"I take it pets have to be left outside?" queried Jack.

"No, I don't think so," replied Bench.

Jack smiled and watched the cogs turn slowly inside his head. There was no point explaining the little dig to him. He would never get it. Bench was a man hired purely for his muscle.

"Is the Guv'nor inside?"

"Who?"

"Your boss, Gregor Banks."

"I don't know."

"So, what are you doing here?"

"Just enjoying the fresh air."

Jack shook his head. He had a feeling that his life was ebbing away. He didn't have long enough to live to be wasting it talking to Bench. He shook his head and moved around his large frame, only for the thug to step across the doorway.

"Don't even bother, son, or you're getting pinned for every unsolved crime in this city. If you've heard the tales of unscrupulous coppers, they're true. Mess with me and you'll be going down."

Bench thought for a moment and glanced back at the restaurant. He adjusted his shirt, forcing his fat fingers into the tight collar. It was like watching a mechanical process where his brain was trying to instruct his body to act. After a couple of grunts, Bench stepped aside and allowed Jack to pass.

"Very wise," confirmed Jack, whose heart rate had increased by twenty beats.

Jack never took his eyes off Bench for a second. He stared at the ogre until the restaurant door was closed firmly behind him. It was too easy for something to be cudgelled across the back of his skull and for him to become another of York's missing. Once inside, Jack slipped the latch to prevent anyone from following.

It was quiet inside. The restaurant was set out for dinner, with every table covered with crisp white linen. As many as twenty-five tables filled the main eating area, with a bar running down the side of the room. It was cosy, perhaps the sort of place he would have brought Mary if he was looking for something special. With no tables set for one, it was now out of bounds for a single middle-aged detective.

Suddenly, Jack heard a wail from the back room. It was long and slow and came from the depths of a man's body. It was one forced out through physical means. Gregor Banks was in the house and the self-styled businessman was negotiating in the way he does best. Jack took a deep breath and was treated to a repeat of the noise. His response was to move a little closer.

Jack was on edge. His eyes flitted around, aware that somebody could strike at any moment. Gregor Banks was not someone who saw merit in a clean fight. He preferred to pounce from behind and ideally when flanked by some thugs. Jack knew it and braced himself to react.

He eased the kitchen door open. Inside, there were two men, both with their backs turned away. Jack watched as a meat-tenderising mallet was lifted high in the air. There was a pause and then it was brought down with force. As it crashed to the worktop, the second man released a desperate cry of anguish.

"Gregor, I might need another reminder that you're a businessman," laughed Jack. "It does get hard to remember at times."

Gregor Banks turned around, offering a look of irritation. Beside him, a man in chef's overalls had his face screwed up in agony. His hand was a mess, with fingers splayed out at unusual angles. There was little doubt it was a scene that was meant to have taken place in private.

"What do you want, Husker? I'm busy."

"I can see that. I would shake hands with your colleague but I don't think it would be appreciated. Is this one of your special business deals?"

"Don't get smart with me. Let's go inside the restaurant. I'm done in here."

The relief on the chef's face was obvious. He was in agony and would not have the use of his hand for a while. There were bones to reset and a long period of recuperation ahead.

"I'm working on the basis that your friend doesn't want to press charges. Am I right to assume that?"

"By all means, ask him," shrugged Gregor.

"I'm not sure I'll bother. My card is here if he wants to call me."

Jack threw a contact card onto the table. It was taken by Gregor Banks who tore it up and stuffed the pieces into the chef's mouth. It was done for show, with no resistance offered by a man who would not be making a complaint.

"He's been brought up not to speak with his mouth full," noted Gregor. "Good manners are so hard to come by these days, don't you think?"

"So I'm told," said Jack.

"Shall we leave him to get back to work, Jack? These chefs are like princesses. They don't like people in their way."

Jack walked out of the kitchen while flicking nervous glances over his shoulder. Gregor followed at a distance, detouring to the bar on his way out. He took his time to survey the bottles of red wine. With great care, he chose one and collected a corkscrew and two empty glasses.

"Wine, Jack? The chef said to help ourselves to a good bottle."

"Did he? I must admit I don't speak the language of suffering."

"Are you sure? I thought inflicting yourself on two wives would have made you an expert. I can show you some of the basics if you want."

"I'll pass, thank you."

The pop of the cork made Jack jump. His first thought was a gunshot, with an instinctive move made by his hand to his chest. Gregor Banks looked relaxed and poured two glasses of wine carelessly. He handed one to Jack and clinked it with his own before taking a generous swig.

"They say you should not overfill the glasses to appreciate it more. Something tells me you're not into that pompous stuff."

Jack smiled. For once, they had common ground.

"I presume you want to talk to me," said Gregor.

"That was before I saw you rearranging the chef's fingers," insisted Jack.

"Can you believe the bastard was skimming from me? I will not have thieves in my business."

"I didn't know you owned this place."

"Jack, there is a lot you don't know about me. I may have a certain way in negotiations, but deep down, I'm just a guy trying to make a living like anyone else."

Jack found himself struggling to believe the cheek of the man. He leaned back and took a sip of the wine. The choice was good, a deep oak-flavoured red, with plenty of after-tastes that sat on the tongue. If he could afford to drink wine of that standard, he might even contemplate switching from beer.

"I need some help, Gregor. I've got someone to find."

"Not another missing person. The city will be empty at the rate you lot are losing people."

"This one is different," insisted Jack. "This one needs to be found to go missing."

"Presumably that's some fancy police logic?" queried Gregor.

Jack smiled. A warm sensation ran through him at the thought of having Gregor Banks confused. It made him feel good, not that he would show it to the supposed businessman. In the kitchen, he had seen what he was capable of. With a thug outside, one signal could result in pain being inflicted at his master's bequest. The time was right to do things subtly and see if he could persuade Gregor Banks to help.

Jack explained the details of the couple that went missing along with three of the four members of the tour. Any one of them may have seen the events and yet each now formed part of the missing list. Gregor nodded when they got to the name of Steven Reeves. It gave him the missing piece to his previous conversation. When Jimmy Niven's name was mentioned, a scowl returned to the gangster's face.

"You know him?" asked Jack.

"Yes, he's a small-time dealer. I'm not disappointed to see that little scumbag off the streets. Before you ask, I wasn't involved."

"Why would you be? You're a businessman."

"Do you want my help?" snarled Gregor.

"Sorry."

Jack could see the irritation on his face. Gregor Banks was not happy to be on the wrong side of a joke. He admonished himself, knowing he may have blown his chances. Jack allowed a moment of recovery, which was taken by Gregor's thoughtful words.

"So, we've got the older couple plus Steven Reeves and Jimmy Niven missing."

"That's right."

"Anyone else?"

"Yes, Sophie Neal."

Gregor Banks shook his head, the name unfamiliar to him. He thought for a moment and then frowned at Jack.

"Do you want me to find them all?"

"No. I want to know who the fourth person was on the tour. I think Jimmy Niven knew even if he can't tell us and Steven Reeves certainly did. I'm not so sure about Sophie. For some reason, the girl's identity is being kept from us."

"You think she's someone special, don't you?" Gregor's face lit up as he said it.

"Possibly. Either way, we need to find her before she goes missing. We've got to work on the basis that she is in serious danger."

"Only once her identity is known," noted Gregor.

"Precisely. As soon as we find her, we don't let her out of our sight. The trick, of course, is finding out who she is."

"Which is where I come in," nodded Gregor.

"Exactly," smiled Jack.

"Well, why didn't you say so sooner? If we are done, I think there was something I forgot to tell the chef. Let yourself out, will you, Jack?"

Jack finished his wine and went to stop Gregor before deciding the chef was not his priority.

***

Dan Millings walked through the front door of the station. It was difficult. His injuries were still hampering his efforts. It had been a year since he had been shot and the recovery process had been slow. His position as long-term sick was beginning to grate with his conscious when he knew there were things he could do. Maybe not physically, for the weekly physiotherapy was still a struggle to get through.

It was DCI Lang he wanted to see. He had taken the short taxi ride on the off-chance he might be there. He had to do something to get away from the four walls he was tired of staring at. Too many times, he had flicked through the television channels out of boredom. Now, he needed to regain his sanity.

He recognised nobody at the front desk. It felt like he was walking into a different station. Dan was shocked at how little he remembered. It was a full year since he had set foot in the place and that seemed like a lifetime. His life had been compromised with the bullet he had taken and now he questioned whether there was any way back.

He reflected on how lucky he was to be alive. That was what the experts had told him. It was his fault. He should have waited for backup even if he did not remember the events leading up to being shot. They were all lost memories from a time when life felt so much simpler.

Lang came down to greet him as quickly as he could. He found Dan in a visitor's chair, staring across the station with a vacant expression. Dressed in casual clothes, he could have been anyone to those sitting around him.

"Dan, it's good to see you," announced Lang, thrusting out a welcoming hand.

"You too, sir."

His response was slow as if he was fighting to remember who he was talking to. It was hard not to feel sympathy for the lad. Anyone could have taken that bullet though others may not have survived. It was an exclusive club for which there were very few wanting to join.

"Come through, I'll get us some coffee."

"No, thanks," replied Dan. "That bit I do remember. Has the coffee improved?"

"Not at all."

"Then I'll stick with water."

"A wise choice. So will I."

Lang collected two glasses of water from the cooler and took Dan into a side office. He deliberately chose one away from his own. He wanted Dan kept out of things until he was sure of his motives. He looked well enough but that could be a mask for his true condition. Underneath, Lang had a sense there was still plenty of recovery time needed.

"How are you keeping, Dan?"

"Good, sir. I want to come back."

"Are you fit enough to do so?"

"I think so. Perhaps on lighter duties to start with. After that, I'm pretty much good to go."

"And the physio? How are those sessions coming along?"

"Still ongoing; I'm getting there."

"Are you sleeping?"

There was evasiveness that said he was not ready to answer. He never needed to. The look on Dan's face was enough. The nightmares were just as bad as they had ever been.

"What's the real reason for wanting to come back, Dan?"

Dan fell silent. His eyes drifted down to the floor. In front of the DCI, he melted like a child before a teacher. A nervous shuffle between feet preceded any words he could offer. When he spoke, it was little more than a squeak.

"I need to do something, sir. I can't sit at home any longer. I know I probably won't be able to go back to what I was doing before but I have to do something. I can't stay at home forever."

"Dan, I know what you're going through but I can't have you back unless you are fit. You know the environment you are returning to."

"There must be something."

"Look, we'll do our best. You will have to be signed off as fit to work before you come back. Those are the rules for everyone. I'm sorry."

Dan sighed. He knew the rules as well as anyone. He also knew he was unlikely to ever be signed off as fit. Not to do what he loved and if he was honest with himself, sitting at a desk shuffling bits of paper was never going to give him a reason to live.

"I just wish there was something I could do to help, sir."

"There will be, Dan. We'll work something out when you are signed off as fit."

***

Jack had left the restaurant feeling uncomfortable. He hated being indebted to Gregor Banks, knowing it would come back to haunt him. He could imagine Gregor making the breakthrough and finding the lead that he and others had missed. It sent a chill through his spine. That uneasy feeling did not sit well. It was enough to make him seek out a pub.

His nearest hostelry was The Ebor Arms, a tatty establishment that had deteriorated over the years. It still served a good pint even if the décor was in a poor state. The lack of worthwhile customers made it inevitable it would close. That, like Jack's retirement, was just a question of time.

"Hi Jack, it's been a while."

The greeting was to be expected. He rarely went in and yet the paucity of customers meant everyone was remembered. He smiled at the middle-aged barman who was a throwback to the era Jack was from. He had probably worked there since he was young and then watched the establishment grow old around him. As it did, its appearance had fared little better than his own.

"Pint of best, please, Dave."

A nod was all it took to acknowledge the request. A pull of a pint lever and a splutter of gas told Jack the handle had not been used in a while. He feared the worst and was left wondering whether the drink might be as out of date as the barman.

"Try that, Jack. If it's not right, I'll change it."

Jack sipped the drink suspiciously. He took as little into his mouth as he possibly could. His internal alarm bells said it would be off. He wanted to dislike it and yet a sense of surprise filled him with the first taste. It was undeniably good, allowing the pint to slide down his throat with ease. It was his first for a while and a good follow-up to the wine he had drunk with Gregor. It meant he could relax and allow his mind to rest.

Jack slipped a twenty-pound note onto the bar, a crisp one straight from the machine.

"Have one yourself, Dave and while you're at it, line me up another."

"Don't mind if I do."

Jack eased his first pint down. He was pleased to have some company from someone that expected little from him. Home was empty and still as unwelcoming as the day Mary had left. The thought of her name made him soften and ponder his next move. His heart was telling him that he should get in contact with her. The rest of him knew he had already moved on.

"Do you want a chaser with that, Jack? On the house."

"Why not?" he smiled, allowing himself to ease back against a wooden beam. It brought a feeling of comfort that would allow him to settle in for the night.

CHAPTER 16

FOR TWO DAYS, LISA spent every waking moment tracing through the financial records of the tour party. Jack had offered assistance, enlisting the services of Will to help her. She had declined. Her mindset was on finding the breakthrough alone. It never helped that on both mornings Jack stank of drink. Nobody could find a man attractive when he turned up smelling like he had spent all night as a wastrel in the gutter.

Jimmy Niven was the quickest to review. There were so few transactions to look at. He had one bank account and a permanent overdraft and yet so little went through it. In the past year, he had raised his borrowing limit by four hundred pounds and withdrawn the full amount of cash within two days. It was a classic piece of financial indiscipline.

What was most surprising was the lack of income. The bank accounts were also missing any form of utility bills, suggesting he lived in a world of cash. He was known to skirt the edge of the law. Small-time, he was the type who took advantage when the opportunity arose rather than operate with an organised plan of deceit.

Lisa made her notes and placed an asterisk against the tour company. They had never once paid anything into his bank. Either he was a tax dodger or he had another account. The latter would mean the forensic team had not yet traced it. She put the papers to one side and moved on from staring at the blank statements.

Sophie Neal ticked all the classic student boxes. She had little income except for the occasional transfer from her parents. There were few bills and no credit card payments or much else that was regular. Her mobile phone was her largest direct debit, the one essential item for her generation. It was likely she spent more on that than food.

Steven Reeves was very different. For his age, he was wealthy, with his bank account over-filled with unused cash. He lived off his debit card and paid for almost everything that way. Not that there was much other than bars and restaurants. Lisa scanned the accounts for cash withdrawals and found only two, one of which had been in the last month.

It was the payments into the account which caught Lisa's eye. A regular sum appeared every month, far more than anything he spent. It looked like a trust fund paying money in. The amounts were sending his account to eye-watering levels and yet he seemed to live such a frugal lifestyle. Even his phone appeared to be paid for on a top-up basis.

One of the restaurants attracted Lisa's attention. It was a regular haunt, an Italian just off Castlegate. Lisa knew it. An Italian colleague had taken her there when she first moved to the city.

He had eyes on taking things a step further but that one meal with him told Lisa he was far from boyfriend material.

Every couple of weeks there was a bill. They were in midweek rather than at the weekend. A quieter time, perhaps a moment when two people could be together undisturbed. The size of the bill indicated that Steven never dined alone. All of a sudden, a line of the investigation led in that direction. It was something, perhaps more than they had so far. And yet it was reliant on finding someone willing to talk.

A call to the restaurant put her through to the owner. He sounded like a genuine Italian, his accent authentic rather than coming as part of a franchise. Her mind drifted back to her date. The good food was the one consolation of a particularly lousy evening.

Gino Ashton was effervescent, his personality addictive from the moment he answered the phone. He oozed passion. Lisa struggled to get a word in beyond introducing herself as a detective. She needed to say something just to stop his flow, her mind scrambling to think of anything which might have the desired effect.

"Mr Ashton," she began.

"Gino, please. I like my Italian name better."

"Yes, I must say your surname is not the most..."

"Second-generation. Blame my mother. She married an Englishman and took his name."

"And you don't like it?"

"You try running an authentic Italian restaurant with the name Mr Ashton."

Lisa smiled at the thought of that name etched above an Italian flag.

"I need to see you. Are you free if I pop over?"

"Of course. What is it about?"

"One of your regulars. I need to know who he dines with."

"Anything to help. Who is it?"

"Steven Reeves."

The phone went silent. Lisa pondered whether Gino had hung up. She could hear enough background noise to suggest the phone was still in his hand. Any response had died at the end of the line.

"Gino, are you still there?"

Silence

"Gino?"

"It is not a good time. Perhaps in a few days."

"I'm coming to see you. Do not go anywhere."

Lisa kept the phone to her ear and waited. The sound of the dialling tone cut her conversation off just before she had finished. Everything had changed and Gino's personality had waned as if he was scared of what the conversation might bring.

***

The restaurant was locked when Lisa arrived. She had gone there alone, hoping to keep the meeting low-key. There had been too many disappearances after meetings with Jack to make a lot of fuss about speaking to the owner. Not even DCI Lang had been informed.

She knocked on the door and noticed that the restaurant was in darkness. There was nothing, not even the twitching of a curtain. She rang Gino again. The phone went unanswered before it triggered the answerphone. A glance at her watch told Lisa he would soon be opening for lunch.

Lisa bought a coffee from the cafe next door and sat on the bench outside. It was a warm day, making it the most relaxed stakeout she had ever done. Jack interrupted her once. She ignored the call and waited for a message to be left.

At eleven thirty, a young lad tried the door. It didn't move. His hand rattled the handle a couple of times. He looked up and called out Gino's name. That achieved nothing other than to catch Lisa's attention.

"Can I help?" she asked, offering her badge to assure him of her intentions.

"Not unless you have a key."

"Do you work here?"

"Yes, I do normally. For some reason, Gino isn't opening today."

He showed her his phone. A short text confirmed what he had told her. The lad looked nervous when he thrust the phone towards her. Lisa nodded and wondered what else he knew.

"Why are you here if Gino isn't opening?"

"I left my jacket behind yesterday. Thought I'd pick it up on my way past. He better open up tomorrow because I'm skint."

"Let me buy you a coffee and I might be able to help."

"I'm not sure. Gino wouldn't be very happy about me talking to the police."

"You're only doing me a favour. My coffee's gone cold and they'll think I'm a right saddo if I go and sit inside drinking another one on my own."

He smiled. Her self-putdown appeared to make him relax. Lisa showed no reaction, mindful of the opportunity he presented. She would be gentle with him and extract what she could in a careful manner. Only when finished would she squeeze him for the last few drops of information.

The young lad walked inside and marched straight to the counter. In any other circumstances, Lisa would have told him to sit down. This time, she was not going to allow him out of her sight. He ordered a cappuccino and then made way for her to order a latte. It felt like the right time for Lisa to move in with the killer question.

"Do you want a cake to go with it? I'm having one."

His face lit up like a child's as his eyes scoured the display area. He seemed partially frozen as if unable to cope with such a choice. It took an age before he selected a muffin. Lisa nodded her approval and confirmed she would have the same. She had little intention of eating it. It was all part of getting him to talk.

"That'll be nine pounds seventy-five. I'll bring them over when it's ready."

Lisa smiled, offered up a ten-pound note and took the receipt. All essential police expenses; she had learned that from Jack. It put the lad at ease. His carefree walk to a table signalled that he was starting to relax in her presence.

"I'm Lisa, by the way," she said, taking a seat diagonally opposite him. There was no other choice. To go opposite was too confrontational and it was far too intimate to sit alongside him.

"Mikey."

A hand shot out. It was offered with a brief rise up to greet a lady. Lisa nodded at the formality and urged him to sit back down.

Once seated, Mikey started to look nervous again. The wait for the drinks did not help. Lisa took her time and did not move in with her questioning, knowing it would be easier when he felt comfortable.

"Look, I know you want to question me. What has Gino done? He doesn't close up without a good reason."

"Nothing as far as I know, unless you want to throw something in," smiled Lisa.

"No, he's done nothing," insisted Mikey.

The kid's voice sounded panicked, suggesting she had stumbled into something sinister. That was for another day. For now, she only needed one thing.

"Look, don't worry, he has a piece of information that we need. Nothing big, just the name of somebody who comes in. He may or may not even know them."

Mikey relaxed as if an almighty burden had been lifted from his shoulders. Lisa made a mental note to get one of the junior PCs to do some follow-up work. He had to be hiding a secret. His fear told her there was something untoward in his life.

"Who is it?"

"That's what we are hoping to find out."

Their conversation was interrupted by the arrival of their order. Lisa was relieved at the timing. It offered a welcome break from the suspicion surrounding her questioning. It broke things up nicely, with the lad going straight for his muffin. Lisa wondered whether it was the first food he had seen for days.

"So why doesn't he just tell you the name, if that's all it is?" garbled Mikey. His voice was muffled by the mouth full of cake.

"I'm sure he will but seeing as he is not here, how about you tell me instead? The guy who pays the bill is Steven Reeves, the councillor's son. The question is, who does he go out to dinner with?"

The enjoyment of the muffin stopped immediately. Crumbs spluttered out of Mikey's mouth as he coughed in response. He looked worried. His hand reached for a napkin, to wipe up the mess. Lisa allowed him to compose himself and took a small sip of her latte. When he had recovered, it would be time to get the answer she needed.

"Sorry," he muttered. "I didn't realise I was about to cough."

"That's fine. Are you okay now?"

Mikey nodded. "Yes, thanks."

"So, you were going to tell me who Steven Reeves dines with."

"I'm not sure I know him," offered Mikey feebly.

Lisa placed a picture of him on the table. There was instant recognition etched across his face.

"I would say you are going to need to do better than that. He's pretty distinctive, isn't he?"

Mikey's eyes flicked away in the silence.

"Mikey, who does he dine with?"

"He comes in with many different people. He's very sociable."

"I thought you didn't know him."

Mikey blushed, giving himself up with his reaction.

"I think I might have seen him a few times. As I said, he comes in with lots of different people."

"No, he doesn't. He brings the same person every time."

The tone of the lad changed. His voice lowered several decibels. A glance around confirmed nobody was listening.

"Gino will kill me."

"Trust me; that would be preferable to what I might do."

He stared at Lisa, shocked at her fierce response. Gone was the soft and gentle lady that had bought him a cake. In her place, a stern woman bore down on him. It was not a transformation he liked.

"It's private. They come in as a couple when it's quiet. We are sworn to secrecy."

"I know. Who is she?" demanded Lisa.

"I can't tell you."

"I said, who is she?"

"I can't," he squeaked.

"Mikey, for the last time, who does Steven Reeves dine with? We can do this here or at the station after you have spent twenty-four hours in a cell."

"But..."

"Of course, we could also get a search warrant for the restaurant and your house. I need a name," she growled.

"I..."

"Now!"

"Elizabeth Moss!" shrieked the lad whose hands were too late to cover his mouth.

"See, that wasn't hard, was it? You can have that other cake. I'm watching my weight."

Lisa got up and patted him on the back, leaving Mikey at the table. She felt good and had little sympathy for the lad trembling behind her. With a rush of adrenalin filling her body, she now knew why Jack did things the way he did.

***

At the station, Jack was sitting at his desk in the missing persons' office. It had been a while since he had gone in there, with his investigation leaving little time for anything else. Not that he had tried to make much effort to go into the station when the teasing about Spain was still topical. Some had worked for over twenty years and had not been sent on a foreign trip. Jack wondered whether one or two had even seen daylight.

He felt queasy after two successive days on the sauce. Not just evenings but mid-afternoon sessions running into the early hours. It was the chasers that killed him. His stomach was no longer able to take the strength of the whisky. All common sense told him to stick to beer.

Thankfully, Lisa's call prevented another afternoon of drinking. Already, his head had turned to alcoholic ways to stop his stomach from turning over. Jack suggested a pub as a place to meet only for Lisa to change it to lunch. Even the thought of food made him feel worse. The compromise was a local cafe where at least he could order something light.

The barracking started as soon as he got to his feet. It was early for a lunch break by anyone's standards. It was particularly early for the lifers in the department used to a routine that never changed. Going early was not how things were done. Such a change was seen as a threat and threats were met with spiteful comments.

"Got to move with the times, guys," offered Jack. He then wondered why he even bothered to respond.

It was met with some crude retorts, not that he cared. Jack was pleased to have an excuse for fresh air. His hangover had made for a long morning and the headache tablets were no longer having their usual effect. He needed a sharpener and more than anything, he needed it now.

He stopped off in the first pub he passed. A half was downed in three quick gulps. It was a struggle to drink it. Jack's stomach fought him and offered to return the beer to where it had come from. If he kept it down, he would feel better by the time he met Lisa.

Briefly, he contemplated another. A growl from his stomach confirmed that would not be wise. Jack left the empty on the bar and continued towards the cafe. It was a walk that would normally clear his head. Today, every step was a challenge.

When he got to the cafe, he saw Lisa sitting on her own. He could see her in the window, with the glass frontage affording him a full view. She was attractive even in her work clothes and a complete contrast to Jack. He straightened his collar and brushed his jacket down without improving his appearance. If he had a comb, he might have brushed his hair and still not managed to make a difference. It was hard enough seeing Lisa. It was even harder seeing his aged reflection in the window. At least she smiled when she saw him walk in.

"What have you got for me?" asked Jack.

"Charming, I don't even get a hello anymore."

"Sorry, it's just it sounded urgent. I'll get you a coffee."

"Thanks. Are you alright, Jack? You look terrible."

"Maybe that's why you don't get a hello. I'd hate to see you when you're not on a charm offensive."

It was Lisa's turn to feel embarrassed. Her face flushed red with the bluntness she had shown. Jack had already moved on. He was asking for two coffees and requesting someone to take Lisa's lunch order. For once, he felt peckish himself. The half-pint was starting to take effect and would provide enough lining if he kept the order simple.

Lisa had left Jack the seat in the corner. Never liking his back to the room, he always wanted a full view. He squeezed past her, conscious that he was not at his best. He moved slowly while trying to avoid brushing against her manicured appearance.

"Coffee is on its way. What do you fancy eating?"

"I'll probably go for one of their salads. And you?"

"It won't be any of that green stuff. You don't get a figure like mine from eating salad. I'll give one of their toasties a try and hope it doesn't come with garnish."

"I think they call them paninis these days."

"Call them what you like; they're still a bloody toastie."

Lisa smiled. That felt like the Jack she knew and liked. Not loved, though her feelings had grown in the year she had known him. Even off-colour, he always found ways to amuse her. The stubbornness in the man was a challenge to be met head-on.

"You said you had something for me."

"Oh yes, and I have a feeling you might like it."

A twinkle sparkled in Lisa's eyes. Jack could not fail to notice it, nor the excitement radiating across the cafe table. He sensed she wanted to tease him and dangle it for him to go after. Jack would play her game as long as he got the information.

"Okay, I'm hooked. How about a little side bet? If it's worth it, I'll buy lunch. If not, it's your treat."

Eagerly, Lisa reached out and shook Jack's hand. She could not help but notice he felt cold. She was unsure whether he was under the weather or was just a man crying out to be looked after. That was for another time. Now was about one name.

"How about the name of a regular dinner date for Steven Reeves for the past year and a half."

"How regular?"

"Every couple of weeks; sometimes more."

"I take it we are talking about a mystery female. Perhaps one that might fit the description of a fourth person on a ghost tour?"

Lisa nodded. A smile filled Jack's face. It lit him up. In that brief moment, he looked in better health. His appearance became that of a man with energy pulsing through him. With his reaction, Jack suddenly looked alive.

"In that case, you can work on the basis I'm buying lunch and I might even throw in dinner as well."

The waitress interrupted them to take their order. She placed their coffees down and took a notepad and pen from her pocket. A smile in Lisa's direction confirmed that she was ready.

"Tuna salad for me, please."

"And for you, sir?"

"A ham and cheese panini, please," confirmed Jack.

"A panini rather than a toastie, sir? We do both."

"Oh, definitely a panini. They are so much better than a toastie and make sure there is some garnish with it."

Lisa struggled to keep a straight face. The bare-faced cheek of Jack was sometimes beyond belief. He winked at her while the order was written down. His eyes then drifted onto the waitress long enough for Lisa to offer one of her sternest looks. Mikey had capitulated under such a stare. Jack just smiled back, taking her wrath in his stride.

"Got to move with the times," he laughed.

"Particularly when a panini costs a pound more and you're paying."

"Only if the name is a good one."

"How does Elizabeth Moss grab you?"

"Like this," laughed Jack, making pincer movements with both hands.

"Jack! She's young enough to be...oh, forget it. I meant, how does that name sound as a date for Steven Reeves?"

"You mean the Tory councillor's daughter?"

Jack's face looked stunned, perhaps for the first time since Lisa had known him. He was genuinely speechless, with his brain struggling to process the information he had been given. Twice, he shook his head and then looked across for confirmation. When Lisa nodded, Jack puffed out his cheeks and sat back.

"Well, that is a turn-up. I take it nobody knows."

"Just the restaurant. All the staff are sworn to secrecy."

"And her father?"

"I don't know, but I would work on the basis he probably doesn't. I am guessing you would like to be the one to tell him."

"I wish I could be," confirmed Jack. "Somehow, we are going to have to speak to Elizabeth without him finding out. Let's face it, we haven't got a very good track record of speaking to people without them going missing."

"You mean, you haven't."

"That's a fair point. Come on, let's enjoy our lunch first. After all, I've got a delicious panini to get through and if I'm lucky, there will be plenty of garnish to go with it."

CHAPTER 17

ELIZABETH MOSS HAD BEEN expecting the call. For over a year, she had been waiting for the inevitable knock on the door. She had experienced nightmares of being woken by a dawn raid and being led from the house in shame. It had led to her wearing pyjamas, the thought of being taken out in a nightshirt too much for her to bear. Not that she had slept much since that fateful night when her mind was awash with sinister thoughts.

It had been Steven's idea to keep her identity a secret. The two others had little idea who she was. To the tour guide, she was just another faceless guest, given the same made-up stories for a few pounds. The student was another young airhead, likely to be wasting three years of her life.

Steven had suggested going on it as a change from their normal dinner date. She was surprised he was interested and only went along to be with him. Half-listening, she clung to his arm. Of course, she had been scared at times. That was the whole point even if it was a made-up script.

Now Steven was missing, it was different. Thoughts of the night kept coming back to haunt her. She had seen the van and the couple's disappearance. She should have gone to the police but she couldn't. In any case, Steven had told them everything they both knew. It was not that she did not want to help; it was just her father. It was always about her father.

"Is that Elizabeth Moss?"

"Speaking. Who is this?"

"I'm DS Lisa Ramsey from York police station. We need to speak to you as a matter of urgency."

Elizabeth went quiet. She felt her whole world closing in around her.

"Elizabeth, are you still there?"

"Yes," she muttered softly.

"We need to speak to you."

"I don't know anything," she offered desperately.

"We still need to speak to you."

There was a pause and then Elizabeth let out a deep sigh in defeat.

"Fine."

"Can we come and collect you?"

"No, my Dad's here. Can we meet somewhere?"

Lisa's thoughts turned to the disappearance of the others. If she had managed to find Elizabeth's name, it was only a matter of time before somebody else did. Only Jack and Lisa knew at this stage but what did that matter? Whoever was behind the disappearances appeared to be one step ahead of the game.

"How soon can you be ready?"

"I can get out in about an hour. I'll come to the station."

"I'd rather send a car."

"Elizabeth, your dinner is ready!"

Lisa heard the booming voice at the other end of the phone. The tone was aggressive and drowned out Elizabeth's voice. She feared an overbearing father who might intervene. She had to get to the girl before he did and prevent another disappearance.

"I'll be there as soon as I can; I've got to go. Bye."

The phone was hung up before Lisa could respond, leaving her with a sense of regret. Something felt wrong as if she was missing an obvious point. She sat and thought for a minute and then sent an unmarked car to keep watch on the house. It was discrete and instructed to maintain a low profile. Inside, was a father who would be easily spooked if he sensed that somebody was watching. It left Lisa to pace impatiently and wait for Elizabeth Moss to appear.

***

In the hour that passed, Lisa spoke to Jack three times. Twenty minutes before Elizabeth was due, Jack came to the interview room to sit with her. She wanted him there, knowing they were in for a difficult conversation. It could define their case. All their hopes rested on Elizabeth and the account she could give of the night.

Elizabeth Moss never came to the station. Instead, a smart gentleman in a pin-stripe suit called at the front desk. He looked official, perhaps from the legal profession, with his hair slicked over in a perfect sweep. To Lisa, who kept watch, he was just another visiting suit. To Jack, he was something a whole lot more sinister than anyone could have imagined.

"Oh no," he muttered as soon as he set eyes on the man.

"Problem?" asked Lisa.

"That's the barrister from the Banks case," groaned Jack.

"What's he doing here?"

"Who knows? It can only mean trouble and I have a feeling that it's going to involve us."

James Thakins arrived with all the arrogance Jack would have expected from the man. He looked pompous, his natural dislike for him not helped by the court case. Even without it, he was someone Jack would openly detest. Just watching him go about his work made his skin crawl.

A brief exchange took place. The reaction from Thakins told Jack and Lisa the first answer he received was not what he wanted. A few harsh words were exchanged and were followed by the desk sergeant making a phone call. There were no pleasantries or kind words offered. James Thakins stood looking utterly bored.

"You have no idea how much I'd like to punch him," said Jack.

"I've got a feeling there might be a queue," laughed Lisa.

"It would cost me every penny I have ever earned and more by the time he was finished with me. Something tells me it would still be worth it."

"What do you think he is here for?" asked Lisa.

"I don't know for certain but something tells me David Moss might just know the identity of our fourth person."

"Do you think Elizabeth is alright?"

"She'll be fine. He's many things but he isn't the type of guy to hurt his daughter."

"Are you sure?"

"Not really. I'm just doing my best to convince myself."

DCI Lang appeared a minute or so after the call. There was a brief shake of hands in front of the desk. Lang took James Thakins into a meeting room and shut the door behind them. Jack and Lisa waited, knowing it would not take long. Barristers charge too much by the hour to spend time on social niceties.

It took six minutes for the door to reopen. When it did, Thakins strode purposefully to the exit. He never looked around once. His fee had been earned by meeting Lang, who was now looking more than a little peeved.

Jack's mobile rang as soon as Lang got back to his office. Both he and Lisa had ducked down when he passed. They did not want to be seen watching the meeting. Jack pressed the button and waited for the inevitable question.

"Jack, where are you?"

"Just back in the station, sir."

"And Lisa?"

"I saw her earlier. I think she's in the station as well."

"Well, go and find her and come straight to my office."

"Okay, we'll be there in twenty minutes."

"Make it five."

"See you in ten. I've got to find her first."

Lang rang off before Jack could end the call. He looked at Lisa who already knew what he would say.

"Lang wants to see us."

"Come on then. Let's go and face the music."

"Certainly not," stated Jack. "I said ten minutes, so we need to keep him waiting. Let's grab another coffee and head up in fifteen."

"You're impossible at times, Jack."

"Not impossible; just bloody difficult unless you know how to play the game."

Lisa sighed. No matter how long she knew him or how close she got, she wondered whether she would ever know the rules of the game he played.

***

Exactly fifteen minutes later, Jack and Lisa walked into Lang's office. The DCI was reading through a letter clutched in his hands. He beckoned for the two of them to come in, glancing at his watch as he did so.

"Sorry, sir, it took a while to find her," offered Jack.

Lisa flushed red with embarrassment. She hated the insinuation that it was her fault they were late. She made a mental note to kick Jack under the desk. That would wait until they were alone.

"Okay, you're here now. Pull up a chair."

Jack sat down opposite Lang, allowing Lisa a little more space. Lang's chats could be uncomfortable and were best accompanied by a hot drink.

"Not going to offer us a coffee, sir?"

"No, this is important."

"So is coffee, sir."

"Jack, stop playing the fool. Have a look at this."

Lang turned the letter to face the two detectives and slipped it across the desk. It looked official, a mix between a letter and a formal statement. It was on headed paper and signed by David Moss. It had been delivered by James Thakins and was written by someone of significant legal standing.

They read quickly. It offered a statement that detailed the council leader's version of the facts. His daughter was a friend of Steven Reeves but had only ever had dinner with him on rare occasions. There was no relationship and no contact before or after his disappearance. It stated that their friendship only went back a matter of months. Jack was the first to respond.

"So what? We just ask her for the truth."

"Read the second sheet," insisted Lang.

James Thakins had set it all out, a complete statement of everything Elizabeth supposedly knew. Then came the punchline, the final twist of the knife, that said she would not be making any further statements. She had signed to say that she had told them everything and was feeling harassed by the officers. It was a marker and a clear warning that Elizabeth Moss was now out of bounds.

"We have to stay away," sighed Lang.

"She's the fourth member of the tour party. She was the girl who was with Reeves," said Jack.

"Not according to this," replied Lang. "Her statement says that she only met him a few months ago."

"Bullshit!"

"Jack, we are both old enough to know we are heading down a dead end. This line of enquiry ends now. If she won't speak, we are wasting our time."

"I could speak to her," offered Lisa.

"No," said Lang.

"So that's it," snarled Jack. "We're done on this case. That was a waste of taxpayers' money."

"Don't be like that, Jack."

"Why not? We've got our first decent lead on the case and we're giving up and going home, just because some councillor has a fancy lawyer."

"Says who?"

"You just have."

"Oh no. All I've said is that the Moss girl is off-limits for the moment. That just means I've got to take the brakes off you and let you do a bit of tree-shaking elsewhere."

A smile spread across Lang's face. It was the type of smile which sent Jack's pulse racing. He had no idea what Lang had planned and yet he already had a feeling he was going to like it.

***

Jack could hardly contain his excitement on the journey to see Alice and Jamie Johnson. His body tingled with the thought of shaking them until they made a mistake. He had been let off his leash by his superior. Lang had told him he could do anything short of arresting them, with Lisa primed to step in if he overstepped the mark.

Jack had not liked the pair from the moment he first met them. They had been difficult, indeed confrontational, as if it was the police who were harassing them. Now, he would show them what police pressure amounted to. His blood was pumping through his veins at the thought of raising the stakes.

Of course, there was regret about Elizabeth Moss. She was the one they really needed to speak to. DCI Lang was right. Any immediate advance on her would tie the whole force up in an expensive legal wrangle. Yet Lang had still offered encouragement with his choice of words. 'For the moment' meant exactly that. The David Moss hurdle would be overcome even if the route of approach might be a little circuitous.

"What's the plan?"

Jack glanced across at Lisa when it was safe to do so. He never had much of a plan. Charging in was what he did best.

"Just as the boss says. We go and shake some trees."

"Which means?"

"Let's just say we are going to put them under a little bit of pressure. Bagsy playing bad cop."

"Don't you always?"

He smiled. If he had said it to her, she would have jabbed him. Jack had felt enough of her digs to feel the psychosomatic pain in his side. Ever the gentleman, he said nothing as he turned into the road where the Johnsons lived.

"Seriously, Jack, what is the plan?"

"There isn't one. We go in and stir things up. Just keep me on a reasonable leash if I get carried away."

"Don't do anything stupid, please, Jack."

"Do I ever do that? No wait, don't answer that."

It was Lisa's turn to offer a smile.

As Jack parked up, the front door opened. Jack and Lisa were barely out of the car when the harsh voice came. It was a screech rather than any welcoming offering and set the tone for the meeting they would have.

"What do you want?"

"And hello to you too, Ms Johnson," replied Jack. "Have we come at a bad time?"

Alice Johnson stood at the door in an old pair of tracksuit bottoms and a paint-covered t-shirt. It was obvious she had little underneath even from the distance Jack and Lisa were looking from. A large brush was gripped in her hand and a small smudge of paint coated her cheek. Both detectives tried to look past her into the house.

"Yes, you have. I'm decorating."

"Never mind."

Jack approached and pushed past her. She never moved and forced the collision. It caused Jack to stumble, his hand catching the hallway wall. It was wet. Jack's immediate reaction was to pull back. He saw the light blue colour covering his full palm.

"Oh great," hissed Alice Johnson. "Don't worry, I'll repaint that wall."

"And I'll use your sink."

Jack marched forward, turning off the hall to enter the kitchen. In a flash, he was gone, leaving Alice fuming on the doorstep with Lisa.

"Hang on, I never said you could come in."

"He's got to get the paint washed off," said Lisa. "I better go and make sure he's alright."

She, too, pushed past. This time, Alice stood aside to let her in. Lisa was more careful to avoid the paint, which was perfect except for Jack's handprint. Behind her, Alice touched up the damage and then stood back to ensure it was covered. Once satisfied, she chased after the pair of intruders.

Jack was at the sink and was scrubbing his hands to within an inch of their life. The paint had washed off quickly but Jack wanted to have his back to Alice when she came in. It would give him a little more time to throw in a couple of grenades while Lisa could play the calmer role.

"What the hell is this about?" demanded Alice. "I never invited you in."

"I just came in to wash my hands," insisted Jack. "Only reasonable, seen as you were careless with the paint."

"Careless? You put your hand on the bloody wall!"

"Did I? I think you'll find you caught me with the paintbrush when you answered the door. I can check the wall if you like."

"I painted over it."

"That's convenient."

"And what's that supposed to mean? I'm hardly going to leave it and stare at your handprint forever, am I?"

"Have you got a towel?"

"I beg your pardon?"

"Normally when you wash your hands, they come out wet. You can check if you want. My guess is I will need something to dry them on."

Lisa could hardly contain her laughter and put her hand to her mouth to stifle her giggle. It was Jack at his irritating best, a master in the art of winding somebody up. She had been on the wrong end of it, so to see the artistry from his side was something you could only admire.

Defeated, Alice marched from the room. She was gone for a moment and returned with a towel. It was thrown with force in Jack's direction. He allowed it to hit him, offering her a small window of satisfaction before he returned to the traits that served him best.

"Yes, I was right. They are wet."

"You've got a towel, use it."

Jack picked the towel up and wiped his hands. He took his time as if producing a work of art. It was obvious he would not accept questions while he was doing it. Each finger was individually dried. Alice seethed and readied herself to strike. Jack and Lisa were going to be thrown out the door.

"Seeing as you are putting the kettle on, mine's white without," said Jack.

"I wasn't making any tea."

"Good, I prefer coffee. Lisa, do you want one?"

"I would love one, Jack."

Alice filled the kettle in a manner that implied she had been asked to build a time machine. She resented every minute and, more so, the implication that the police intended to stay. Part of her wanted to throw them out and yet common sense told her she was only delaying an inevitable meeting. It was better to do it over a cup of coffee than get dragged to the station.

"Is Jamie in?" asked Jack.

"Yes, he's in bed."

"Not helping with the decorating?"

"No, he's bloody hopeless."

Jack laughed, the approach familiar with his own. He had successfully convinced two wives he was incapable. In doing so, he had removed the requirement for him to ever try.

"Do you want to ask him to come down? That saves us having the same conversation twice."

"About what?"

"Let's get him down first. Do you want me to pop up to get him?"

"No!"

The response was a little too quick, offering the suggestion that something was being hidden. Lisa reflected on Jack's previous thoughts of whether they were more than brother and sister. Her stomach churned and a shiver tingled through her spine. It was all she could do to quell the sick feeling inside her.

"I'll go and get him," snarled Alice. "You can finish the coffee."

Lisa completed the honours and handed a cup to Jack. For Alice, going and getting him consisted of standing at the bottom of the stairs and bellowing his name. It was followed by an insult about his level of activity. There was no response other than for

Alice to return and make a fourth cup of coffee. It seemed strange to assume that he would come down after so little reaction.

"That was effective," said Lisa.

"He'll come down now he's awake."

True enough, Jamie emerged having thrown on a pair of track-suit bottoms and a t-shirt. His feet were bare except for a pair of flip-flops designed for the beach. He nodded at the detectives and then at his sister who handed him a coffee. Lisa went to introduce herself and was interrupted by Jamie. He knew who they were and didn't need any fancy introductions.

"Alice, go and put some clothes on. You can see everything in that outfit," barked Jamie.

Jack and Lisa were shocked. Their exchanged glances confirmed how uncomfortable they both felt. Something was going on. Jamie's attention seemed unduly taken by a matter that should not have concerned him. Both detectives stared into their coffee, waiting for the issue to blow over.

"Stop worrying, I'm sure these guys have seen it all before."

Lisa said nothing while Jack could not help thinking that it had been too long since he had.

Jamie took a swig of his coffee. It seemed to wake him and he visibly bristled in their presence. He felt irritated, first by the disturbance, but more by there being police in his house. He had given what information he could. The matter was over as far as he was concerned. And yet two officers were in his kitchen determined to rake over old ground.

"Have you found our aunt and uncle in Spain yet?" he growled bluntly.

"We haven't looked recently," offered Jack.

"I thought you lot wanted to track them down."

"There's no point; they're not missing."

"I thought you reckoned they were."

"That was before we received some new information."

They relaxed and remembered the postcard taken in by Alice. The siblings smiled at each other and took another sip of their drinks. It was good to hear everyone was on the same page.

"Of course, the postcard," noted Jamie.

"You mean the fake postcard," offered Jack, his eyes watching for the faintest flicker in response. "No, we didn't mean that. We've got a witness."

"A witness for what?"

"A witness who saw the abduction of your aunt and uncle. They saw the vehicle and the driver and are happy to testify. Any biscuits, by the way? I do like a biscuit with my coffee. Do you, Lisa?"

"Get out! Get out of my house, right now!" shrieked Alice.

"You mean your aunt and uncle's house. Oh sorry, it's yours now they're dead."

"Get out and don't you dare touch the paint on the way out!" There was pure hatred written across Alice's face.

Lisa remained quiet. She took a final sip of her coffee and handed the cup to Jamie as she followed Jack out of the front door.

The door slammed hard behind them. Jack could hardly contain the grin on his face nor the warm feeling pumping through his body. Behind him, Lisa had a hand over her mouth, trying to stifle the amusement she felt. Two suspects had been suitably wound up, leaving them provoked to strike or make a mistake. It was Jack's rules now and that was how the game would be played.

"What now?" asked Lisa.

Jack looked at his watch. The day was coming to an end. That meant drinking time and a chance to pour some more nectar down his eager throat. There would be no shots, just good honest beer that would send him slowly into his stupor.

"We wait."

"Really?"

"Well, we go to the pub and then we wait."

"Don't tell me, The Cellars?"

"No, I feel like a change tonight. Do you fancy a drink in The Red House?"

"That's on the other side of town. The Cellars is only a few hundred yards away."

"The walk will do us good."

Lisa knew Jack better than to think he had turned into an exercise freak. No amount of convincing would tell her he had good intentions. There would be a reason for his choice of pub. Lisa's challenge was to work out what that purpose was before it was too late.

"Yes, I'll tag along. We could get some food there."

"Let's grab something on the way. I'm not sure we'll be in the mood for eating when we are there."

They settled on an Italian restaurant at the midway point of the walk. A quiet restaurant, it had none of the authenticity of

Gino's place. The menu was good but displayed the hallmarks of a chain even if they were trying hard not to show it.

Jack hardly touched anything. Lisa gorged herself on pasta while fighting her guilt. It told her she would regret it on the scales in the morning. Jack pushed a lasagne around the plate. He seemed preoccupied with other matters as if the weight of the world sat upon his shoulders.

Lisa wanted to ask him about it, knowing their relationship may be the issue. She could not help but notice the reciprocation of the attraction she felt. Jack seemed unwilling to do anything about it. If it was going to happen, it would have happened in Spain. Back in York, the awkwardness between them had returned.

"You've got a healthy appetite," smiled Jack. It broke the silence, much to Lisa's relief as she fought to get the final pieces wrapped around her fork.

"It's not good for the waistline. My skirts are getting a little tight."

"Just buy bigger skirts. Problem solved."

It was a refreshing attitude in a man. There was no suggestion she should watch what she ate. She liked that about Jack. He was different from the others even if a myriad of faults were never far from the surface.

"You were going to tell me why we are walking all the way to The Red House."

"Was I?"

Lisa nodded.

"An old friend drinks there, someone I've been meaning to bump into for a while."

"Good or bad?"

"Bad."

It was said with such frankness, it felt like the norm. Jack seemed indifferent to what 'bad' might bring.

"You had better eat your dinner then. You can't do 'bad' on an empty stomach."

"I'm not that hungry."

"I am."

Jack pushed his plate across the table, offering it to Lisa. She tried to remain restrained and declined. That was until the smell of the lasagne wafted past her and temptation overcame her resolve.

"I'll have a try."

"Dig in. You can always buy skirts which are two sizes bigger."

***

Jack's reason for picking The Red House was apparent the moment they walked through the door. Lisa recognised David Moss in an instant, the Tory leader holding counsel at the bar. Jack had been quick to advise Lisa to sit down. That was met with a refusal when she saw where he was heading. A meeting between Jack Husker and David Moss meant trouble and she was not going to stand back and watch.

"What are you doing in here?" snapped Moss.

"Just popping in for a drink. Fancy seeing you here."

"Yes, fancy. This is not your usual drinking den."

"No, I thought I would broaden out a bit."

"So, you picked my regular. Funny that, isn't it?"

"Call it a coincidence."

"I think I'd call it something else."

Jack turned towards the bar for a moment. He ordered a glass of white wine and a pint. Unusually, he never asked Lisa what she wanted. The landlord looked across at Moss as if confirming it was okay to serve the intruder. It was a brief stand-off, with three people waiting to see who blinked first. Eventually, David Moss broke away and offered a slight nod of his head.

"Right you are," said the landlord.

"How's the family, David?" asked Jack.

"Very good. How's yours?"

It was a topic Jack knew he could not win. His situation was well-known around the city. There had been two failed marriages, including one that had been played out in public. It never stopped him from going on the attack.

"How's Jennifer?"

"None of your business."

"And Elizabeth?"

"That, too, is none of your business, as I believe was explained to you earlier today. Of course, I could phone my lawyer and ask him to consider a case of harassment."

"Harassment? You mean walking into a public bar and, by co-incidence, meeting an old friend and asking him how his family was. You mean that harassment."

ALEX ROBERT

"Coincidence, my arse!" growled David Moss.

CHAPTER 18

JACK FELT GOOD ABOUT the morning. It was the first time he had woken feeling clear-headed for a good few days. He rolled over, the stream of sunlight bursting through the window of his bedroom blinding him with the brightness. Normally, he would have pulled the curtains across to hold onto the darkness. This morning was different.

To his side, he saw a heap of crumpled clothes. The other half of the bed was empty, long since made so by the departure of Mary. He had pondered the place being taken by Lisa. Yet the longer he left it, the less likely he felt it would happen. Work and pleasure never mixed well even if there was an undoubted attraction.

The memory of the previous evening's events brought a smile to his face. Indeed, it was hard to contain his satisfaction. First, the Johnsons and then David Moss, who had done everything except plant his fist into Jack's face. It was obvious he wanted to. Only the surroundings and the implications of doing so had prevented it. Jack had pushed him to his limit until finally, Lisa took his arm and sat him down at a table.

It was nice to know she cared enough to do so. That had left him feeling contented and with no need to visit The Cellars on his way home. He had slept well, without tossing and turning in bed. Life felt better with the benefit of sleep and now he felt positively hungry.

He glanced at his watch to confirm he did not need to hurry. Not that he would anyway when his time for rushing had long since passed. A cooked breakfast beckoned as a reward for a night of non-excess. He contemplated inviting Lisa before deciding he might be better off seeking an alternative companion.

Jack thumbed through his contacts. It never took long. The half dozen numbers he had bothered putting into his phone were quickly scrolled through. Two were gangsters, not ideal breakfast companions, including one who had been inside for a couple of years. That only left Dan, his old partner, a man in need of a catch-up. That worked. Jack could treat him as long as he was eating unhealthy foods.

"Dan, Jack here. Heard you were back on the job."

"Not really. Lang has relented and put me on some ultra-light duties. To be honest, I'm sitting around doing bugger all."

"Good, well not good actually, but never mind. Fancy a bit of breakfast?"

"Okay, where are you thinking?"

"How about the greasy spoon off Kings Square? That's probably the biggest breakfast around here."

"Are you sure you're going to eat it, Jack? I've never known you manage a breakfast this early in all the time I've known you."

"I'm a new man, Dan. Body a temple and all that."

"Body a dilapidated ruin, more like. I'll see you there in twenty minutes."

***

They arrived at the same time. Dan opened the door for Jack who went straight to the corner table. He sat looking across the cafe while the waitress came over to serve them. Dan beckoned for Jack to go first and he was not one to hold back in any way.

"I'll have the big breakfast and stick two fried slices, some black pudding, an extra rasher and another slice of toast on, plus a pot of tea."

"Are you pregnant, Jack?" asked Dan.

"Certainly not, or I'd want peanut butter on it as well."

The waitress smiled and looked across at Dan who sat waiting to be asked about his order.

"And you, young man?"

"Just a normal full English for me, plus a tea, please."

She scribbled on her pad and placed down two sets of cutlery before returning to the kitchen. It was quiet, with just the two of them sitting down. The remaining customers were take-out, leaving with their hands weighed down with coffee and pastries.

"How's it going, Dan?"

"Not good. I'm bored and I just can't get back into the job. With Lang keeping me out of the firing line and no case to work on, I might as well be back at home."

"Are you fit to work?"

"Not really. Physio sessions are still once a week but mentally, I'm shot, if you'll excuse the pun. Any loud noise makes me jump a mile."

"I'll remember not to drop my cutlery."

"I'm not sure I'm that bad. I suppose my heart is not in it anymore."

Jack clung to the words, remembering the kid who was so keen when he first arrived. Like Jack, he was one of the force's big hopes, a fit young lad with the will to succeed. For different reasons, they had both fallen by the wayside and were washed up before they had reached their prime. At least Dan had his injury whereas, for Jack, it was a mixture of drink, women and an increasingly bad attitude.

"Are you going to stick with it?"

"Probably not. I'll get myself fit on the rehab scheme. After that, I'm going to do something else. You won't tell anyone, will you?"

"Of course not. I'm not a grass."

"What about you, Jack? How's life treating you?"

"I'm okay. I'm on my own, which will be of no surprise to anyone. At the moment, I am concentrating on work and drinking too much."

"And how's the Johnson case going?"

"Not great. We think we know who did it but we can't get near the key witness. Let's just say Daddy has stepped in with a rather swish barrister. I probably only need five minutes with her to get what I need."

"Who is she?"

"Elizabeth Moss."

"As in the Tory leader's daughter?"

"That's the one. Do you know her?"

"Of course I do. I see her most weeks. Her mother goes to the same physio as I do. She's recovering from a horse-riding fall. Elizabeth takes her there for her weekly sessions."

"Do you get time to talk to her?"

"Yes, we have a chat when we can. She's a cracking lass if I'm allowed to say that. That's one girl I wouldn't mind getting closer to."

"Well, Dan, I think you might have just found yourself a new job."

Dan smiled. A feeling of purpose went through him and was heralded by the arrival of two large breakfasts.

"Remind me, which one of you was the one with extras?"

"He is," laughed Dan. "The one expecting twins."

***

Gregor Banks had also made progress. A body count of injuries lay across the streets of York. Nothing permanent, just some superficial bruising, with a couple of broken ribs thrown in for good measure. When Gregor had met Jack, he left with no real intention of helping him. Yet the longer he thought about it, the more the questions all seemed to be leading to the same place.

Something intrigued him about the mystery girl. It allowed him to answer a question the police had failed to for a year. And then there was Jack. There was always Jack, nagging away in the background while desperately clinging to the right side of the law. They both knew there was little difference between them other than the badges they chose to wear. In time, they would probably both end up on the wrong side, maybe even sharing a cell behind bars. Then, who would be the man? Not Jack, for sure. He would need him for protection. That made him smile, the thought that Jack would have to plead for every bit of help he required.

The streets had not been slow to talk. They never were. Through a combination of fear and desperation, Gregor was able to get what he needed. Everyone knew that it was better to be on the right side of Gregor Banks than hold out and have the information extracted. They all knew the stories; the kids that had gone missing after crossing the Banks family. First, his father and now Gregor had a reputation for causing harm. Over time, those stories got embellished and the number of disappearances went up.

It was one of the unwashed who identified the girl. A young lad, perhaps in his late teens, maybe early twenties, had spoken up. Homeless and looking unkempt, he was covered with facial hair that masked his features. Gregor Banks had never needed to do anything to him, for the lad was eager to find a friend. He was not a lifetime down and out, just a well-spoken lad who had found the need to run away from home.

"Kid, I hear you have some information for me," said Gregor softly, offering the one conciliatory approach the youngster would get.

Gregor Banks stood over him, flanked by two of his ogres. They stayed a respectful distance, offering the lad the benefit of the doubt. He was hardly a threat and yet you could never be sure when a tatty grey blanket would be able to conceal a knife with ease. All pairs of eyes never moved from the lad's hands. One sudden movement was likely to bring nothing except pain.

He nodded.

"What have you got?"

"I know who the young lady is. We were educated together."

Gregor looked shocked and nodded appreciatively, knowing you could never judge a book by its cover. Even in his sorry state, the lad was well-spoken and forming sentence structures far more complex than his own.

"And you're going to tell me her name, aren't you?"

He nodded again.

"It's Elizabeth Moss, the councillor's daughter."

There was no attempt to bargain with the information. He was keen to help and knew the vulnerability of being there alone. There was a code if you got into trouble and he had not been slow to learn it. You were on your own and nobody else ever saw anything that happened.

"Are you sure?"

"Yes," he confirmed. "I went out with her on a date once."

"Lucky man. What's your name, kid?"

"Harry. Harry Borthwick."

"How long have you been on the streets, Harry?"

"Eighteen months or so."

"And I'm guessing you left a pretty good home."

"You could call it that. I called it hell."

"Why?"

"Let's just say I had a father who was a bit keen with a belt. I couldn't face seeing my mother beaten again, so I left. Ran away like a coward."

"You're not a coward, Harry. I can help you if you want."

"How?"

"Give me your father's name and I will get you back home."

The insinuation was obvious and it left the threat hanging in the air. The kid shuddered and looked down. In a muttered tone, he rejected the offer he had been given.

"I don't want any more violence, Mr Banks."

"Your choice. Here, take this."

Gregor reached into his pocket and counted out a few notes. He made sure there was plenty and pushed it down into the lad's hand. Harry took it and nodded in appreciation. The transaction was complete and Harry Borthwick returned to being nothing in the gangster's life.

"Take care of yourself, Harry."

"Thank you, Mr Banks."

***

Jack's mobile rang just as he forced the last piece of toast into his mouth. Twice, it had circled the plate, mopping up every last morsel. Dan had long since finished, his stomach unable to cope with the greasy food. For Jack, it was heaven-sent and finally gave an under-filled stomach what it so badly craved.

He looked down at the phone and saw one of the few numbers in his contact list appear. To see Gregor Banks come up surprised him, more so, that he would ring on a recognisable number. Normally, they were throwaway phones that could not be traced back. This time, Gregor seemed happy to make an official call.

"This could be interesting," said Jack, showing the phone to Dan.

"I didn't know you two were best friends."

"I can't say we are. He certainly won't be ringing me for a chat."

Jack pressed the phone to his ear. A feeling of uncertainty filled his thoughts.

"Gregor Banks, what an unexpected pleasure."

"Good morning, Jack. I'm flattered to have my number recognised. I know you haven't got any friends, so it must be a pretty exclusive list of contacts I'm on."

"It is. Just criminals."

"Jack, don't be like that. I thought we were getting on better these days given we now run little errands for each other."

"Just be clear, I don't run errands for anyone."

"That's fine. I'll work on the basis that you don't want the name I've got for you."

"What name?"

"I thought you didn't want it."

"It depends on who it is."

"Let's just say I know who your mystery person is. A little love interest for Steven Reeves."

"Old news, sorry, I'm not interested."

Gregor Banks's tone changed immediately. Gone was the tactical interplay, replaced by a stern voice that burned from inside. Jack was playing with him and trying to be the big man. Gregor never liked anyone doing that to him.

"Don't mess me around, Jack. You know there will only be one winner."

"I told you, I don't do favours for anyone. We've already exhausted the lead on the girl. She saw nothing, not a jot, so we're barking up the wrong tree with that one."

"I'm sure I could get something out of her. Tell me, Jack, is she a pretty one?"

"I'm not telling you anything."

"Surely not another one of your exes. Soon a man won't be able to date anyone in this city without you having ruined them first."

"You go anywhere near her and I'll..."

"You'll do what, Jack? You're nothing. You never have been and you never will be. Face it, you're a washed-up old drunk."

"And you're a scumbag that I'm going to put inside with your father."

The phone cut off, with Gregor Banks not even bothering to respond. He was irritated, not only with the wasted time but also with the tone. He and Jack had unfinished business, the type where only one of them would walk away. Maybe not soon, but one day he and Jack were going to finish things for good.

"Was that wise?" asked Dan.

"Probably not. I was just trying to put him off the scent. We need to get to the Moss girl fast. If Gregor Banks gets wind that she might be useful to us, we, or more importantly, she will have a big problem. He doesn't play nice with anyone."

"I'll see what I can do to get both our physio sessions brought forward. What are you going to do, Jack?"

"First job is another cup of tea. That breakfast hit the spot."

***

Lisa's morning had been quiet. Up early, her twenty-minute yoga routine had been motivated by Jack. His words had been said in jest, yet something fuelled the devil inside her. Perhaps she was putting on weight and what exactly was the healthy appetite he referred to? Was that his polite way of telling her she was fat?

In truth, it was the kick she needed. When she had bought the yoga outfit and mat, she promised herself she would use them three times a week. That had lasted precisely four sessions. After that, the clothing was consigned to the back of a drawer while the DVD remained within the player.

Whether it was her mind playing tricks on her or a genuine change in shape, the outfit seemed so much tighter. It felt like her hips needed to be wriggled from side to side to pull the leggings up to her waist. Lisa scowled as she did it, her irritation directed towards Jack. It was only for a few seconds, for she found it hard to remain cross with him for any amount of time. Jack was Jack and a throwaway comment was exactly that to him. It would be forgotten as soon as he said it while others stewed on what he meant.

Lisa had enjoyed the show he had put on and his bare-faced cheek in antagonising David Moss. How did he do it, to be so downright obtuse and yet keep a straight face? He was a master of the art of irritation and yet something in her said he would make boyfriend material. It was madness to even think about that with Jack.

From the outset, the yoga routine was tough. It emphasised how long it had been. Any suppleness had gone and her legs burned when she stretched them. There were two positions she found unachievable after such a long break. Lisa admonished herself, promising new resolve in her endeavours. They were just words which were never going to be honoured.

It was some relief when she finished. She had a shower and went out for an early walk. It allowed her to gather her thoughts and think about the day ahead. Like Jack, it offered the chance to find a cafe for breakfast. It had been earned, an early morning exercise routine always meriting some calorific intake.

Lisa walked through the streets. To think, in an hour they would be bustling with workers hurrying to their offices. She headed towards the Minster, knowing there were a couple of the more quirky cafes hidden in the old buildings. They were a little expensive for a detective's budget and yet still an affordable treat.

Lisa surveyed the first cafe, noting the lack of room to sit. Not suitable, she moved on and took in a little more of York's cold morning air. It was worth it when she saw the second cafe filled with a window full of cakes. More importantly, there was room for an army to sit. Just one gentleman sat in the corner, quietly reading his paper between stares into his teacup.

Her time at the counter was brief. She ordered a latte and a muffin, a large blueberry mound over-spilling its case. For once, she was pleased that Jack was not there, his words still ringing in her ears. There would be another rude comment about something as soon as she sunk her teeth into it.

"I'll bring it across, love."

Lisa took a seat in the corner as if her choice had been learned from Jack. It gave her a view of the other tables and offered a direct line of sight to the counter. The order came quickly and was carefully placed in front of her. Already, she was savouring the thought of the cake she had earned.

Her peace was disturbed by a man entering. He looked vaguely familiar as if she should recognise him. He glanced across twice and then walked to the counter. His order was one black coffee to take away. Lisa watched him and noted his distinct appearance. His hair was scruffy, his jeans and shirt long overdue for replacement and yet she could not place him in his rightful location.

Still, he gazed at her until Lisa began to feel nervous. It was not a seedy, lecherous look, but one that said he was formulating a plan. Instinctively, she reached for her phone, ready to call in help if needed. Something about the man felt wrong and it nagged away in her mind.

He took his coffee and walked away. Then he paused directly opposite her seat. It felt uncomfortable. He had recognised her, leaving her at an obvious disadvantage.

"It's Lisa, isn't it?"

"That depends on who is asking."

"May I sit down?"

"That would also depend on who is asking."

"You don't remember me, do you?"

"I must admit I am lost for a name."

He smiled, holding out his hand and sitting down in the same motion.

"Andy Hutton, York's leading journalist."

Suddenly, there was recognition. Lisa's eyes stared at the slimy man Jack so detested. She had seen their run-ins and then been told so much more. He was bad news, a worm, a maggot and many other things all rolled into one.

Andy Hutton offered a limp handshake. He felt clammy and he clung to her hand a little too long for comfort. She wanted to yank it away without appearing overly rude. Unable to do so, she allowed it to linger before withdrawing and asking him what he wanted.

"Just saying good morning. No agenda."

Lisa knew that was a lie. She was yet to meet a journalist without an ulterior motive. She would play along without lowering her guard for a second.

"Fair enough. I wish you a good day."

Hutton went to get up. He smiled across at his new friend and then paused to suggest a thought had entered his head. He dismissed it and continued before changing his mind at the last minute. As he spoke, he sat back down in the chair and allowed his hands to come together in front of his face.

"Actually, there is something. It's not one for now though. At some other time, I could do with a chat with you."

"A chat?"

"Yes, I want to do a feature on your colleague, Jack Husker. He's done a lot of years of loyal service for the people of York and I'm concerned about a minority trying to sully his reputation. Some horrible things are going around as rumours about him. Of course, we would never print such rubbish."

"Of course not."

"It would just be good to put something out there as a positive article about him. You know, we could balance the rumours. We do hear a lot of negativity from unofficial sources."

"Unofficial sources?"

"Yes, you know the sort of person. They say a lot without being prepared to put their name to it. Naturally, we don't engage in such tittle-tattle. However, we do worry about the reputation of somebody who has put so much in for the good of the city."

"Do you? How kind-hearted."

"We try to be. Will you give us something to use?"

"Let me think about it."

Andy Hutton smiled. He made a mental note that he had her on the hook. Maybe not today, or tomorrow, but in the fullness of time, he would take her out of his pocket and bounce her up and down like a little ball.

"Thanks, I think Jack would appreciate it."

"If you promise you can keep a secret, I'll tell you something now, off the record. It's something I know he would appreciate."

Hutton's eyes lit up, his tongue licking his over-moist lips. He leaned forward and brought his head close to Lisa's mouth.

"What is it?"

"This is strictly between you and me."

"Yes, yes."

"Listen carefully. I'm only going to say this once."

"What is it?"

Lisa looked left and right before lowering her mouth to within inches of Hutton's left ear. Her words were whispered menacingly.

"If you print anything about Jack or claim to quote me on anything, I am going to rip off your nuts with my fingernails and stuff them down your throat. Is that clear?"

Hutton jolted back. His face drained of colour with the fire in Lisa's eyes. In response, she took her muffin and ripped it in half violently. She took the first piece and stuffed it into her mouth. Lisa chewed frantically. She could swear his eyes looked watery and never left her teeth for a second. Any threat he carried had long since dissipated from his body.

"I said, is that clear?"

"Crystal," he muttered, pushing the chair back in a hurry. Any deals with Gregor Banks were off and he would take his chances with him rather than risk the wrath of DS Lisa Ramsey.

Lisa smiled and gazed down at the muffin. It no longer held any guilt or regrets.

CHAPTER 19

DAN ARRIVED EARLY FOR his session of physiotherapy. The plan had been set and the appointments moved using the full persuasion of the law. He had even insisted that no one followed the second session, leaving him more time to work on Elizabeth Moss. Something told him she might prove difficult to convince.

Dan had dissuaded Jack from going with him. Too forthright in his approach; it was a task that required subtlety and understanding. That meant Lisa. Her role was to pose as a friend while keeping a respectable distance until a breakthrough had been made. She would be unleashed once Elizabeth was on her own.

After getting through his session, Dan walked back to the waiting area. As soon as he emerged, he saw them sitting together. Jennifer Moss, the patient, and Elizabeth Moss, the loving daughter, escorting her mother for her rehabilitation. He smiled at both of them, just as he would at any other time.

"How are you getting on?"

"Very well," replied Jennifer. "Another four or five sessions and I should be back on a horse. How about you?"

"Making progress. I've just started working again."

"Really?"

"A few light duties. It's hardly a proper job. I'm just helping out where I can."

"You're a policeman, from memory," recalled Jennifer.

"That's right."

"Jennifer, we're ready for you."

"If you'll excuse me, I won't be long. Nice to see you again, Dan."

She rose to the call of the physiotherapist. Her ability to get to her feet was much improved from the first time Dan had met her. That day, she had needed two crutches. Without them, she would not have been able to get upright.

"Good luck," smiled Elizabeth.

"Go and get yourself and Dan a coffee. I'm sure you two young 'uns have plenty to talk about."

"Fancy one, Dan?"

"Yes, that would be perfect. I'm not rushing off anywhere."

"I thought you were supposed to be working," offered Elizabeth mischievously.

"I don't think the taxpayer will mind me stopping for a quick coffee."

As soon as Jennifer had disappeared from view, Dan sent a text to Lisa. She was poised outside, ready to walk in unannounced. The instruction had been clear; not to enter until Dan said she was okay to do so. Only then could the two of them begin to work on the daughter of David Moss.

"You're just milk, aren't you?" called out Elizabeth.

"Yes, that's fine," replied Dan.

Lisa timed her entrance perfectly. She walked in at the moment the two of them sat down with their drinks. She smiled and acknowledged Dan. Elizabeth Moss briefly displayed a sense of irritation.

"Hi Lisa," said Dan.

Instinctively, Elizabeth edged a few centimetres away from Dan, offering a show of separation. In reality, she barely moved even if her body language said something totally different.

"Are you going to introduce me?" barked Elizabeth.

"Sorry, I'm being rude," said Dan. "Elizabeth, this is Lisa, a work colleague of mine. Lisa, let me introduce Elizabeth."

"A work colleague?" queried Elizabeth.

"Yes, I'm not supposed to be driving, so Lisa said she would pick me up to take me in. Light duties, remember?"

"Of course, pleased to meet you, Lisa."

All of a sudden there was a radiance back in her look. Elizabeth offered a hand and then smiled back at Dan. Any frostiness was gone with the introduction.

"You too. Sorry, I'm early. I thought I had better come in."

"Have you got time for a coffee, Lisa?" asked Elizabeth.

"As long as it's a quick one. You know, these suspects don't interview themselves."

She waited until she had a coffee in her hand and the three protagonists had settled back to their relaxed state. This time, Elizabeth made no effort to put distance between herself and Dan.

"Are you a police officer as well, Lisa?"

"Yes, I'm a detective. I came down from Newcastle a year or so ago to help out when Dan got injured and well, I'm still here. It must be all the crimes he left unsolved."

They all smiled even though Lisa could sense some tension at the joke she had made at Dan's expense. She had a feeling that she was an intruder in someone else's space.

"I'm sure Dan will be out catching all those villains again soon," offered Elizabeth.

"I certainly will," confirmed Dan.

"Elizabeth, I'm sure you sound familiar," said Lisa suddenly. "Have we spoken before?"

"She's not murdered anyone," laughed Dan. "Or I hope she hasn't."

"I'm pleased about that. Your voice is strangely familiar. I've just got that feeling that we've spoken on another occasion."

"You might have heard of me because of my father. He's the council leader."

"That's it!" exclaimed Lisa, offering the words as if some form of revelation had been made. "We've spoken on the phone."

It was Elizabeth's turn to look surprised. She remembered the conversation they had shared and the outcome. Her father had stopped her from responding to Lisa's call.

"I can't talk to you," said Elizabeth abruptly.

She rose to her feet. Dan reached out and placed his hand on her arm to offer reassurance. He sensed she was about to run for the door and if she did, the conversation would be over.

"Sit down, please," said Lisa. "Look, we're all friends in here. Sorry, I didn't mean to worry you. I just realised that we had spoken before. Don't worry, I'm not going to start grilling you."

Elizabeth paused and weighed up her options. Her watch told her that she still had fifteen minutes to wait. Often her mother was early, which would reduce the time further. It could be as little as a few minutes. Or it would be if Dan had not asked the physiotherapist to extend Jennifer Moss's session by a further twenty minutes.

Offering all the reassurance Elizabeth needed, it took Lisa ten minutes to regain the girl's trust. From a short conversation about her mother's accident to her father taking control of the council, the matter drifted on to the night of the disappearance. In that time, Lisa could hardly fail to notice the eloquence with which Elizabeth spoke. Her privileged upbringing was at odds with her own in Newcastle. It was hard not to feel sorry for her, knowing the world such innocence was about to be drawn into.

Elizabeth spoke fluently about her childhood. She offered a hint of the claustrophobic nature of her relationship with her father. In many ways, he was the father that most girls would aspire to have. Yet the reality of living under his control was something more difficult to accept. Lisa found herself listening to a girl torn between parental loyalty and the need to break out of his stifling grasp.

A boyfriend was mentioned at the end of her schooling. It had not lasted for any significant length of time. Her father had exerted pressure and made it too difficult to continue. He had not known about Steven and perhaps some others, none of them ever likely to be good enough for his darling princess.

"Mummy's a saint, you know, with what she has to put up with."

Lisa smiled. It was the first direct show of defiance or willingness to offer any words against her father. Dan kept quiet and allowed Lisa to probe as delicately as she could.

"You must introduce us when she comes out. I would like to meet her. Does she give you more freedom?"

"I suppose. She goes along with my father mostly."

"And how do they react when you bring friends home?"

"They're okay, as long as they are of the right standing."

"And dare I ask about boyfriends? My parents were terrible when I brought my first boyfriend home. They made it impossible for both of us. The poor lad scarpered at the first opportunity."

Elizabeth only offered silence.

"They wouldn't let one in the house," laughed Lisa. "Not unless he stood on a mat."

A small smile emerged from Elizabeth's mouth.

"Look, we know all about Steven. I can understand why you kept him quiet. That might have taken too much explaining, given political allegiances."

"Sorry, I need to go," insisted Elizabeth.

"No, you don't. We can help you find him."

This time, it was Lisa who placed her arm on Elizabeth, a reassuring touch offered in support. She glanced down for a few moments. Then her face disappeared into her hands. As soon as it did, the tears welled up in her eyes.

"We'll do everything we can," said Lisa. "We need your help."

"I can't. Daddy told me to say nothing."

"Elizabeth, only you can help. You know that."

"No."

"Steven is in serious trouble."

Her eyes exploded with tears. Her sobs soon turned into a wailing cacophony of noise. Lisa looked across at Dan and beckoned for him to find some tissues. He was not gone for long, perhaps thirty seconds in total. While he was away, Elizabeth did nothing but cry.

"I love him," she wailed.

"I know and we want to help him," said Lisa.

"What exactly did you see on that night, Elizabeth?" asked Dan as he sat back down.

"I saw it all," she sobbed. "The van, the couple, the man bundling them into the back. He grabbed them, threw them in and drove off. The others were listening to the tour guide. I was cold and bored and watched it happen."

"Would you recognise the man?" asked Lisa.

She shook her head.

"It was foggy, I didn't get a look at his face. The van was pretty distinctive. It had a damaged bumper on the back. I don't want to get into trouble."

"Elizabeth, you're not going to get into trouble. This is about finding Steven and whoever took the Johnsons."

"Do you think it was the same person?"

Lisa nodded. The tears that were offered in response told her that it might have been nobler to lie.

The rest of their conversation was calmer. By the time it was over, Elizabeth had dried her tears. Once settled, Dan and Lisa made sure to leave before Jennifer Moss emerged. They thanked Elizabeth and walked out of the building to find Jack. He was sitting on a bench, huddled down to avoid the cold wind biting into his flesh.

"You took your time," he offered.

"Good things come to those who wait," insisted Lisa.

"Yes, and they come quicker if you ask the right questions."

"You mean blunt ones," laughed Dan.

"They work for me."

"As do many things I could not recommend to others," interrupted Lisa. "Let me tell you what we have got."

Jack was excited when he heard the news. For nearly an hour, he had waited outside the building. Twice, he had entered the front door before discretion had taken over. It was torture not being able to go in and interview the girl himself. He knew why it had been done that way when the girl was likely to be scared off by the first sign of pressure.

"Are you sure she'll help us?"

Lisa nodded. It made Jack's eyes light up with excitement. They were close, he could smell it. It was just a question of triggering the final move.

"What are we going to do to flush them out?" asked Dan. "She hasn't got enough to identify who it is."

"We need to find the van at the very least. We also need to find a body or two," said Jack.

"We could organise a tail," said Dan.

"Or we could just use Elizabeth as bait to entice them out."

"No," insisted Lisa. "Lang will never go for it and we are not going behind his back."

"As if I would. Just arrange for her to meet us at that cafe Reeves went missing from."

"Jack..."

"I only want to buy her a coffee."

Jack, stop it!" barked Lisa. "Come on, we need to get back to the station."

"What's the hurry?" asked Jack.

"This is," said Lisa as she thrust her phone at Jack to allow him to see DCI Lang's curt message. "I think we have been ratted on."

***

DCI Lang stood in his office with a face like thunder. Jack and Lisa sat opposite him, their positions that of naughty children summoned to the headmaster. His face had reddened and was threatening to explode in a moment of rage. All it needed was one of Jack's wisecracks to be the trigger.

The two detectives knew better than to say anything. They sat in silence from the moment they entered his office. Lisa knew they were in trouble while Jack made little effort to show that he cared. It had been Lisa's idea to send Dan back to his desk. Light duties did not mean getting a dressing-down from the DCI.

For over sixty seconds, the stand-off continued. Lang bit his lip and sat with his palms face down on the table. His body was tense, with anger flowing through him. It was unlike him to hold onto such rage rather than offer up what he was thinking.

Lang wanted one of them to say something. Even one of Jack's flippant offers to get coffee would have done it. Yet there was not one sound; not even a murmur that he could go at. It forced him to break the impasse and go on the attack.

"What the bloody hell were you two thinking?"

Lisa looked at Jack who shrugged.

"Well?" demanded Lang.

When Jack did not speak, Lisa felt the need to explain.

"Sir, we..."

She was cut off in her prime. Her few words were broken up by Lang's rage. It was punctuated with profanities, his normal well-spoken manner replaced with that of a raging tyrant. While the explosion happened, Jack sat waiting for the right moment to offer his version of an explanation.

"I told you two not to go anywhere near Elizabeth Moss."

"But sir, we..." continued Lisa.

Again, she was interrupted. Her face filled with colour, a combination of guilt, embarrassment and tension all wrapped up in one dangerous parcel. Lisa hated the arguments and that feeling of having done wrong. What she hated more was the way it washed over Jack.

"And have you got anything to offer?"

With a quick twist, it was Jack's turn in the spotlight. Lang's full fire had been turned on him. Jack looked so calm and so indifferent to their boss's ire. It was hard to know if he even had a pulse.

"Not that you will want to hear."

"And what the hell does that mean?"

Jack paused, allowing a moment for the words to sink in. If he responded quickly, he too would be given short shrift. Lang was set for an argument, no matter what was offered. That was something Jack was not going to give him the satisfaction of having.

"It means there is a simple explanation."

"Which is?"

"Give me two minutes and I'll tell you. Coffee, sir?"

Jack got up and walked nonchalantly from the room. Even Lang struggled to comprehend the audacity of his detective. Every part of him wanted to scream at the man. Yet nothing would come out and, in the absence of correction, Lang sat quietly with Lisa. It increased her discomfort as she wondered how he found the nerve to do it.

"I guess that's Jack for you," she smiled, feeling obliged to offer something in his absence.

"This had better be good for both your sakes. Do you want to get us started while Jack is away?"

"I think we should wait for Jack. He has all the facts."

"You mean he is better at making up a story."

Inwardly, Lisa nodded. She looked away from Lang, hoping her face did not betray her. All she could do was pray that Jack would come back quickly. That was if he came back at all, for Jack was unpredictable at best.

He returned twenty minutes later. They were twenty of the most uncomfortable minutes in Lisa's life. Lang did nothing to hide his impatience as Jack continued to defy him. He had kept Lang waiting for as long as he possibly could. A quick visit to the toilet was followed by a catch-up on telephone calls. Finally, he reappeared holding three coffees.

"Did you go to Colombia for them?" asked Lang.

"Peru for these, sir. You get a far smoother blend in my opinion."

"Jack, I don't care. Put the coffee on the table and let's hear it."

"Hear what, sir?"

"You are testing my patience. Either you tell me why you approached Elizabeth Moss after I expressly told you not to or both you and DS Ramsey are suspended."

Lisa slumped in her seat. Her heart was pounding in her chest. She had worked hard to achieve her rank at such a young age and did not need a stain on her career. Alongside her, Jack never even flinched with the threat.

"We didn't," shrugged Jack.

"You didn't what?"

"We didn't approach Elizabeth Moss. I told you it was a simple explanation."

"So, you just happened to bump into her?" queried Lang, raising his eyebrows noticeably.

"That's right."

"That's some coincidence."

"I know. We were just saying we should pick some lottery numbers while we're on a streak."

"Don't push it, Jack. I'm not stupid."

"I never said you were, sir. I'll work on the basis that you don't want to be in the syndicate."

"And would you like to add anything?"

Lang turned to Lisa who was still staring down at her feet. Her discomfort was obvious and she made no effort to hide it. Lang looked at her, knowing he could make things as difficult for her as he wanted. It would make no difference when Jack was the one that he needed to tame.

"Look, sir," interrupted Jack. "How were we to know she would be at Dan's physio session?"

"You wouldn't unless he told you."

"He didn't know who she was."

"Yet you just happen to turn up the week she is there. Dare I ask why?"

It was Lisa's turn to grow in confidence. It was a question she could answer and that offered her a chance to climb out of the hole she had dug herself into.

"To give him a lift."

"But only this week."

"Yes, it's the first week he is back on light duties. I thought it would be nice to offer some support."

Jack nodded in admiration at the little piece of factual detail she had thrown into the mix.

"And I suppose you could not help but ask her about Steven Reeves?"

"We never got a chance," replied Jack. "She started talking about him from the moment she found out we were from the police."

"And what about the night the Johnsons went missing?"

"She spoke about that as well. She went straight from talking about Reeves to the Johnsons."

"Wow, she was pretty talkative for a girl who was adamant she would not speak to us."

"You know what women are like once they get started," laughed Jack.

This time it was Lisa's turn to scowl.

"Just get out...both of you! And do not go anywhere near Elizabeth Moss. That is a direct order."

Jack and Lisa left the office with Lang's words ringing in their ears. He had made his point clear by instructing the two of them to stay away from Moss. Already, he was contemplating dealing with David Moss's fancy lawyer. The only thing more inflated than that man's ego was the rates that he would be charging for his work.

"What do you reckon?" asked Lisa when they were safely out of Lang's line of sight.

"Sounds like plan B," sighed Jack.

Lisa stopped on the stairs, a little surprised at Jack's response. She had known him for a year and never once in that time had he deviated from his intention. Despite Lang's harsh words, she never expected Jack to waver. He would do what he always did best and charge into the battle. Warning or no warning, Jack was one to act in the way he believed was right.

"Which is?"

"We go and meet her in that cafe."

"I thought that was plan A?"

"No, that is plan B."

"But it's the same as plan A?"

"Yes, and that's what makes it so clever," winked Jack.

***

Elizabeth Moss was scared. She was too scared to meet the detectives and even more frightened of not doing so. If the police could find her, it was only a matter of time before the kidnapper followed the same lead. He had got to the Johnsons and he had got to Steven. She would be no harder to deal with.

Did she trust them? That was a question she kept asking herself. Dan seemed kind and the type who genuinely wanted to help. She was less sure about Lisa who appeared to have a tougher attitude. It was Dan who had been the one to put her at ease. It was Dan who she would be prepared to talk to.

He had arranged the meeting in a cafe off the side of Fossgate. Elizabeth had insisted that Dan would be there to accompany her while she spoke. Not her mother and certainly not her father. It was Dan she looked to in her moment of need.

As she walked to meet them, she kept telling herself everything would be alright. Of course, the relationship would be out in the open and laid bare to the detriment of her father's political career. She would put it all on the table and find a way of tracing

Steven. It was hard to imagine they could be a couple again. It was too late for that. All she wanted was for him to return home safely.

All of a sudden, Elizabeth stopped. She had a feeling that someone was following her. A van drove slowly behind her, idling along some hundred or so yards back. It was white and seemed to hold position before turning off down a side road by the river.

She felt vulnerable in the isolated street. Until she met up with the police, she was on her own. The daylight was good and yet what did that matter in a quiet part of town? Without tourists or office workers, there was no blending into the throng. Dan had promised her protection and now it felt like she was more vulnerable than ever.

The devil in her head began to play tricks. What if Dan was the kidnapper and had been tracking her down to extract the information he needed? First Steven and now her, he was in the perfect position to do it. Maybe, he was not even a detective and his ID was a fake from the internet. Anyone could learn a few key phrases and pose as somebody a vulnerable girl could trust. Maybe it had all been done to get at her father.

Elizabeth looked around. Her head was spinning and unable to make sense of the thoughts inside her. Could she trust anyone or was everybody intent on causing her harm? Where was her father when she needed him? His overprotecting presence was now exactly what she wanted.

Befuddled, she sat down. She lowered herself onto a low wall that ran by the side of the road. Tears welled up in her eyes, blurring her vision as her lungs began to tighten. She couldn't breathe and her heart was threatening to explode out of her chest.

"Are you alright?"

Above her stood a woman. Her face was cold and yet she offered a kindness that wanted to help. Elizabeth said nothing and concentrated on regulating her breathing. She was barely ready to offer a response.

"I saw you stop and thought you were going to fall over."

"I'm fine. Thank you."

The politeness was an afterthought. It came out as a separate sentence in its own right. Elizabeth did not look up when she responded. The woman stood over her, offering barely a flicker of emotion. If Elizabeth had gazed upwards, she would have seen a face as dull as the late afternoon sky.

"Where are you heading?"

"The cafe up there," whispered Elizabeth, pointing vaguely with a weak arm.

"That's where I'm going too. I'll walk you there."

The stranger held out an arm and placed Elizabeth's upon it. It felt odd as if the woman was a little overbearing.

"You don't have to."

"It's fine," she said coldly. "It's only just up here and the pavement is uneven. We don't want you getting hurt."

Elizabeth felt the stranger take a firmer hold of her arm. She pulled her up to her feet. They set off in the direction of the cafe. Every part of Elizabeth wanted to say something, for an uneasy feeling was beginning to fill her thoughts.

"How far is it?" she asked nervously.

"A couple of hundred yards. Careful!"

The stranger jolted Elizabeth to one side. Instinctively, she glanced down to understand the cause of the commotion. There was nothing other than a few leaves blowing across the pavement. It left her feeling even more confused.

"You almost tripped over that cat."

"What cat?"

"Didn't you see it? We need to get you to the cafe. Just keep hold of me and you'll be fine."

Elizabeth did exactly as she was told despite her brain telling her there was no cat. There never had been and the pavement was flat. Yet the stranger was insistent on treating her like an invalid. Something was wrong even if she was not capable of understanding what it was.

The pace was quickened. The lady offered a couple of glances over her shoulder. Both caught Elizabeth's attention. She was looking for something or more likely somebody. Elizabeth thought she was about to be mugged.

The pair of them continued to move forward. Elizabeth saw the sign for the cafe and some familiar figures in the distance. Her eyes had cleared and the sight of Dan getting out of an unmarked car was welcoming. Alongside him, it was harder to make out who the others were. Perhaps one was Lisa. With her, was a shorter middle-aged man who was scruffy and in need of some new clothes.

"Here is fine, thank you. Those are the friends that I'm meeting."

The stranger looked into the distance and panicked. She turned around sharply, yanking Elizabeth's arm towards the road. In a chaotic few seconds, she was on her phone and shouting instructions. It was a shriek that demanded action.

"Now! It has to be now!"

In a blur, a white van screamed alongside them. Out jumped a man before the vehicle had barely stopped. Elizabeth pulled away only to find the woman's grip was not offering her an inch. Then came the darkness of a bag thrown over her head. It was traumatic and brutal as she was dragged unwillingly into the back of the van. She heard the doors open and felt the pain of her body hitting the metal floor before the van sped off and a foot pressed down on her neck.

"Move and you're dead!"

CHAPTER 20

"THAT WAS HER!"

Lisa's voice pierced the breeze. Jack and Dan heard the squeal of tyres from the van while their colleague's hand pointed frantically towards it. The vehicle sped towards them, offering the temptation to jump out and stop it. It would mean an instant trip to the morgue.

The three detectives leapt back in their car. Lisa drove while Jack rang in the number plate from the van. He called for backup, fighting the bumpy ride as he spoke. Lisa was in pursuit and tailing the van as best she could.

"Don't lose him!" cried Dan, with the feeling of adrenalin flooding through him. It had been a long while since he had enjoyed the exhilaration of a chase. In the back seat, his body was thrown around by each crude movement of the wheel. For the first time in a year, he felt alive and it was an experience he had missed.

"Put your seat belt on. You're supposed to be on light duties, not chasing bad guys," said Lisa.

"Did you get a good look at them?" asked Jack.

"Not really. I recognised Elizabeth; I didn't see much of the others."

"I'm sure that was Alice Johnson," said Jack. "I couldn't swear to it but she had the right figure."

"Trust you to remember that bit."

Jack blushed and wiped his face with his hand. It was only to cover any colour that had flushed through his cheeks. He put his own seatbelt on to protect himself from some of the bumps. Lisa's driving was almost as erratic as the van in front.

"Anyone got any travel sickness pills?"

Jack's barb was met with a swift backhander from Lisa's left hand. It was enough to deaden the muscle and remind her colleague that she did not like comments about her driving.

"Do you want me to slow down and lose them?"

Neither Jack nor Dan offered a response. It was Lisa in charge and she was not about to spare her right foot.

Despite her speed, Lisa struggled to keep up. The van stretched away, driven to its reckless limit. Pavements were mounted and pedestrians were sent scurrying. With each dangerous manoeuvre, Lisa's car fell further behind.

Jack rang for backup again. His description was detailed and supplemented with a street-by-street commentary of where the van was heading. Cars were mobilised to head for the northwest of the city. Jack feared it might be too late by the time anyone caught up with the van.

"Any idea where they are heading?" asked Dan, with his hand gripping the overhead handle as tightly as he could.

"I would guess the same place they took the others."

Lisa saw the van turn left into Water End. Her foot pressed down hard to reach the turn. When she got there, she yanked the car around the corner. The van was gone, leaving a feeling of desperation churning inside.

"Oh no, I've lost them."

"Keep going," urged Jack. "If they are hiding down a side road, we've got them."

Progress was slowed. The car's speed was eased down to allow all the streets to be checked. No matter how hard they looked, there was nothing to find. The mood felt sombre. Lisa could already sense the meeting she was going to have with DCI Lang.

"Oh bugger," she cursed.

"Now what?" asked Dan.

Jack puffed out his cheeks. "We will have to get the uniforms to find them. We should put a watch on their house."

***

Elizabeth Moss could hardly breathe. Her body was bruised and the foot across her throat forced every jolt of the van through the side of her face. She gasped for air, fighting the bag that restricted what little she could take in. At first, she had screamed and then the threats had been clear. Two kicks into her side had made her whole body feel cold and numb. In her pocket, she still had her phone but any movement towards it would mean certain death.

Her captors had said little. In the commotion of her being bundled inside, her memory of them was limited. She was certain it was the fake Samaritan that was pressing down on her neck. It was a woman who made the threat but it was hard to know if it was the same one.

The mounting of the pavement had been particularly painful. The metal of the floor had cracked into the side of her face. She had bitten her cheek and left the taste of blood in her mouth. When Elizabeth coughed, it brought more firmness to the foot. Whoever it was had no sympathy or compassion in their body.

Briefly, there had been a moment of hope. The speed of the van confirmed the chase. The pursuer had got closer and then the sound of the siren became distant. That was when the van had slowed and she knew it was over. Now, calm had returned and they would be making their way to Elizabeth's final destination.

A flicker of optimism flashed through her. Would it mean that she could see Steven for one final time? Dead or alive, Steven would be there waiting for her. Maybe they would be killed together and die united in one another's arms.

A change of terrain sent another shudder through her side. It was a rough track and the vehicle had mounted a kerb to get onto the dirt. Branches scraped the side of the van, offering the distinctive noise of wood on metal. It had the feeling of the vehicle being squeezed through a gap. To Elizabeth, it was an attempt to take it out of sight. They hadn't been driving long enough to get out of the city.

Elizabeth had counted to ten when the van came to a halt. The speed was low, making the distance travelled no more than twenty or thirty metres. The scraping never stopped in that time, putting their location somewhere deep in the trees. In her captive state, Elizabeth's thoughts turned to the sinister end game she was about to unwillingly take part in.

She straightened her leg a little to ease the pain. The movement was met with more pressure applied to her neck. The surging pain suggested something was about to snap. Elizabeth knew her life was close to being ended.

"I said, don't move," snarled the woman.

Elizabeth's body stiffened. There was a bang as the driver's door was thrown back with force. Dull footsteps moved down the side of the van. They were cushioned, perhaps on the damp ground outside. Elizabeth prayed she might be left in the van only for her hopes to be destroyed when the door was yanked open.

"Couldn't you have driven any worse? I'm black and blue," growled the woman.

"Do you prefer to get caught? This bitch has the police on her tail."

It was a short conversation finished by the male voice. It ended any hopes of escape. Outrunning them both would be impossible and she was not going to outmuscle the woman, let alone the man. Elizabeth laid still and prepared herself for the worst.

"Let's get her inside. We need to get rid of the van and check her pockets for a phone."

"Crypt?"

"Yes."

As her phone was taken from her, Elizabeth processed the information. A crypt meant a church somewhere on the outskirts of the city. It also meant somewhere dark and unwelcoming. At least the foot had been lifted to offer relief to her neck. That moment of hope was destroyed by two rough hands grabbing her and lifting her out of the vehicle.

"I'll walk, just give me a moment."

There was no response. Her knee cracked against the edge of the van. She winced in pain and tried to reach down to nurse it. When they dragged her, she let out a wail, which was met with more cruelty from the woman.

"Shut it, or you're dead."

It was too much for Elizabeth to take. The tears were pouring down her cheeks. The bag caught most of them, leaving it stuck to her sodden face. When they placed her on the ground, her legs could take no weight. Twice, she fell, only to be dragged to her feet. It was a tortuous few steps they forced her to take.

"Walk, bitch. We're not carrying you."

Elizabeth's last memory flicked between a set of stone stairs and a dark musty smell. Her brain was telling her the two were the same thing. She tried to focus on the hope she held in her head. It told her she would soon be back in her bed. Any such illusion was lost when she was pushed forward roughly, sending her body crashing to the floor. With the impact came the sound of a heavy door slamming closed behind her. Then the lock turned, to seal her into the darkness.

***

Lisa was the first to react when the radio sprang to life.

"We've had a call from a lady who has spotted a van in the undergrowth at Saint Stephen's Church in Acomb."

"We're on our way!" she shouted.

Lisa pressed the accelerator hard to the floor. They were minutes away, their detour to drop Dan off at the station having taken them out of the area. It was Jack's idea to go there, done under the guise of needing to brief Lang. In truth, Jack had concerns about taking Dan into battle.

He knew the flack would be flying, They were already in too deep to get themselves out. Dan was still convalescing and able to claim he was not part of the mistakes. It would probably finish Jack's career, with a last shameful error seeing him packed out of the force. Lisa would be sent back to Newcastle, with a black mark on her record but with no long-term damage from the charge.

"I'll direct you," said Jack. "I know a quick way into Acomb."

Even with local knowledge, it was painful. Those minutes seemed like an hour. Each minute which passed reduced the chance of Elizabeth Moss being found alive. They had seen her snatched in a manner that held little concern for her well-being. She would now be close to death.

"Keep your foot down; I want to get there before the uniforms do."

"There's not a lot I can do with that."

A delivery van blocked their way. It was another online electrical item being delivered to a waiting household. It was no time to mourn the loss of the high street. Jack had too much on his mind as his brain raced through the potential scenarios that faced them. He had been there before and it never stopped the blood from pumping through his veins. With excitement came danger or possibly the other way around. Jack was never able to tell the difference.

"Just drive on the pavement."

His phone rang when they were less than a mile from the church. It was Lang, whose voice was racing to get his words out. Dan had briefed him and it had spurred the DCI into action. Any potential irritation he held had been curtailed by concern for his team.

"Don't do anything stupid, Jack. This is not a time for heroes."

"No plans to. We just need to get to the Moss girl."

"Uniforms will be there as soon as I can get cars summoned."

"That may be too late."

"Where are you, Jack?"

"Lisa, turn left. We're a quarter of a mile away; maybe half at the most."

"Wait for backup."

"We'll see what we find."

"Jack, you wait for backup. That's a direct order."

"Okay, I heard. Get someone over to the Johnsons' house. If they aren't at the church, we need to pick them up."

"Will do, but Jack…"

"Yes," he interrupted eagerly.

"Be careful."

"Anyone would think you cared, sir."

"Maybe I do, despite my best intentions."

Jack pressed the handset to cut Lang off. His focus was on the church, which Lisa was approaching. She slowed the vehicle and surveyed the perimeter. Jack pointed to a side road as somewhere to stop. There was no sign of the van, just an old church with an overgrown graveyard alongside it, surrounded by a high brick wall. It looked like any other, with a slightly unkempt appearance to an outsider.

"Where's the van?" asked Lisa.

"Park up and we'll do a walk around. Make sure you've got your vest on."

"And you, Jack?"

"Always ready."

It was obvious he was unprotected. His dismissive tone was that of someone who hardly cared. Did he have no concern for his safety or was it just bravado? It was hard to know when Jack was a mystery to everyone.

Lisa slipped the vest over her head. They were never comfortable, with her frame not equipped to take the weight. The whole thing had been made with a larger man in mind. It made her feel better to know it was too big even if it compromised the safety it offered.

"Do you want to split up?" she asked.

"No, we stick together on this one."

Lisa felt reassured. Whether he was just being protective, she did not care. It was no time to be heroic when anything could be waiting for them. With churches came shadows and the overgrown trees only added to that feeling.

Step by step, they worked their way around the outside. At times, it felt like Jack's hand was almost taking hold of Lisa's arm. His concern did not go unnoticed. Lisa was pleased with the reassurance when her body was riddled with tension. It was too quiet for her liking and the perimeter brick wall was too high to see in. The only glimpse it offered was where its poor state of repair allowed glints of light to shimmer through the missing mortar.

"Where was the van seen?" asked Lisa.

"Around the side."

The two detectives continued until they saw a gap in the wall. It was a small gateway made bigger by the crumbling brickwork to each side. Branches hung over the void, a horse chestnut coming into full leaf. It drooped down to cast dark shadows across the space.

The flattening of the grass was the first giveaway. A vehicle had been through the gate in recent hours. The grass was pressed down and a couple of tyre tracks were fresh. Above them, a broken branch was hanging limply from the tree.

"I'll get this rung in," said Lisa. "We need to find that van."

"I'm going inside," announced Jack.

"No, wait!"

Jack set off at pace. Something told him there was more to find. Any thoughts of safety had been cast from his mind. Inside, he knew Elizabeth Moss was there.

"Jack, I'm coming with you."

They rushed through the graveyard, past the collection of headstones, some angled over at perilous degrees of incline. The place looked like it had been left to go wild, with the bodies beneath long since forgotten in all but the families' minds. It offered a glimpse of the temporary state of life itself except it was no time for either of them to be philosophical.

The church door had been left open. It was ajar as if someone had exited in a hurry. Jack peered in as Lisa caught up with him. She appeared troubled while Jack looked like a gundog primed to get his teeth into its quarry.

"We should wait," insisted Lisa.

"No time; I'm going in."

Lisa was scared. No part of her would let a colleague go in alone. It would be the same with any partner, but with Jack, she knew he was vulnerable. With one carefree move, he would be gone. She adjusted her vest, took a deep breath and followed him inside the church.

It was eerie. Even during the day, the light was dim. The windows were ill-equipped to allow the sun in. A wash would not do any harm. With such effort, it would still be hazy inside. There were not enough windows for the place to be anything other than gloomy.

Jack crept slowly, each footstep echoing around the large space. His heart pounded inside an ever-tightening chest. There was no mistaking the danger from what was concealed in the shadows.

"Come on, Jack, we need backup here," said Lisa, her voice more of a plea than a statement.

"There's no time. I do think we should announce ourselves. I'm not getting jumped as we walk. Are you ready?"

Lisa nodded without even convincing herself.

"Police, come out!"

There was no response.

"This is your last warning or we're coming in. Please identify yourself."

Again, there was nothing.

"Empty?" asked Lisa, more in hope than expectation.

Jack shook his head. His brain told him something was wrong. He sensed a presence lurking, perhaps someone watching their every move. If they turned their backs, the threat would strike in an instant.

"You go around to the left and I'll circle right. Don't go out of my sight."

"Yes, Dad."

It was no time for jovial wisecracks. Jack appreciated it all the same, his sense of unease turning the acid in his stomach. He knew they were vulnerable, their lack of support not sensible. And yet he had that urge to bring the search to a conclusion.

Jack and Lisa circled the church. Lisa screamed when a mouse shot across her foot. Jack turned only to see a sense of calm return. Lisa walked forward, watched by Jack, whose eyes tried to cover everything.

"Up or down next?" asked Lisa.

Jack thought for a moment. "Let's go down first; then we can try the tower."

A side door led to the crypt. It was heavy oak, with an old key broken off in the lock. It took a firm shove to move it, Jack's shoulder pressing hard above the handle. Inside, smelt damp, a smell not too dissimilar to a student flat. Both Jack and Lisa could sense the eeriness the place exuded.

"Is there a light, Jack?"

He reached towards the wall, fumbling at an array of switches. Each looked ready to give the user a nasty shock. Bare wires were on show above one, with Jack's appetite to touch any of them limited. Yet he knew he could not go on without putting some light into the space.

Jack clenched his teeth and pressed the first switch. There was nothing, not even a flicker. The second caused a sharp bang; a brief flash of bright light before the bulb exploded. It left the switch with the wires exposed, the least welcoming of all on the stone wall.

"Nothing ventured," he grimaced, pressing his thumb against the crumbling plastic.

The result surprised him. A light flickered into life at the bottom of the stone stairs. Though far from bright, it was better than nothing. Coupled with torches, it would illuminate their descent.

"Steady on the stairs," noted Jack. "They are pretty uneven."

"I'm not an old lady. Remember, I'm the youngster out of the two of us."

Lisa's words were interrupted by her stumbling on the first step. Only Jack grabbing her arm prevented her from tumbling downwards.

"Sorry, I missed that. What were you saying?"

Lisa said nothing. The two detectives eased down the steps. Headroom was limited, not that it was a concern for either of them. Jack was barely five foot eight and even that was only on a good day.

Inch by inch, they moved down into the crypt. It felt unpleasant, the type of place there was no reason to go. Cold, damp and uninviting, the dead of the past were welcome to occupy it. It was a painful reminder to Jack of his mortality.

At the bottom, the stairs turned right. There was another door, this time protected from the external elements. It looked just as solid except for a small amount of dampness rising from the floor. Tentatively, he tried to open it. The handle was tough to turn and the lock prevented the door from moving.

"Got a key?" asked Jack.

"Of course. I carry church keys in my handbag everywhere I go. Just in case I need to break into one in the middle of the night."

Jack released the handle and looked around at the featureless space. There was nowhere to hide a key, no obvious frame or ledge to tuck it in behind. And yet, he doubted it was the sort of place you would take a key away.

"What about the one in the top door?" asked Lisa.

"It was snapped off; no use to anyone. There must be one here somewhere."

"Unless it has been taken away by the Johnsons."

"That's a fair point, though why would they take it away? What is the church to them?"

"Maybe nothing, but that assumes there isn't something behind that door."

"You're right," said Jack. "Somewhere they can come and go as they please. Why would anyone ever go into a crypt? Not even a vicar would bother coming down here."

The urge to get inside was growing by the second. Frustration was also growing, a locked door normally presenting little in the way of an obstacle. This was different. It was inches of solid English oak, designed to put a heavy door in the way of anyone trying to get in. Church doors were made to last, the number of originals remaining in York paying testament to their strength.

"Let's call in a specialist team," said Lisa.

"There must be a key."

Jack shone his torch around the small damp area. There was hope when he saw a small indent in the wall. Without a thought, he thrust in his hand. His fingers were met by cobwebs and the feeling of a rotting rodent. He shivered in disappointment at his failure and wiped his hand on his side.

Beneath his feet lay stone slabs. His torch followed the lines between them. Each had an inch gap, deep crevices unfilled when the stones were laid, perhaps with the thought that one day they would be levered back up. Maybe bodies were buried underneath? Jack's mind wandered back to the Johnsons and whether it could be their final resting place. It was the thought that filled his mind until his torchlight reflected on something metal in one of the crevices.

He bent down and pushed his fingers into the crack. In the dim light, he could sense it was rusted metal. The coldness to the touch confirmed his thoughts.

"What is it, Jack?"

"I think it is a key. It looks like it has been there for a while. Yes, it is. Someone has dropped a key and has not been able to get it out. I just can't reach it."

"I'll try. I've got smaller fingers."

Lisa reached down and, like Jack, could touch the edge of it. It was too far in to drag out. She could not get her fingers down the side. Lisa glanced back at the door and was confident it was of the right proportions.

"I can't get it," she sighed.

"Have you got any wire?" asked Jack.

"You mean in the same handbag as the church keys?"

"Or anywhere else."

"Only in my bra," she laughed, leaving her thankful the dim light did not offer up her reddening face.

"Perfect. Can you pull a piece out?"

"No!"

"I can help if you want."

"Jack! I'm not dismantling my bra to go ferreting for a key."

"Not even if it will solve a case?"

"You're priceless, you are. Give me a minute and turn your back."

Lisa turned away from him and slid her hands under her vest. She fidgeted for a minute, cursing at the difficulty of the task. There was a pause and a moment of silence, then another series of expletives before she dragged out her hand and put her finger to her mouth. She could taste blood on the tip where the wire had pierced her skin.

"Would it help if I shone my torch across you?"

"No, it bloody wouldn't!"

With dogged determination, she dragged out a wire. Lisa could feel the shame burning through her when she handed it to Jack. Instinctively, her right arm clamped firmly across her chest. Whether it was imaginary, she suddenly felt less supported.

"Don't you ever say I am not committed to the job."

"Would I? Mind you, it's not very long. I might need another piece," said Jack.

"Don't even think about it."

Jack took the wire and pushed it down inside the crack. The devil in him appeared, the chance to have a moment of fun at Lisa's expense. He tried to focus, only for it to get the better of him.

"Buggar, I've dropped it. Can you get another one out?"

"Jack, for Christ's sake!"

"Just kidding," he grinned.

He turned to face her and was met by a look of thunder. The time for jokes was over. Jack pushed the wire down into the crevice. After two failed attempts, he looped it under the metal. With surprising dexterity, he dragged out a sorry-looking key.

"Is that it?" asked Lisa.

"It might look past its best but it will get results, just like me. Now, do you want your bra back?"

Lisa smiled and took the wire from him, without knowing what she would do with it. She was hardly going to put it back in, nor was she about to let Jack keep it. By the time she had it in her hand, Jack had moved on and was working the key in the lock. It did not sound like a great fit. The lock was stiff and was offering stubborn resistance.

Suddenly, Jack stepped back and put his finger to his lips.

"Did you hear that?"

"Hear what?" asked Lisa.

"A noise behind the door."

"Jack, this better not be one of your wind-ups."

"I promise you, it isn't. You better brace yourself."

"Jack, this is stupid. Uniforms will be here soon."

"No way. I'm going in."

It was too late to argue. A shoulder to the door was timed to coincide with the turning of the lock. There was no subtlety, just the crash of her colleague through the door. Jack tumbled inside, his body stumbling into the crypt.

The smell was terrible, like decaying flesh. It came from sheets that were covering a series of mounds. Lisa's first instinct was to cover her mouth. Jack's response was the same. As their stomachs turned over, their eyes were drawn to a figure on the floor.

"There's movement!"

They rushed to a body laid before them. It was a dishevelled girl covered in dirt and blood. She groaned and partially turned over. When she did, they recognised her immediately.

"It's Elizabeth Moss!" exclaimed Lisa. "She's alive!"

"Which is more than I can say for these poor sods."

Jack pulled back a sheet to reveal the decaying corpse of a man. There was no doubt he had been there for a while.

CHAPTER 21

"How long do you think we've got?" asked Alice Johnson.

Jamie knew the answer was not long, not that he was ever going to admit it to Alice. She scared him. Her likely response was to lash out, her violent side something he struggled to cope with. He had seen her at her worst. The venomous spite she had displayed when she ended the life of young Steven Reeves had chilled him to the bone.

Deep down, he still loved her. He always had, long before she had first suggested killing their aunt and uncle. Of course, he had argued against it. She had called him weak, leaving him no choice but to go along with her plan. If only there had been no witnesses, they might have got away with it. Then there was the meddling copper, the one who ignited such rage in Alice.

"They won't go inside the crypt for a long while. That will give us plenty of time to collect our things and get out of here."

"And the van?"

As soon as we have packed up, we'll dump it. If we set light to it, it'll never be traced back to us."

Alice smiled. She felt reassured that Jamie had a plan. He was clever like that, always thinking about things well ahead. He was both the brains and the brawn in their little gang. He was right. They would go home, pack a few things and then the two of them could disappear to a warmer climate. They could visit Spain, maybe even Nerja. Her aunt and uncle had spoken so fondly of the place.

Jamie drove as quickly as he dared through the streets of the city. He was relieved to get away from the church. The whole place gave him the creeps. He had never been comfortable with them, not since he was dragged there as a little boy. There had been the incident with the vicar and ever since then, churches sent a shudder through his body.

His brain told him to press his foot down hard. And yet it would attract attention. Time was limited before their secret was discovered. Elizabeth had hit the floor hard but that single blow was unlikely to have killed her. Indeed, she would probably be awake and screaming her lungs out. Hindsight told him they should have ended her life right then.

"Do you want to keep the van running while I go in?" asked Alice.

"No, I'll come in with you. I'll park it around the corner. We can walk the last couple of hundred yards."

"I might not want to walk."

"Okay, I'll drop you off and I'll walk."

Typical Alice, always difficult right up to the last moment. He would drop her off at the gate and then take the vehicle away from the house. The neighbours might see them. By the time they reported it, they would be gone. Off into the sunset to enjoy the rest of their lives. It was a shame to leave the house behind but it was too late to come up with a plan to sell it.

Jamie pulled the van into their street. It was quiet. Thankfully, spaces abounded in front of the house. A few cars were parked at regular intervals, all quite smart though not ones he recognised. They were the commuters who left their vehicles before heading into the city. Too mean to pay for proper parking, they forced the residents to compromise on kerb space.

"Why don't you just leave the van outside? Nobody will notice."

Laziness got the better of Jamie and he parked outside the house. It was a careless move. At this stage, he hardly cared. His focus was on collecting his things and getting on the road to their new life. By tomorrow, they would be gone and York would be a memory of their distant past. It was just the two of them, ready to go on an adventure together.

Alice was first out of the van. She strode across the pavement to the gate, with Jamie moving swiftly behind her. There was a stillness in the air as if the world had been paused. Then they struck and chaos filled the street. The two of them were grabbed from behind in a whirlwind of action. Neither saw their captors approaching or offered any resistance when it happened.

"Stop, police! DS Dan Millings. I am arresting you for the abduction of Elizabeth Moss. You do not have to say anything, but anything you say may..."

"Stop!" screamed Alice. "I have something to say."

"What?" asked Dan.

"Fuck off and leave us alone!"

***

Two hours later, Jack, Lisa and Dan sat in DCI Nick Lang's office. His smile was broad and a jug of high-quality coffee had been poured into china cups. Biscuits had been offered around, with the mood eased significantly from previous meetings. A call from the Assistant Chief Constable had already interrupted them.

Alice and Jamie Johnson were in custody. Crime scene investigators were in the process of recovering five bodies from the crypt. Two had been dead for a long time while three were more recent. Each corpse varied in its state of decay.

Elizabeth Moss was alive. Her condition was being monitored in York General Infirmary. She was not badly hurt, despite the violence she had faced. A severe blow to her head was the greatest concern while her father had already advised that he intended to sue. In time, Lang hoped his mood might ease even if the Assistant Chief Constable was less concerned.

"If he does, we'll prosecute him for obstructing an investigation. He was hardly helpful in the matter."

It was a long shot but it would be enough for him to drop the case. The publicity was unlikely to be good for his political career. He had got what he wanted. They had secured the return of his precious little girl, removing the need for him to pursue the matter any further.

"So, what next, sir?" asked Jack.

"Take some time off. You deserve it."

"And then what? Back to missing persons?"

"No, Jack. You can work on the basis you are back in service."

Jack smiled. He felt relieved at getting away from the desk job.

"And me?" asked Lisa.

"Well, after you take some leave, Jack is going to need a partner. Someone has to stop him from doing something stupid."

"I thought Dan would want his old partner back."

Dan smiled. A resigned look filled his face.

"With all due respect, Lisa, I don't think I'm ever going to be fit enough to do the chasing around after Jack. As much as I enjoyed arresting the Johnsons, I think I'm going to need something a little bit more sedate even if that is outside the force."

"There is a vacancy in missing persons if you are interested," noted Lang.

For the first time in a long while, Dan could see some sense. It was a genuine job and, as Jack had shown, one that could lead to results. Of course, the department would need a shake-up and the pace of work would have to increase. With those changes, there was the possibility that he could make it work.

"Would I be in charge of the team?"

Lang smiled at the latent ambition. It was the first clear sign he might have the old Dan back. Gone was the lethargy and in its place was the eager young lad he remembered.

"I think we might be able to swing that."

"In that case," smiled Dan, "I think we might have a deal. Do I get the same time off as Jack and Lisa?"

"Dan, you've just had a bloody year off," snorted Lang. "Look, have a couple of days off to get yourself sorted. Then, I want you back in. It will take a few weeks to get the place ship-shape. You haven't got much of a team in there, has he, Jack?"

"Not really. I would do what you can with that young lad, Will. He shows plenty of ambition and no shortage of tenacity."

"Thanks, Jack. Just make sure you tidy up your desk before I take over."

"I'll do that first thing in the morning before I go on leave. Now, is anyone coming to the pub for a celebratory drink? I'm buying."

"Yeah, I will," said Dan.

"Sorry, Jack," said Lisa. "I've got my parents down and they are going back tonight. I'll see you in the morning."

"And I've got a mountain of reports to sign off," sighed Lang.

"Looks like the old team is back together," smiled Jack as he walked out of the station with Dan.

It only took them a few minutes to reach The Cellars, helped by Jack hailing a taxi. He was not in the mood for walking and he justified the expense by it helping Dan. As the streets shot by, Jack reflected on the chaos of the day's events. It was good that Lang was satisfied with the result and that Jack was back as an acceptable person within the station. The prospect of seeing Dan return was encouraging though whether he would last long in a dead man's world was another question. Even a couple of weeks in there had been enough to have Jack contemplating retirement.

"Do you think you'll take the job in missing persons?"

"I'll give it a go. Let's be honest, I'm leaving anyway, so what have I got to lose?"

"Your sanity. It's like a departure lounge in there, all queuing up, waiting to leave or die."

"Remember, I will be making one or two changes."

"Seriously, I'd give Will a go. He did some great work for me on the Johnson case."

"I'll bear that in mind."

"I would. Now, more importantly, what are you going to be drinking?"

"No, Jack, this is my shout. It is only fair the arresting officer gets the drinks in."

The two men walked through the front door of The Cellars. For Jack, it was good to be going in with some company. Too many nights had been spent drinking alone. Even Alf's caring face had grown weary after a while.

"Pint of best for me, as always."

"And a chaser?"

"No, not this time, Alf. I'm just here for a quiet pint with a friend."

For once, his usual seat was occupied, an indication that he had been there less in the past few days. Jack settled down away from the door. He had never sat there before, with the view of the room not as comprehensive as he was used to. He did not mind. His thoughts had turned towards taking some time off. The only view he needed was of Dan returning with two glasses in his hands.

"Are you off the medication?"

"Why?"

"You're drinking."

"I thought I would have one. Got to break the rules occasionally, haven't you, Jack?"

Jack smiled and settled back in his chair. He took a small sip of his drink. The urge to gulp down a third of the glass with the first swig was not there. Instead, he would take his time and enjoy a steady pint. It had been a while since he had consumed a drink for a reason other than self-harm.

As Jack relaxed, his peace was disturbed by a tap on the shoulder. It made him jump. The two detectives swivelled hastily. It was Nigel Reeves, or what was left of the man after the strain of losing his son.

It was hard to know what to say when no words could make up for his loss. Jack paused and wondered whether he blamed the police for Steven's demise. There would always be the feeling that the authorities could have done more to save him. Jack forced a half-smile to offer some form of greeting.

"Look, I'm sorry," said Jack.

Nigel held out his hand and shook Jack's limply. He held it there for longer than he might, gripping Jack's palm as best he could. There was no strength left in his body. It had been taken from him and some twenty years added to his physical age. Jack could do nothing other than feel sorry for the man.

"Thanks, I knew I would find you in here. I just wanted to thank you for all that you did. I know you tried everything."

"We were just doing our job. I'm sorry we couldn't do more."

"No, you did more than I could have expected. I know it won't bring Steven back but it wasn't for the want of trying."

Finally, he allowed Jack's hand to go free. The released hand patted Nigel on the back in comfort. In front of Jack stood a man whose life had just been ruined.

"Let me get you two guys a drink," insisted Nigel.

"No, you don't have to."

"I want to."

Before they could decline, Nigel Reeves was at the bar and asking for two pints to be poured in honour of the officers. Jack shrugged at Dan, knowing it was important for Reeves to undertake the act.

"It looks like you're breaking the rules twice now," said Jack.

Dan smiled and took another sip from his pint. The glass was still half full and already he felt light-headed. His lack of drinking had made him vulnerable to the effects, not that he had any reason to fight it.

Suddenly, Jack gave his colleague's arm a nudge. A subtle point of the finger directed him towards the door. An imposing figure entered, flanked by a couple of stooges, putting Jack on the edge of his seat.

"Here comes trouble."

David Moss arrived with a face looking like thunder. His manner told him he had come to The Cellars intent on causing trouble. He spotted Nigel Reeves at the bar and then flicked his eyes at Jack. He offered indecision as to which of his foes he would go at first.

"Should we step in?" asked Dan.

"No," shrugged Jack. "We're all just guys having a relaxing drink after work."

That theory lasted less than a few seconds. A heated exchange broke out at the bar. First, David Moss launched an angry tirade at Nigel Reeves before life returned to the previously crestfallen man. The rest of the conversation was brief and ended with Moss shoving Reeves in the chest. The response was a straight left jab that caught David Moss square on the nose.

His knees buckled and then the blood started to run. It forced him to scramble for a handkerchief to stem the flow of red. Reeves looked shocked at what he had done before concern turned to pride. All of a sudden, his chest pumped out as if he was a strutting peacock attracting a mate. In front of him, David Moss clutched his nose and moved swiftly over to Jack. Under the reddening cloth, the anger was hard to miss.

"Did you see that, Plod? Did you see that? He assaulted me."

Jack gazed up from his pint, offering a look of indifference. It was all he could do to hold back a grin that was threatening to break out. Dan sat quietly, pleased that his view was limited from where he was sitting.

"Can't say I did. What happened?"

"You're a bloody disgrace, Husker. You should have been thrown off the force after that to-do with Gregor Banks. He's still going to have you, Husker. You're a dead man walking, a relic from the past that needs putting out of its misery."

Jack rose and, with one big swing, landed his right fist flush across the jaw of Moss. It knocked him backwards, with his body sending two stools flying on his journey to the floor. It was a solid connection and far harder than he had been hit by Reeves. Once over the shock, Moss's two gofers struggled to contain the smile invading their faces.

David Moss lay sprawled across the floor, still clutching his handkerchief to his nose. It had little effect, with the force of Jack's blow sending blood across his face. He was stunned and had been humiliated in the public arena. He needed to get out before the story made the local news.

"You two, don't bloody stand there doing nothing. Help me up."

Jack winked at one of them as they walked forward to assist their floundering leader. Moss looked dazed and struggled to get off the ground. It was Alf who offered the final insult by sending him on his way with some stinging words. He had no doubt it would be a while before they returned to drink in his establishment.

"And don't bring that kind of behaviour in here again or you'll be barred."

It was said with tongue in cheek and accompanied by a sly smile towards Jack. His next task was to push a free pint in front of each of the protagonists. There was little which shocked him in the game anymore. This had been one of those occasions. It never mattered how well you knew someone, they always had the capacity to surprise.

CHAPTER 22

JACK WOKE WITH A surprisingly clear head, thanks to keeping his intake to less than four pints. An early night had helped as had his decision to have just one more after Dan had left. It had been good to see Dan back in the game and enjoy a simple drink with him. There were signs of the old colleague returning even if he would never be quite the same.

Some things never changed in Jack's life and brought a feeling of continuity. The cupboard was empty except for a jar of instant coffee. At least it was a good brand and not the muck from the corner shop. Then there were the headache tablets, propped up alongside the jar. Jack took them out and eased the strip of tablets out of the packet. He thought for a moment and then decided he would go without them. It might make it a long day but the time had come to sail his boat without the need for support.

His clothes were the usual shabby affair and held little joy. Yesterday's shirt and a pair of trousers fresh from the laundry basket went with the obligatory pair of unmatched socks. At least he remembered where he had left his shoes, the advantage of going to bed sober. With time off to come, he vowed to do some shopping and get his clothes situation sorted. It had been too long since Mary had left for him to live the life of a man waiting for her to return.

Jack wandered out onto the streets with a sense of optimism in his stride. York felt different and his walk to work was both refreshing and done without any stress. He felt relaxed and was looking forward to some long overdue leave. Jack could hardly remember the last time he had taken a proper break.

Indeed, he had not had a holiday since his last marriage ended. Now felt like the time to recharge the batteries and get his life back on track. First, he had to close off the files he had been working through and then hand them over to Dan. After that, he was done and free to fill his time.

Lisa had awoken in a similar frame of mind. She, too, would be taking two weeks of leave. Whether she would head back to Newcastle, she was unsure. Her parents would be happy to see her but they had only just visited, leaving her with the flexibility to avoid any firm plans.

There was no doubt she would see Jack at some point and there would be conversations about the future. Their paths had become intertwined even though nothing had happened. It was no more than flirtatious banter, leaving her to wonder whether anything would ever come of it. She had pondered that question on many occasions and was no closer to having an answer.

Lisa put on some casual clothes and brushed her hair. There was no need for work clothing when her purpose in the station was just to tidy a few things up. That should have made it easy to decide what to wear and yet it only made it harder. Each item she chose was swiftly replaced by another. She asked herself, why should she care? It was only Jack. No matter what he did, he was always in her mind.

Jack arrived at the station first and he quickly put a few files into the cupboards. It was done methodically to leave Dan with an empty desk. The lad would have enough on without having to clear up Jack's mess.

"You leaving us, Jack?"

Dick Foster's words lifted everyone's heads from their stupor. No one ever left the department, other than to retire or be carried out in a box. Dick had no plans to go anywhere and had a little notepad on his desk to tick off the days until he reached maximum pension. He was sitting there waiting to die and Jack was relieved he would not be there alongside him.

"Back to the front line for me, Dick."

"Rather you than me, son."

It was probably the longest conversation Jack had shared with him in the miserable time he had been in the department. Not a man he found particularly pleasant, Jack had made sure they spoke only when needed. There were others he felt a little sorrier for, guys who could do so much better with their careers. For most, it was their choice to stay there and grow old before their time, rather than make something of their lives.

Carefully, Jack continued to put away his files. He took care to ensure the order was logical for someone else to follow. With his desk clear, he sat back and took in the room for one final time. After a last check of the drawers, he would be heading off on leave. Jack pulled them open one by one and gazed at the usual array of detritus. Tatty stationery filled most of the space other than one item in the bottom drawer which left him in a dilemma.

Everything he had on the Timmy Jackson case was there in one file. It was something he had worked on in his own time and he was close to having the evidence to prove Gregor Banks had made him disappear. The lad had been seen getting into Gregor's car and all that was missing was a body. Until that was found, Timmy Jackson was just a missing person.

The warnings from Gregor had been clear when Jack stuck his nose in. Then a deal had been struck where Jack had promised to leave the case alone. He had agreed in a moment of desperation when faced with finding a killer. That agreement now rankled with Jack when he knew Gregor Banks had got away with murder.

As he sat there, Jack pondered his next move. If he took on the case, he knew the gangster would snuff him out in an instant. It meant somebody else had to stumble upon it for justice to be served. A missing person review would be something Jack would not be part of.

Jack took out a folder and typed up the headings to open a case file. Once complete, he slipped everything inside it that he had. Gregor Banks would face justice eventually and that ticking time bomb would explode in his face. It might take years to come to light or be opened by Dick Foster in a moment of boredom. That amused Jack to know that Dick would think he was getting the better of him by nailing the one man Jack couldn't. It would be perfect to have unsullied hands and see Gregor locked up with his father.

Carefully, Jack slid the folder into one of the drawers. Not in its rightful place but squeezed in at the back. It could be years before it was seen or, if Dan got to work on reorganising the team, maybe sooner. That was the thrill, to know it was just a matter of time before Gregor Banks was nailed.

"You look a little too happy," said Dick Foster. "What are you up to?"

"It might be the last time we see each other for a long while, Dick. That gives me every reason to be happy."

"Sod off, Husker."

"You too, Dick."

Jack banged the drawer shut. It was his last sight of the Jackson file and he swept up his jacket with a flourish. His work was done and it was time for rest and recuperation. It felt good to have the chance to clear his head of the complications that had been building up.

Jack skipped down the stairs and was on his way out of the front door. There was no sign of Lang and the station appeared almost empty. It was a good sign that no last-minute hiccups would affect him. An inconsiderate murderer could soon scupper Jack's restful plans.

"Are you trying to sneak out without me?" came a voice from behind him.

At the front door, Lisa was a few paces behind Jack. She had tidied up her loose ends and was due on leave for the same duration. She looked happy and full of energy, all things Jack had never been at any recent point in his life. He smiled and allowed himself to soften a little in her presence.

"Of course not. Are you done?"

"Yes, schools out for a fortnight. I can't wait."

Jack felt the uncertainty flash through his head. It was the same demons that had chased two wives away and more recently, Mary. It was fighting him and dominating his mood, filling his head with an urge to run away. He needed space or there was a danger he would be forced to show some commitment. That cold shiver that went through him visibly changed his demeanour. Any relaxation he felt was quickly evaporating from his body.

"Are you alright?" asked Lisa.

"Yes, I'm fine," said Jack, fighting to regain control.

"So what happens next, Jack?"

"You tell me," he forced out with difficulty.

"Why don't we go for a drink and see where it leads?"

Jack smiled as a sense of relief lifted the uncertainty from his body. The decision could wait and the demons could be dispelled for a little longer. Any need to commit was gone and the prospect of two free weeks returned to being favourable. He knew exactly what Lisa meant and there was only one suitable response.

"Now you are talking my language. How about The Cellars?"

Lisa rolled her eyes, shook her head, and smiled. "Where else, Jack? Where else?"

ACKNOWLEDGMENTS

Every book has more people to thank than it is possible to include. Some people offer insights into characters and provide inspiration for the traits they demonstrate. Others play a more immediate role by offering ideas for the story. All I can do is thank all of these people for their help.

One person, I would like to make specific mention of is Gillian, my cover designer. I worked with her for the first time on Death Sketches and I was delighted when she agreed to do the same on its sequel. She is a talented designer and offers something that I could never hope to. So, thank you for another fantastic piece of design work.

I would also like to thank my wife. She has put up with me for more years than she would care to remember. I won't name her but suffice to say, she provides a great deal of feedback about my books. I have offered to give her a role in the next one but she has no desire to have Jack Husker investigate the gruesome ending I might dream up for her!

Available Now

Death Sketches

A university student is found hanging from a butcher's hook in the Shambles. Her body has been stripped and her bloodied form sketched by her killer. When she is found, it is the marks on her body that catch the detectives' attention. They are not there by accident but have been carved meticulously into her body.

DI Jack Husker is the detective tasked with finding the macabre killer before another student goes missing. He must put aside his own problems and the distractions from his past. Will he solve the case before the killer strikes again or will more of the brutal artwork be found across the city?

Set in the beautiful city of York, this is DI Jack Husker's debut outing as he tries to solve the toughest case of his career.

"Now my beautiful sculpture, please be quiet. I need silence for my work."

DEATH SKETCHES

CHAPTER 1

He pushed her forcibly up the stairs. Her slow, stumbling steps in the narrow staircase hindered her progress. Around her, she sensed an old building, its distinctive damp smell hanging in the air. She could see no part of it, the hastily tied blindfold masking her main sense and yet he offered her no concession for her lack of progress.

She tripped on the fourth step, her tied hands unable to break the fall. The tread of the stair above it cut into her shin. It felt broken. Numbness filled her leg. Her loud cry was met with a heavy grab of her shirt, dragging her back to her feet. She stumbled again, her leg unable to take the weight put on it. She needed a moment to rest but he had no compassion. Why should he? It was her weakness and he despised it.

Once more, he lifted her. His strong arm wrapped around her to prevent her from falling for a second time. There was barely room for the two of them in the stairwell. Still, he expected her to move forward. Her sobbing grew louder but it would do her no good. He was immune to emotion and unable to comprehend why anyone would plead. Pleading was what you did if you were hurt and he had barely started.

"Get up!"

She recognised the voice. No matter how hard she concentrated, she could not place it. She wanted to rip off the blindfold to reveal her tormentor though he had tied her well. Too well.

"Please, who are you?"

There was nothing.

She could sense they were near the top of the stairs. The climb had exhausted her. Blood was running down her leg and her body felt weak. She was never good with such things, prone to fainting at the tiniest sign of a scratch. Mummy had always said she should be braver. For once, she was thankful for the blindfold.

A lock. She heard him fumbling with a lock and a key. She memorised the time it took for him to turn it and the sound it made. An old building, a narrow staircase and a heavy-sounding lock. There would be blood on the fifth or sixth step, her blood, and then there was the familiar voice. They were all things she could tell the police about her abductor. The modern policemen would find him from the smallest detail. They were good at things like that. All she had to do was get through her ordeal and try to be brave.

He opened the door to a distinctive thud. The door needed a push, perhaps out of shape for the frame. Again, more evidence, more information to find the place, a damp corner somewhere in the middle of the city.

She sensed light as it opened, the sun streaming into the room to hit her face. A shove to her back pushed her to the wooden floor, bruising her knee. Why did he have to be so rough? She would do as she was told. It was her best hope. Then she would reason with him and he had to listen.

The door closed behind her. The turning key sounded more sinister from the inside. He was locking them in, trapping the two of them in the room. Her mind raced, her breathing more erratic than ever.

"What do you want?"

Again nothing, just footsteps walking across the room. His weight on the wooden floor vibrated through her body. How could he be so calm?

"Please, just let me go. I'll do anything."

Silence.

Suddenly, the room plunged into darkness. The curtains were pulled across the window with force. He flicked the switch to her side, providing a dim light by which he could see. Beneath the blindfold, there was just darkness and a sense of desperation in her thoughts. She was truly alone.

For the first time in her life, she prayed. She prayed she was back in Durham in the comforting presence of her parents and her dog. In front of the warm fire in their large house, she would be safe. From her position on the rug, she could see the top of the cathedral and the university where her parents had wanted her to go. Instead, she had chosen York, as much to exert her independence than for education. Now, she wished she had followed their path.

"Please, I'll scream."

A single strike to her head forced her to drift out of consciousness. The sweet taste of blood in her mouth was her last memory as she slipped away from the world.

***

She was the obvious choice. He had watched her carefully over those past few weeks. Indeed, he had studied her shape and she was perfect. Perfect in almost every dimension and he could change those parts where she was not. Why did she have to threaten to scream? Why could she not play along like the good girl he thought she was? Did they all have to be that way?

He walked around her lifeless body, watching her, studying every inch of her form. She was beautiful and at peace with the world. It was his favourite moment and he had prepared for it. He had followed her so many times. Now, he could get as close as he wanted. He could stare at her, touch her and taste her. She would taste so sweet when he ran his tongue across her face. He knew she would.

"Why did you scream? We were getting on so well, weren't we?"

She never answered.

It irritated him. Why did she ignore him? She had been so keen to talk when they climbed the stairs. Yet now, she was silent. It made no sense. Nothing ever did.

"Get up!"

Still, she ignored him, defiantly. For how long? They never ignored him for long.

"I said, get up!"

He hated rejection. It had been the watchword of his life. First, his father and then his mother. He would show them both and they would be proud. He would make them proud.

He dragged her to her feet. She felt limp. If she would not stand up for him, he would make her do it. Then he would sketch her.

"Take off your clothes."

She defied him again, ignoring his commands as if to spite him. He had tried hard to be friendly. He hooked her hands onto the large metal hook in the beam above her head. So convenient and perfect to hold her in place. He would strip her and he would not be nice. Oh no, he had tried that and she had ignored him. He had brought knives and he would use them. He would cut her clothes from her and if he hurt her, it was her fault. Not his. She had brought it upon herself.

Carefully, he laid the three knives on the floor. Each so different, they demanded to be examined. Just the way they glinted in the light, offering her reflection to him. All spotless, they had been cleaned well, making it a difficult choice between the three. He had his favourite; the one that always made the first cut. He smiled and held it up, feeling the adrenalin pumping through him. It was time and he could wait no longer.

The act did not take long. The sharpened knife sliced the clothes from her body in seconds. He wished he had taken more time and savoured it but he had work to do. He had no wish for delays and she would not help him. And now she looked perfect.

Just as he had imagined she would. Her beauty was screaming at him in the most artistic of ways.

With a smile on his face, he moved away from her body and stood behind his easel. The position was perfect, the single bulb illuminating her naked figure. He needed to work and get every last detail right. It had to be just as he wanted if his work was to be admired.

"Now my beautiful sculpture, please be quiet. I need silence for my work."

AFTERWORD

My aim for this book was to create an enjoyable experience for the reader. It is not a history book or designed as a guide to the city of York. Indeed, there is commentary in it that would paint York as a dark place. Having lived close to the beautiful city for most of my life, it is anything but. Like most cities, York has great variety and that is its charm. There is something for everyone from the history it presents to the modern vibrancy that brings it alive.

Are your books an accurate depiction of York?

In some cases, yes. I have tried to take some of the features of the city and blend them with some creativity. Where buildings are in the wrong place or do not fit how I want them to be portrayed, I have simply moved them. As an example, I wanted a university in the city, so I used the location of York St John University rather than the more remote campus that is the University of York. For me, the most important thing is the story is enjoyable and if that takes a little bit of artistic licence, then I am happy to use it.

Why don't you give the addresses of where the characters live?

For privacy reasons. While I use streets in the book, it would be wrong to name a specific real-life address where someone lives. Who wants to wake up to someone staring at their bedroom window expecting Jack Husker to be looking out?

Are your characters based on real-life people?

All characters are fictional. Of course, I have used some of the traits of people I have met over the years. Some characters have been given two or three traits from different people, though they remain fictitious characters. There is certainly no character who is a direct representation of anybody in real life.

Is Jack based on yourself?

Definitely not! I can confidently say that Jack is not an alter-ego of mine. Indeed, I would struggle to find anything in common with him, both good and bad. Okay, maybe I am protesting a little too much and I might share his sense of humour.

Will there be more books in the series?

Definitely. Jack Husker is a long way from being finished, be it through retirement or meeting a grizzly end. There is plenty more out there for him, so make sure you look out for new releases. This book was always going to be the continuation of the journey and it is a journey that does not have an obvious ending.

Printed in Great Britain
by Amazon

24161459R00202